Praise for the Washington Whodunit Series

LARCENY AT THE LIBRARY

"Kit and friends sample the capital's best restaurants and ogle the Library of Congress's architectural splendor. Fans of light traditional mysteries will be amused."
—*Publisher's Weekly*

"The book has a great flow and the dialogue is crisp. The mystery is full of twists and turns and kept me captivated from beginning to end."
—*Escape with Dollycas Into a Good Book*

"Former Library of Congress executive Shogan delivers a sequel to 2019s Gore in the Garden that educates while it entertains. Not only does this engaging traditional mystery offer insight into Washington, D.C.'s inner workings, but it also takes readers on armchair tours of Ford's Theatre, the National Portrait Gallery, and several of the library's exhibits. The conceit is clever, the MacGuffin is marvelous, and Kit's list of likely culprits is as varied as it is long."
—*Mystery Scene Magazine*

"These books are a tribute to what makes our nation's capital so special. I love that they give an insider's look into our country's most historical buildings with none of the politics—just an appreciation for the rich history the places hold. Kit is a great protagonist and I always love going along on her adventures."
—*A Cozy Experience*

Other Books in the Washington Whodunit Series

Stabbing in the Senate

Homicide in the House

Calamity at the Continental Club

K Street Killing

Gore in the Garden

Larceny at the Library

Dead as a Duck

Dead as a Duck

A Washington Whodunit

COLLEEN J. SHOGAN

Seattle, WA

A Camel Press book published by Epicenter Press

Epicenter Press
6524 NE 181st St.
Suite 2
Kenmore, WA 98028

For more information go to:
www.Camelpress.com
www.Coffeetownpress.com
www.Epicenterpress.com
www.colleenshogan.com

All rights reserved. No part of this book may be reproduced or transmitted in any form or by any means, electronic or mechanical, including photocopying, recording, or any information storage and retrieval system, without permission in writing from the publisher.

This is a work of fiction. Names, characters, places, brands, media, and incidents are either the product of the author's imagination or are used fictitiously.

Cover design by Scott Book
Design by Melissa Vail Coffman

Dead as a Duck
Copyright © 2021 by Colleen J. Shogan

IISBN: 978-1-94207-832-6 (Trade Paper)
ISBN: 978-1-94207-833-3 (eBook)

Library of Congress Control Number: 2021932526

Printed in the United States of America

This book is dedicated to my friends, especially those who spent time with us on the Outer Banks over the years. Thank you for the memories!

Chapter One

I T WAS A BALMY NINETY DEGREES OUTSIDE. I was only a short walk away from the gentle breeze of the Atlantic Ocean, but instead of frolicking in the sun with a cold drink in hand, I was staring down a dimly lit narrow corridor inside the municipal building of Duck, North Carolina. Such was the regrettable hand dealt to a senior congressional aide whose boss was contemplating a run next year for the United States Senate.

"Kit, the meeting is inside this room." My boss motioned for me to follow her. A military veteran who had served in Iraq and Afghanistan, Representative Maeve Dixon was a natural-born leader. When she spoke, people listened. At least I did. As her chief of staff, following her direction was the most important aspect of my job.

We walked inside a large multipurpose room that had been arranged for a typical town hall meeting. Rows of folding chairs filled the room, all facing a small stage outfitted with two podiums. I heaved a sigh of relief as I flopped myself into one of the uncomfortable seats in the front row. It had been a long, hot August. Thankfully, today was the end of the trail, at least for now.

Dixon stood near the edge of the stage, fiddling with her smartphone. Even though the oceanside town of Duck in the Outer Banks was the last stop on her "exploratory" Senate campaign sweep through North Carolina, my boss still wore her standard, fitted black pantsuit. She had replaced her conventional one-inch pumps with dark, heeled sandals, and her brightly printed blouse had a hint of beachside flair to it. Maeve Dixon relished the political game and she'd do well if she decided to declare herself a candidate for the open United States Senate seat, but even she was ready for a much-deserved break from the hustings.

I heard the door in the back of the room open and turned around to see who had arrived. A middle-aged man with a deep, copper tan and sandy brown hair strode confidently toward the stage. I stood to intercept him and introduce myself, but he blew right past me. He walked up to Maeve Dixon and thrust his hand out.

"Chairwoman Dixon, I'm Ronan Godfrey, the mayor of Duck, North Carolina, otherwise known as the best vacation spot on the entire eastern seaboard." He smiled widely at her, smoothing his crisp, stylish light brown linen pants and blue sport jacket with his other hand.

Maeve returned the greeting with a firm shake. "Pleased to meet you, Ronan. I've heard a lot about you from my contacts in state and local government."

If Ronan had been a lighthouse, he would have beamed so brightly it would have blinded passing ships. "What a tremendous compliment," said Ronan. "It is certainly an honor to meet our next senator from the great state of North Carolina."

Dixon's face was impassive. "Let's not get ahead of ourselves, Mr. Mayor. I'm only on a preliminary listening tour around the state. I haven't decided whether I'll run for the Senate yet. That's why I'm talking to voters."

Godfrey chuckled. "Don't delay too long, Madame Chair. I always found decisiveness was important, both in business and politics."

Maeve's lips formed a tight line. She motioned me to join her. "I'd like you to meet my chief of staff, Kit Marshall. She has accompanied me the last several weeks on our trip around the state."

I stepped forward and offered Ronan Godfrey my hand. He politely accepted it. "Welcome to Duck, Ms. Marshall. Have you been here before?"

"Not until this morning," I said. "Since this is the last stop on the campaign . . ."

Maeve shot me a dirty look. I wasn't supposed to be calling it that.

"I mean, listening tour," I corrected myself quickly. "I'm meeting my husband, brother, and several friends for a weeklong vacation after the town hall meeting is over."

Ronan's eyes sparkled. "What terrific news! The end of August is a perfect time to soak up the sun and enjoy our beach. Do you have any four-legged friends joining you?"

"As a matter of fact, my dog Clarence and my brother's girlfriend's dog Murphy will be on vacation with us," I said.

"We're the number one beach in the United States for dogs," said Ronan proudly. "You'll want to stop by our Duck Dogs store to stock up on beach necessities for them."

Like scuba gear? A doggie swimsuit? A canine floatie? My mind drifted and I had to suppress a giggle when I thought of our chubby beagle mutt, Clarence, wearing a rubber ducky inner tube, bobbing up and down with the ocean waves. Little did Mr. Mayor know I'd already purchased Clarence's swimwear for his first-ever ocean excursion. Still, it was my job to play nice. Who knows if we'd need this guy's help in the future?

"I'll be sure to visit the store," I promised. "However, before vacation starts, we have the town hall discussion to get through. Are there any specific issues Chairwoman Dixon should be prepared to address?"

Ronan waved his hand dismissively. "There's the usual squabbles, like any small town. The bottom line is that everyone who lives here loves it." He paused for a moment. "I don't like to brag, but I'm a very popular mayor."

Dixon's face remained blank. I'd worked for her long enough to surmise her thoughts. Politicians who had to tell you about their supposed popularity usually had something to worry about. I'd hoped this last stop on the listening tour would be an easy one so I could slide peacefully into vacation mode. Something told me I might be mistaken.

Maeve pursed her lips. "That's terrific to hear, Ronan. If that's the case, this meeting will be smooth sailing. I'd appreciate if you tossed any questions of national significance to me. Of course, you will handle the local matters. That's your territory."

Ronan's forehead wrinkled. "There may be a few questions about some of the business decisions we've made lately. Of course, you know my background." He stared expectantly at Dixon.

"I do," said Dixon. "You were a California tech entrepreneur who sold his company a few years ago for millions of dollars. You left Silicon Valley and decided to settle in the Outer Banks of North Carolina. Last year, you were elected mayor of Duck."

Before she was a soldier, Maeve Dixon had been a Girl Scout. She was always prepared. Clearly, she'd studied the two-page background memo I'd written for her the night before. Like the former Speaker of the House Tip O'Neill, my boss knew that all politics was local.

Ronan nodded enthusiastically, clearly impressed. "That's correct. Since I've been mayor, I've made a few key changes to improve Duck's prospects as a vacation spot."

"Seems like it's doing pretty well from my perspective. The traffic to come across the Wright Brothers bridge onto the island was worse than the Washington, D.C. Beltway during rush hour," I said.

Ronan ran his fingers through his expensive haircut. "We're moving in the right direction. But we could really boost the type of vacationer who spends time here in the summer. If every tourist spent more money, it would benefit our small business owners. I'm always looking out for them."

Maeve looked skeptical. "We certainly want all North Carolina residents to enjoy our valuable coast real estate," she said. "That will be my standard reply if I'm asked directly."

Ronan waved his hand, too dismissively for my taste. "Don't worry about it. I can handle any questions related to town business matters. After all, we're here to introduce you to voters for a statewide run next year."

"Potential run," corrected Maeve again. "I don't want to make any headlines in the Outer Banks. That's not the purpose of my visit."

The door in the rear opened again, and I turned away from the conversation to see who had entered the room. To my delight, it was my husband, Doug, and my best friend, Meg.

"Please excuse me for a moment," I said.

I broke away and jogged down the aisle of seats to embrace Doug first and then Meg. It had been a long three weeks on the "listening trail," and I'd missed the comforts of my normal life.

"Why are you guys here?" I asked. "I was planning to come to the house we rented after we're done with the town hall meeting."

"We wanted to support you and Congresswoman Dixon," said Doug. "Besides, I missed you." He gave me another tight squeeze.

"How sweet," I smiled from ear to ear. Then I looked around. "Where's Clarence?"

"Sebastian and Lisa have him, along with Murphy," said Doug. Sebastian was my younger brother, who moved to the Washington, D.C. area about a year ago. He worked in technology for a non-profit, but in his spare time, he enjoyed protesting for leftist causes. Environmentalism, corporate greed, and workers' wages were popular with him, although he wasn't really picky. The more noble the cause, the more attracted Sebastian was to it.

Meg chimed in. "Trevor's at the rental house, too. Although I doubt he's wrangling with the dogs too much."

It was a minor miracle that Trevor had joined us at all. A former colleague who had recently become Meg's exclusive boyfriend, Trevor had never been on a beach vacation before. If we had successfully lured Trevor to the ocean, there was a first time for anything.

"I hope he's put on sunblock," I said. "Trevor is as white as ghost. No offense, Meg."

My best friend nodded. "He bought S-P-F 125. I didn't even know they made it that high."

I shook my head in disbelief. "Neither did I, but I'm not surprised Trevor found it."

"Both of us are eager to see Maeve Dixon in action. I mean, *Senator* Dixon." Doug smiled mischievously.

"Don't say that." Both Meg and I spoke simultaneously and laughed.

"Old habits die hard," said Meg. "I still think like a congressional staffer." This past spring, Meg left her job as the legislative director in Maeve Dixon's office to become the head of congressional relations at the Library of Congress after we helped solve a murder there.

"That's a good thing," I said. "It can only help the Library with its Capitol Hill dealings."

I was still getting used to not working with Meg every day. Her new office was only across the street, but I missed our morning coffee breaks and our frequent consultations. Nonetheless, I knew that Meg had accepted a bigger and better job with more responsibilities and room for growth. Life moved on, and it was best to change with it.

Meg leaned closer to me, the sides of her blonde bob clipped away from her face with a colorful barrette. "Who is that guy?" She gestured toward Ronan.

"That's the mayor of Duck," I said. "His name is Ronan Godfrey, and he'll answer questions alongside Maeve today at the town hall meeting."

"Have you vetted him?" Meg wiggled her perfectly sculpted eyebrows in a questioning manner.

"I did," I said. "He's a tech mogul who relocated to the Outer Banks and quickly became the mayor. He's got a businesslike approach, but he seems clean. No red flags."

Meg stepped back and adjusted her stylish white jean shorts. Even when dressed in casual beach attire, my best friend looked like she'd just stepped out of the pages of a fashion magazine.

Doug leaned close and whispered in my ear. "No work this week after this town hall is over."

I giggled. "You won't get any argument from me. I'm ready for a vacation."

Our private moment was interrupted by another middle-aged man. This guy's look was distinct from the mayor's. He had bushy, slightly unkempt hair and was dressed in a worn t-shirt, brown cargo shorts, and Birkenstock sandals. "Am I early for the political rumpus?"

We turned to face our guest, and I focused on his shirt, which sported a rainbow-colored logo of a pony with the words, "SAVE THE COROLLA HORSES."

Doug pointed to the shirt. "Why do the horses need to be saved?"

The man put his arm around Doug's shoulders. "You must not be from the Outer Banks."

Doug, whose professorial habits die hard, stiffened upon the unprovoked physical contact. He adjusted his glasses. "I am not, sir." He swung around with his right hand and untangled himself from his newfound friend. "Doug Hollingsworth. My wife Kit works for Maeve Dixon from the House of Representatives. She's your guest this afternoon."

"Excellent," he said. "Gary Brewster's the name. I play many roles around these parts, but what's relevant for this afternoon's meeting is that I'm the President of the Corolla Horse Foundation." He handed me a business card, and I provided my own in return.

The pieces clicked together in my brain. When I'd prepared the short briefing memo for Dixon, I'd read about federal legislation concerning the wild horses who lived on the Outer Banks.

Time to go to work. I interjected myself into the conversation. "Gary, my name is Kit Marshall," I said. "Maeve Dixon has supported the proposed bill concerning the wild horses. But she doesn't serve on the committee in the House of Representatives where it's been referred." This was technical jargon, yet I needed to explain to him that Dixon had done what she could at this point for his cause.

Gary blinked several times. "What's your name again? Did you say Kit Marshall?"

I gulped before nodding. Sometimes, my reputation preceded me. I couldn't imagine how I'd created an enemy on the Outer Banks, but I'd covered a lot of territory in my political career.

"Are you related to Sebastian Marshall? I remember he mentioned a sister who worked in Washington, and I thought he said her name was Kit."

A wave of relief washed over me. Gary knew my younger brother. "Yes, that's him. How do you know Sebastian?"

Gary grinned. "We've been front line environmental activists for years together. The last I heard, he'd given up on California and moved east to live closer to his older sister."

"I'm *slightly* older," I said, in a partially defensive, partially humorous tone.

Gary ignored my comment. "Is Sebastian in town? I thought I heard you mention a vacation when you were chatting with your friends."

"As a matter of fact, he is. Several of us from Washington rented a house in Duck for the week. He's there now, unpacking with his girlfriend and watching our dogs."

Gary whistled softly. "In that case, I'm going to text my good buddy. He won't want to miss this meeting."

Before I could ask Gary what he meant, he sprinted to the door and left the room.

"What did he mean?" asked Doug. "Why would Sebastian care about a small-town civic meeting in the Outer Banks?"

"There's going to be a few surprises is my guess," said Meg. "Haven't you watched the videos that have gone viral on social media? Local meetings can be downright deadly."

On that sunny summer morning at the beach, Meg had no idea how prophetic her words would become.

Chapter Two

My gut told me Meg was right about the town hall meeting, which was scheduled to start at noon. My pulse quickened. I needed to warn my boss. She was good on her feet, but everyone deserved a fair warning if a hurricane was approaching, especially given our seaside location.

However, Maeve Dixon wasn't inside the large public hall anymore. Mayor Godfrey was no longer there, either. Drat. Now I'd have to kick into high gear to find her. I'd hoped that the last stop on her exploratory Senate tour would be relatively uneventful. After all, Duck was the smallest town we visited on the swing through the state. We came here because I'd convinced her it made sense to visit a coastal community and a beach visit would make for some scenic publicity shots. When she started barnstorming North Carolina weeks ago, reporters had followed every speech, breakfast, and photo opportunity. Now we were old news, and I figured several informal photos on the beach, perhaps showing off Maeve's athletic side, would at least generate a couple hundred "likes" and "retweets" on social media. Maeve hadn't argued. As hard-nosed as she was, I think she secretly looked forward to spending a day or two in a more relaxed locale.

"We gotta find Dixon," I said, glancing at my iPhone to check the time. "The town hall starts in about an hour."

"If there's going to be trouble, she won't want it sprung on her at the last minute," said Meg.

"Precisely," I said. "Follow me."

We exited the large multipurpose room we were in and looked down a long hallway. The restrooms were located to the left and the entrance lobby was on our right.

"Doug and I will head to the lobby," I said. "Can you check the women's bathroom, Meg?"

"Sure thing," she said. "If she's there, I'll tell her you need to speak with her." Meg paused. "After all, I don't work for Maeve Dixon any longer."

I put my hand on Meg's arm. "Of course," I said. "She's not your responsibility. I'll take care of it."

We split up and went our separate ways. Doug and I scanned the entrance foyer, but it was empty. It was decorated with a smattering of old maps, historic pictures, and artifacts. Doug waved me over to look at a display.

"The first English child born in the New World was Virginia Dare in 1587." Doug pointed to the map. "The location was Roanoke Island, which isn't far from here."

"Fascinating," I murmured as I scanned the entryway again for Maeve Dixon. Doug had entered historian mode, but my congressional staff duties were more pressing.

"Even more historic is the Wright Brothers' first flight, which happened only a few miles down the road." Doug's voice teemed with excitement. "We need to visit that memorial during our stay."

After three weeks of endless press events, town halls, and photo ops, I'd planned to split my days between three places: the beach, the pool, and the hot tub. Historic landmarks hadn't made it onto my list. However, I was married to a historian and marriage oftentimes required compromise.

"Sounds intriguing." That was a perfectly supportive response purposefully devoid of commitment. Perhaps I'd been spending too much time around politicians.

Doug pulled at my sleeve. "Kit, you'll love this." He pointed to a display titled "The Lost Colony."

Normally, I would have gladly indulged my historian hubby,

but I needed to find Maeve Dixon before the seats of the town hall started filling up and she went into charming politico mode.

"Right now, the only lost thing I care about is my disappearing congressional boss," I said.

"She'll turn up soon enough," said Doug. "Look, people are starting to arrive." He pointed toward the hallway, which was no longer empty.

"I'll have to pull her away from the voting public of North Carolina to brief her," I said. "Believe me, she won't like it. Every one of these people matter." I pointed to the town residents streaming inside the hall and sighed. "At least from an electoral perspective."

Doug laughed. "Spoken like a true chief of staff whose boss is running for higher office."

"*Exploring* higher office," I said.

"We certainly hope it's more definitive than that," said an unfamiliar voice from behind me.

I whirled around. A fit man in his early sixties, clad in a brightly colored Hawaiian shirt, sandals, and a baseball hat emblazoned with the three letters "OBX" stared at me with a bemused look on his face. When I failed to respond to his comment, he thrust his hand in my direction.

"Tobias Potter. You must be a staffer for Congresswoman Maeve Dixon," he said.

"Yes, I am." I accepted his hand and gave it a light shake. "Are you a resident of the town?"

"Resident and town council member," he said, his chest out and shoulders back. "Almost twenty years in my elected capacity."

"That's quite impressive," I said. "This is my husband Doug. We're staying on for vacation in Duck after the town hall meeting today."

Potter grinned. "Excellent choice. Perhaps Maeve Dixon will make this her annual vacation spot after she's our next United States Senator." He winked.

I didn't want to tell him that if Maeve was lucky enough to run and win, she would likely have to divide her vacation time carefully amongst all the touristy areas of North Carolina. She wouldn't want to play favorites.

"No matter what happens, I'm sure the congresswoman will always remember Duck," I said lamely. It was the best I could do under the circumstances. "If you'll excuse me, I need to find her before this afternoon's program begins." I nodded politely at Tobias and hustled down the hallway with Doug in tow.

I peeked inside the large gathering hall. It was filling up and others were milling about. The discussion was scheduled to start in fifteen minutes. Mayor Godfrey was greeting guests as they arrived. But Maeve Dixon was nowhere in sight.

Meg was standing on the sidelines, tapping her foot nervously. "You didn't find her either?" she asked.

"No luck." I sighed. So much for gently easing into a relaxing vacation.

"Why don't you text her?" asked Doug.

It was a perfectly reasonable idea. Even though my boss was younger than most members of Congress, she wasn't the most technically adept. She checked her messages when she felt like it and didn't always feel the need to keep in touch every waking moment.

"I can try," I said, grabbing my iPhone out of my purse. I typed out a short message.

15 minutes until showtime. Need to speak w/ you.

To my complete surprise, three dots appeared. That meant she was writing back.

@DD. Back in 5.

I showed my phone to Meg and Doug. "What does that mean?"

"No idea," said Doug.

Meg shook her head. "Sorry, Kit. Nada." She patted my back. "Don't worry. Her text said she'll be here in five minutes. Why don't you go wait for her at the entrance of the building?"

"Great idea, Meg," I said. "You guys should grab seats." I looked around the crowded room. "Or else you might have to stand."

As far as I knew, Maeve had never visited the town of Duck before. A number of possibilities raced through my head. *Department of Defense? Dolby Digital? Donald Duck? Dungeons and Dragons? Dunkin' Donuts?* None of these options made any sense. I hoped it wasn't military code for a distress signal and I'd failed to understand her desperate plea for help.

I'd reached the foyer when I heard a familiar laugh. Sure enough, Representative Dixon had arrived. To my surprise, she was had a smudge of chocolate on the side of her mouth. With a white paper bag in hand, she was accompanied by an attractive woman in her forties with long flowing brown hair.

"Have people started to arrive?" she asked nonchalantly.

"Yes, Congresswoman." I tried to hide the annoyance in my voice. "I've been looking for you. Where did you go?"

Dixon licked the end of her finger. "Duck Donuts, of course. Where else would you go in Duck?"

Had aliens arrived on Earth and replaced my boss with a doppelgänger? "You're eating doughnuts?"

"Not just any doughnuts, Kit. The world-famous Duck Donuts. You haven't heard of them?" asked Dixon.

"I can't say I have," I said. "I wasn't aware you ate doughnuts." My boss adhered to a strict exercise regimen and a diet consisting of protein bars, vegetables, grilled chicken, and low-fat dishes. I wasn't even aware she knew what a doughnut was.

The woman standing next to her spoke up. "I'm afraid I introduced her. I'm Thalia Godfrey. I believe you met my husband Ronan earlier."

The mayor's wife. "Yes, we did." I offered my hand and introduce myself.

"Ronan was too busy to take the congresswoman to our most famous establishment, so I offered to do so," she said. "I do believe she enjoyed it."

"Made-to-order doughnuts," said Maeve. "Really, Kit. I can't believe you haven't heard of them."

I guess I've been too busy trying to get you elected to the United States Senate. Suppressing my inner voice was often a wise move.

"I will make sure I visit during my vacation," I said. "I'll be in Duck for a week after the town hall meeting."

Thalia beamed. "How lovely. Be sure to come to my yoga class. I host it every day at noon on the lawn in front of this building. It's

completely free to the visiting public."
Not on my list of three places. Not even close.
"Thank you, Thalia. I will tell my family and friends about it," I said. If Dixon lost her Senate bid, maybe I had a future as a diplomat at the State Department.

Speaking of family, I wondered if Sebastian had taken Gary Brewster's call. I certainly hoped not. My one and only sibling frequently caused trouble at the most inconvenient moments. If discontent was already brewing, I didn't need to add Sebastian to the mix.

"Congresswoman, can I speak with you before you head inside for the meeting?" I asked sweetly.

Dixon shot me a puzzled look. She knew I wouldn't make such a request so close to the start of an event unless something was up.

Maeve turned toward Thalia. "I'd better catch up with my chief of staff before the discussion begins. Thank you for your time."

Thalia smiled warmly. "Anytime. And I'd better say hello to my husband before he goes on stage."

I motioned for Dixon to follow me down a hallway that was out of the flow of incoming town hall attendees. "Listen, I think there might be some fireworks at this meeting."

Dixon sighed. "Haven't we seen it all, Kit?"

"We have, but just because this seems like a lazy beach town, it doesn't mean there's not controversy over local issues."

Maeve smoothed her brown hair. "I appreciate the warning." She motioned toward the restroom. "I need to touch up my makeup. I'll see you inside."

I exhaled deeply, my duty as a conscientious congressional aide fulfilled. I couldn't always prevent disasters, but at least I could send up a warning flag. In two hours, I looked forward to hauling my suitcase inside our beach house and starting a week filled with relaxation, reading, and recreation. Noticeably absent from the list was politics, campaigns, and voter strategies. Even I needed a break every once in a while.

The meeting hall was now completely full. Every seat had been filled, which was either a very good or very bad sign. It might mean residents were excited about the prospect of a Dixon campaign for Senate and they wanted to see the young, upstart military-veteran-turned-politician in person. On the other hand, if Gary Brewster's allusion to controversy were correct, then a packed crowd might mean we were in for a rough ride.

As I was about to take my reserved seat in the front row, I saw a tall, lanky guy enter the meeting hall wearing a t-shirt advertising the phrase "The Solution Is Less Pollution." His bushy dishwater blond locks stuck out from underneath a tattered baseball hat. Of course, this was no stranger. It was my brother, Sebastian Marshall. While I certainly hoped everyone was here to see my boss in action, the nefarious motive for the high-volume attendance had just become the likelier explanation. There was no time for me to tell Sebastian in person that he needed to behave. But I could rely on modern technology to make sure he got the message. I pulled out my iPhone and texted him.

Please keep it to a dull roar, little brother.

I stared at the screen, hoping he'd at least acknowledge my plea. Sure enough, he wrote back instantly.

Relax, big sis. I'm here to support an old friend.

Famous last words. But at least Sebastian wasn't planning anything big. My brother had a lot of tricks up his sleeve but lying wasn't one of them.

Maeve Dixon and Ronan Godfrey entered the room to polite applause from the crowd. Godfrey took the podium first and began speaking.

"Thank you, residents of Duck and others who have joined us from neighboring towns on the Outer Banks. It's a beautiful summer day, and it's encouraging to know so many of you decided to spend your time getting to know your elected representatives a little better." He took a breath. "As you know, I'm the mayor of Duck, and it's my privilege to introduce you to Congresswoman Maeve Dixon." He licked his lips playfully. "Who knows, someday, she might be Senator Dixon."

Godfrey motioned for Maeve to take the podium. "Without further delay, let's give her a warm Outer Banks welcome." He motioned for applause. Several people began to clap, but stopped when a short woman with tight, curly auburn hair stood up.

"Not so fast, Ronan," she shouted, her fist in the air. "You need to pay for what you've done!"

There were audible voices of support from the crowd. Obviously, the woman had not come to the meeting alone. She'd brought reinforcements.

I turned my attention back to the stage. Maeve had started to stand, but instead sat back down in her seat. I motioned with my hand for her to stay put. If she tried to interject herself, the crowd would end up turning against her. It was best to stay out of the line of fire and let the so-called "popular" Mayor Ronan handle it.

Godfrey gripped the sides of the podium so tightly I could see the whites of his knuckles. Clearly, he hadn't anticipated a surly crowd.

"Now, Jean, this isn't the time or the place to discuss personal business," he said. Although he might have been right, his tone was patronizing. I sank back into my seat. So much for a sleepy beach town. This place was a hotspot, and it had nothing to do with the balmy temperature outside.

Jean wasn't about to be cowed. "It certainly is, Ronan. When the mayor of this town uses his influence to force a business owner out of her rented space, it's perfectly relevant for a public forum."

There was a low buzz in the crowd as people whispered to each other. Ronan cleared his throat. "There has been plenty of discussion about the investment we need to make in this town if we want to make it the number one beach destination in the country." He pointed his finger in the air. "We must feature the right businesses in the right locations to attract vacationers who want to spend serious money here."

"Even if it means ruining the businesses which have been here for years?" countered Jean.

Before Ronan could respond, a younger African American woman stood and raised her voice. "And what about the rumor you want to restrict dog access to our beaches?"

A collective gasp could be heard throughout the crowd. I glanced on stage. Maeve looked like she wished she'd eaten two doughnuts instead of just one. It would have been time better spent than sitting on stage while Mayor Godfrey got skewered alive.

"Now, Lacy, you know that's not a firm proposal," said Ronan. He wiped a bead of sweat off his forehead. "As a businesswoman, you know we need to figure out the best policy for a premier destination resort town such as Duck. We all want to stay the number one choice for people vacationing with dogs, but we may need to tighten up our policy in the future."

An older woman who was sitting next to me bristled. "Premier destination town? This place is fine the way it is," she muttered.

A younger man I hadn't seen earlier stood and waved his hand. "If you want to increase tourism in Duck, what does that mean for the environmental footprint?" Heads nodded in the audience as he continued. "More visitors mean additional strain on resources, like our water supply. Not to mention more trash to haul away."

Uh-oh. That guy had cracked the door open an inch. It was about to get blown apart.

Sure enough, a familiar voice entered the fray. My brother Sebastian didn't bother to raise his hand. He'd had a lot of experience as a semi-professional protester of sorts. In these scenarios, no one asked permission to speak.

"Mr. Mayor, how is this town preparing for sea level rise that will erode the beach in the next ten to twenty years?" Sebastian had his hands on his hips, assembled in a defensive posture.

I glanced at my boss. Her head was slightly tilted to the side, and there was a curious look on her face. She'd met Sebastian once or twice, and Maeve Dixon rarely forgot a face.

Godfrey looked similarly puzzled. "Pardon me, but are you new to Duck? I don't believe I've met you before."

Sebastian didn't miss a beat. He'd undoubtedly faced this question before in other local meetings. "I am new to Duck, but I've been a citizen of the world my entire life. And this problem is a global one."

Several people applauded. Sebastian certainly knew how to turn an argument on its head.

Godfrey stuttered. "We're all concerned about the planet, sir."

He paused for a moment. "That's why I opened an organic wine bar in town."

Jean stood again. "And it displaced my pizza shop from its waterfront location. That restaurant has been in my family for over a decade, and now its future is in jeopardy!"

Sebastian chimed back in. "An organic wine bar is hardly the equivalent of preserving the coastline and its ecosystem."

The mayor scanned the room nervously. He'd lost control, but could he regain it?

"Our guest has come a long way to meet you," he said weakly. "Please join me in giving her a big Duck welcome."

A few attendees clapped, but the damage was done. The oxygen had been sucked out of the room; this town meeting was officially on life support. Maeve walked to the podium and smiled widely. "Thank you, Mr. Mayor. It's been quite a revealing visit thus far."

My boss then launched into her standard stump speech about the policy priorities she supported, outlining her vision for sensible federal spending coupled with a simpler tax system. It wasn't fancy or complex, yet her message had seemed to resonate in the other towns across the state we'd visited earlier in the month.

The audience didn't interrupt her ten-minute spiel. Then she opened the floor for questions about her speech. But the Duckers (was that an appropriate moniker for those who lived there?) had other ideas.

"Maybe you can tell us how you plan to save the wild horses in Corolla?" I turned around to see who was speaking. It was Gary Brewster, the guy who'd invited Sebastian to attend the meeting.

"I'm doing everything I can because I understand the importance of preserving this population of horses for the Outer Banks community," said Maeve. Then she added slyly. "Perhaps in the future I'll be in a better position to advance the cause."

"Better make sure the Corolla horses don't want to operate a business," said Jean, the pizza parlor owner. "Our mayor would sell the land right from underneath them if it meant he could make a fast buck."

Sebastian stood up again. "The pursuit of capitalism shouldn't sacrifice the character of the community and the environment surrounding it!" He raised his fisted hand in triumph, and the crowd responded in thunderous applause.

After the clapping subsided, other attendees shouted out questions and angry thoughts. While the melee continued, I watched as Maeve Dixon slowly moved away from the podium. I saw her gently nudge Mayor Godfrey in the direction of the microphone.

I could practically read Maeve's mind. *You broke it, you bought it.*

"Ladies and gentlemen," said Mayor Godfrey in a shaky voice. "I'll be happy to speak with each of you individually in the near future."

He reached underneath the podium, grabbed a gavel, and pounded the top of the lectern. "This meeting is adjourned!"

The hall erupted in another round of raucous complaints and jeers. Sebastian conferred with the pizza parlor owner Jean. A moment later, a chant broke out amongst the crowd.

"RONAN MUST GO! RONAN MUST GO! RONAN MUST GO!"

It wasn't the most inventive phrase I'd heard from a politically incensed mob, but it certainly rattled the intended victim. The mayor exhibited a glassy stare as he slowly rocked back and forth. I hoped he wasn't going to crumple to the floor and hyperventilate.

Maeve Dixon must have observed his obvious despair. Although my boss was a tough customer, she wasn't heartless. Dixon walked back over to the podium and put her hand on Ronan's forearm, guiding him gently offstage.

I looked around for the mayor's wife, Thalia. Had she left, embarrassed by her husband's political debacle? No, she was still inside the hall. But instead of comforting Ronan, she was chatting, seemingly in an amiable fashion, with pizza parlor Jean, Sebastian, Gary, and the older man we'd met in the foyer who served on the town council, Tobias Potter.

Torn by the myriad of duties which confronted me, I tried to decide whether I should chastise Sebastian for his inciting behavior or alert Thalia to her husband's obviously fragile state of mind. After a moment's calculation, I realized the former could wait. I was spending the following week with Sebastian in our vacation house. That meant there was plenty of time to scold my brother and remind him that siblings shouldn't sabotage each other, even when political protests were involved.

I made a beeline for Thalia and her interlocutors. "Excuse me, Thalia," I said in my most polite I'm-in-the-South-so-I'd-better-turn-on-the-charm voice. "The congresswoman is with your husband, but perhaps you might want to check on him."

All eyes turned to Ronan Godfrey, who still looked like he'd just seen the ghost of his dead grandmother. Politics was no joke. It wasn't for everyone. Godfrey had been a tech tycoon before moving to the Outer Banks and becoming the mayor, which likely explained his business-oriented approach to governance. He might have seen some tough customers in his previous life, but I bet it was pale in comparison to what he'd experienced publicly today.

Instead of rushing to her husband's side, Thalia bristled. Fiddling with her slightly disheveled, cascading hair, she inhaled deeply and closed her eyes. After a moment of what I surmised was self-meditation, she spoke evenly. "Tobias, would you please make sure Ronan has recovered from this afternoon's event?"

The balding man standing next to her nodded. "I can do that." He scurried off in the direction of the mayor and Maeve, who undoubtedly was relieved that I'd sent a reinforcement her way.

Thalia spoke directly to me. "Tobias serves on the town council and will know how to advise Ronan on such matters." She shifted her body and resumed her conversation with pizza parlor Jean as if nothing had happened.

It wasn't exactly the response I'd anticipated, but at least someone besides my boss was speaking to Ronan Godfrey now. Gary pointed across the room and pulled Sebastian's sleeve. "Let me introduce you to some like-minded people." Always eager to meet fellow soldiers in the green army, Sebastian followed Gary's lead.

Maeve Dixon extricated herself from the conversation and walked over to join me. I moved away from Thalia and pizza parlor

Jean since I was positive my boss would want to speak to me privately.

"Certainly not the ending to my listening tour that I'd hoped for," she said.

"Absolutely not." I shook my head. "We carefully researched each stop, and I don't remember any bad press about Ronan Godfrey."

Maeve Dixon waved her hand. "It's not your fault, Kit. Ronan said he recently started this initiative to make changes to the town. He might want to revise his approach."

That was the understatement of the year. "What about the woman who owns the pizza shop? What was that all about?"

Dixon leaned closer and lowered her voice. "I asked him. Apparently, Godfrey convinced the company who owns the real estate to kick her out so he could open his own wine bar on the location."

"Not the best political move in the world," I muttered. "Let's get you out of here. I don't think you're winning any potential votes down the road by being associated with him."

Doug and Meg were waiting for us outside of the meeting hall. "Great job, Representative Dixon," said Meg cheerily. "You were definitely the most popular politician on stage."

Dixon laughed. "That ain't saying much, Meg." She turned to me and placed her hand on my shoulder. "I'm staying at a hotel nearby in Kitty Hawk for the evening and then will join my family in Raleigh for a few days of relaxation." Her face softened. "Thank you for your hard work these past couple of weeks, Kit."

"Have you made a decision about running for Senate?" asked Doug. I shot him a warning glance, but it was too late. It was a sensitive subject, and I knew the choice would be stressful for Dixon. Running for the Senate meant giving up her seat in the House of Representatives. It was a gamble which could either result in a big boost to her career or the end of it. I'd stopped asking her about the decision so she could focus on the events we had scheduled for her listening tour.

Despite the nerve he'd undoubtedly hit, Maeve didn't flinch. "I plan to talk to my family and close friends about it in the coming days." She looked at all three of us. "Everyone should enjoy their vacation. Soon enough, we'll be back in Washington, dealing with killer schedules and more problems than we can fix."

Little did we know that soon enough, we'd feel right at home in the Outer Banks.

Chapter Three

SEBASTIAN WAS STILL BUSY TALKING with his eco-friendly, rabble-alerting friend and others who seemed riveted by the discussion. My reprimand for my little brother would have to wait until we were settled into our beach house. I loaded my suitcase into the Prius, which Doug had driven to the beach with Clarence as his co-pilot, and we turned north on Highway 12 to start our vacation.

I felt the stress of the past weeks leave my body as we drove by cute shops, restaurants, and the famous Duck Donuts. Doug and I took turns pointing out places we wanted to visit during our weeklong stay. Eventually, we turned onto a road lined with beautiful houses that led directly to a tranquil sea of blue water.

"This is going to be so much fun!" I squealed in delight.

Doug adjusted his prescription sunglasses. "I haven't heard you sound this excited since you last solved a murder, Kit."

I giggled. In addition to my job as a congressional chief of staff, I'd assisted the police in solving quite a few Capitol Hill crimes over the course of the past several years. "I think I really need a vacation, Doug."

"Well, you've come to the right place." Doug turned into the driveway of a large light blue beach house. I'd booked the house months ago when Maeve Dixon had decided to move ahead with her listening tour, and now I was delighted to see that it lived up to the photos I'd scrutinized online.

There was a big sign on the second-floor wraparound porch. DUCK DUCK GOOSE.

"What a clever name for a vacation house," I said. "We won't forget where we're staying."

Before we could get my suitcase out of the trunk, I heard a familiar staccato bark. Sure enough, our chunky beagle mutt, Clarence, came charging around the top balcony. He stared down at me from two floors above. "Hey, buddy!" I said.

He was immediately followed by Sebastian's girlfriend, Lisa, and her black Labrador police dog, Murphy. "Welcome to paradise!" said Lisa, who was an officer on the Capitol Hill police force.

Doug hauled my suitcase inside the house, and I braced myself for impact. Sure enough, Clarence barreled down the carpeted stairs. When he was almost at the bottom, he took a flying leap and tried to jump into my arms. Clarence was a big boy and not really as agile as he imagined. Instead, he knocked me backwards and I fell into Doug, who had his hands full with my bag. We both ended up crumpled on the floor with Clarence licking our faces.

Lisa looked down from the top of the stairs. "Are you guys okay down there?"

We signaled with our hands that we were indeed alive. After successfully disengaging Clarence, we managed to stand and make our way upstairs.

The second floor of the house was filled with bedrooms and attached baths, situated along a well-lit, cheery hallway. Doug pointed his finger toward the ceiling. "We've got the master bedroom on the third floor, Kit."

We made it up one more flight of stairs, and I walked past the gorgeous kitchen, complete with sparkling appliances, granite countertops, and a sizable kitchen island. It was certainly state-of-the-art, but other than brewing coffee in the morning and mixing drinks in the evening, I wouldn't be spending much time inside it. I rarely cooked when I was home, and I certainly wasn't going to spend my vacation anywhere near a stovetop.

Our bedroom was a different story. It was airy and spacious, painted a light yellow and decorated tastefully with seashell artwork and other beachside scenes. A king bed with a sea foam bedspread occupied most of the room. Clarence obviously approved. Before Doug could even place my suitcase on the bed, our beagle mutt jumped up and plopped himself in the dead center. He rolled on his back with his tongue lolled to the side.

"Someone is excited to be at the beach." I scratched Clarence's belly. "I missed you, buddy."

"Did you see the balcony, Kit?" Doug motioned for me to follow him to the sliding glass doors situated on the far side of the room.

After opening the vertical privacy blinds and the glass doors, we walked onto an expansive wraparound deck. Doug indicated I should keep following him around the corner. Sure enough, when we reached the rear of the house, I saw what he'd been eager for me to experience. The blue ocean glistened as the sound of gentle waves hitting the sand provided the background music.

I sat down in a wooden Adirondack chair and breathed deeply. "Pure heaven if I ever saw it."

Doug sat next to me. "You definitely deserve a break, Kit. I hope you're able to disconnect from the mayhem for a week."

I grabbed his hand. "I'll do my best."

He smiled as he squeezed my hand gently. "I'm going to hold you to that."

Our peaceful moment of bliss was interrupted by Meg, who appeared on the deck next to us. "Are you guys ready to p-a-r-t-y?" She drew out the last word in a sing-song voice. I'd missed Meg's daily exuberance since we stopped working together in Congress.

Meg's new beau Trevor appeared behind her. We'd known Trevor for years. He'd worked in a Senate office with us, became a high-priced defense lobbyist, written a tell-all book about Washington, and then finally settled into a relatively stable existence as a senior advisor to an important official in the House of Representatives. Trevor was usually clad in a stuffy suit, buttoned down shirt, and tie. In fact, I'm not sure I'd even seen Trevor wearing anything more casual than his usual Brooks Brothers attire.

Today he wore a light blue designer polo shirt, tailored brown shorts, and sandals. I didn't even know that Trevor had feet, but there they were. It was proof that all things were possible at the beach. Trevor had certainly come a long way from his days working in Senator Lyndon Langsford's office when he was more of an annoying nemesis than a friend.

The most unlikely development wasn't his more relaxed attire. It was the fact he'd pursued Meg romantically and succeeded. Their personalities were polar opposites, yet somehow, they'd found love. After a period of tumult last winter, they'd decided to become an exclusive couple and see where it would lead them. Apparently, the answer was the beaches of the Outer Banks.

Trevor nodded politely to each of us. "Kit, Dr. Hollingsworth."

Doug shook his head. "I've told you a million times. You can call me Doug."

Trevor pursed his lips. "Since we are on vacation together, I will abide by your wishes."

Although his attire might have changed, Trevor couldn't completely change his formal demeanor. "Trevor, are you excited to be at the beach?" I asked. Something told me Trevor wasn't exactly a beach bum.

"I don't know how to respond to your question, since I have never been on a beach vacation in my life," he said.

Meg interrupted. "He's excited. I mean, if nothing else, he's excited to be with me for seven days nonstop." She giggled and grabbed Trevor's hand.

"That is very true," said Trevor, with a degree of seriousness usually reserved for taking oaths of office.

"What should we do first?" asked Meg. "Hot tub? Swimming? Beach? Drinks?"

"Yes, to everything," I said. "But maybe not necessarily in that order."

Doug put his arm around me. "I think Kit is in desperate need of a break after that disastrous town hall meeting this afternoon."

"I don't even want to think about it," I said. "Speaking of disasters, where's my brother?"

"While you were settling in, Lisa left and went to the beach for a swim," said Trevor. "I don't think Sebastian has returned from the meeting. I take it from your comment it didn't go well for the congresswoman?"

"That would be an understatement," I said. "But it was a total debacle for the mayor of Duck, Ronan Godfrey."

Trevor raised his eyebrows. "Ronan Godfrey? The tech millionaire who sold his company in his thirties and retired from the business?"

"The one and only. He should have stuck to computers. I'm not sure he's a natural for the political world. He's trying to change the town of Duck and the residents don't seem too happy about it."

"I've only had a brief look around, but this town seems close to perfect already," said Doug. "Relaxed, charming, beautiful landscape. I wouldn't change a thing."

"From what I gather, he wants to make it even more high end. Sort of like a Martha's Vineyard for the Outer Banks," I explained.

Trevor peered down from underneath his glasses. "That seems overly ambitious."

"I suppose you can't really take the tech mogul out of Silicon Valley," I said. "Once a corporate titan, always a corporate titan. He's itching for a takeover."

Doug grabbed my hand. "Too much talk about politics," he chided. "Shall we take Clarence and Murphy to the beach?"

Clarence and Murphy heard their names and began wagging their behinds in excitement. I smiled. "Yes, that sounds like a perfect idea. Perhaps by the time we get there, Lisa will be out of the water and can join us."

"I'll get us some drinks to take while we walk," Meg said. "Three tries to guess what I have chilling in the fridge."

"Prosecco, Prosecco, and more Prosecco," I said, laughing. We loved the Italian bubbly. Meg liked the taste and I liked the low-calorie count. It was a match made in heaven. Well, technically, Prosecco was made in Italy.

Meg laughed. "You know me too well. Eariler in the day, Lisa took me to this lovely place in town called Sweet T's that serves both coffee and wine. That's where I stocked up."

"Sweet T's sounds like heaven," I said.

Ten minutes later, the four of us left the house and turned down the street for the short walk to the beach.

Meg wore a floppy straw hat. With light blonde hair and fair skin, Meg was not a fan of sun overexposure. On the other hand, I looked forward to getting a little color during our vacation. My medium length brown hair blew freely in the ocean air, and I began to feel the tension and stress leave my body.

We walked along the wooden boardwalk and up the flight of stairs to enter the beach area. "I'm so excited to introduce Clarence to the water," I said. "He's never been to the ocean before."

I had visions in my mind of our exuberant beagle mutt frolicking in the surf, chasing a floating yellow ball while sporting a doggie life preserver. I'd gone online and bought the appropriate beach gear for Clarence and made sure Doug had brought it with him. Clarence now sported his bright orange swim vest, and Doug had grabbed the ball on our way out the door.

We stood on the platform on top of the large sand dune which protected the beachfront houses from the surf and looked around. The water glistened a deep shade of blue as the waves gently rolled through. Dozens of sunbathers and swimmers dotted the landscape as far as I could see. I took a deep breath and exhaled slowly. This was perfection.

"Let's go!" said Doug.

As I took a step forward to descend to the beach, I felt a tug on the leash. Clarence had sat down and refused to move.

"Come on, buddy. It's time to go on the beach. You're going to love it!"

I gently pulled in the direction of the stairs leading to the sand. He refused to budge.

Doug, Meg, and Trevor were already strolling on the sand. "Doug!" I raised my voice. "There's something wrong with Clarence."

Doug jogged back to the wooden platform. "What's wrong?"

I pulled the leash. "He won't follow me."

Doug's eyes narrowed. "You baby Clarence an awful lot, Kit. If you lead him properly, he'll follow." He took the leash from my hand

and marched in the direction of the stairs. Clarence watched him but didn't lift a paw to follow.

"So much for that theory," I murmured.

Doug stared at our beagle mutt, who looked right back at him with his big, brown eyes. "I don't think he likes the beach," said Doug.

"How does he know?" I put my hands on my hips. "He's never even been to the beach before."

Doug sighed. He bent down and picked up Clarence, which was no easy task. After descending the stairs, he placed him gently on the sand. Clarence looked skeptical, but immediately started digging.

"See!" I exclaimed. "He's a natural."

Doug shook his head. "I'm not so sure about that, Kit."

It turned out that Clarence's fancy orange life preserver vest didn't serve much of a purpose other than a canine fashion statement. I cajoled, begged, and pleaded to no avail. Clarence wasn't going anywhere near the water.

Meg came over and handed me a pink plastic sippy cup. I looked at it skeptically. "What am I, a toddler?"

My best friend put her hands on her hips. "It's what you use when you enjoy a drink while walking on the beach, Kit. You can't walk down the shoreline swinging a bottle of wine, can you?"

"Sorry," I said quickly. "My mood will improve. I'm upset that Clarence doesn't seem to want to enjoy the ocean. I had such high hopes."

Meg reached down and removed his swimming vest. "First, you need to get rid of this. It's ridiculous."

"But he'll need that if he goes into the water," I protested. "I read about it online. It's recommended for safety."

"Kit, Clarence isn't going anywhere near the water. Didn't you tell me he hates baths and being outside in the rain?"

"Yes," I said weakly.

"He's perfectly happy to stick to land. You shouldn't try to make Clarence into something he's not," she said.

Meg's words hit me. Of course, she was right. Clarence wasn't a water dog. I needed to stop projecting. I took a deep breath and gave Meg a half-hug. "You always know exactly the right thing to say. From this moment onwards, I vow to relax on this vacation."

I clinked my sippy cup with Meg's and took a big gulp. Unfortunately, my vow would soon be broken.

Chapter Four

"Clarence, go back to bed," I said grumpily. I grabbed my iPhone from the nightstand to look at the time. It was half past six, way too early to wake up on vacation.

Clarence ignored my plea. Apparently, he hadn't embraced the concept of sleeping in late on vacation. After intensifying his whimpers, he placed his paw on my face. I opened my eyes.

"Whatever. You win." I got out of bed and threw on a t-shirt and shorts. I finally located my running shoes underneath a beach towel.

Doug turned over. "Where are you going?" he asked in a half-awake voice.

"Clarence needs to go out. I might as well take him for a jog." Clarence and I jogged most mornings when the weather permitted it. Without my running partner for the past three weeks, I'd definitely slackened off my exercise routine. Vacation was a perfect opportunity to get back into it.

Doug mumbled something incomprehensible, although it sounded like, "Bebe werewolf." I took that to mean, "Be careful" or a related derivative.

Clarence's leash and harness were in the kitchen. I closed the bedroom door behind me and was surprised to see Sebastian's girlfriend, Lisa, sitting on couch in the adjacent living room.

"I didn't think anyone else would be up at this ungodly hour, especially on vacation," I said.

"Murphy and I like to go for a run in the morning," said Lisa. "We're headed out now." She saw the leash and harness in my hand. "Can we join you?"

I gulped. Lisa was a police officer with the Capitol Hill force. Slim and sprightly, I imagined she was a first-rate runner. Murphy was no slouch, either. A black lab, he was bigger than Clarence, but served as a professional canine sniffer for the police. He was a working dog and maintained the required physique for his service. However, Sebastian had been dating Lisa for six months, and it seemed serious. I was looking forward to getting to know Lisa better during our vacation—no time like the present, even if it meant a little sweat was required.

"Sure," I said tentatively. "We're not fast runners, though. We're more like . . ." I searched to find the right words. "Lackadaisical joggers."

Lisa laughed. "No worries. We're not training for any races these days." She scratched Murphy's head.

"I'll meet you downstairs in five minutes," I said.

I scurried around to find plastic doggie bags and made sure Clarence had a drink of water. Lisa and Murphy were waiting for us outside the house.

"Let's run around the streets near the beach and then we can double back on the other side of the highway on the Duck boardwalk," suggested Lisa.

We settled into a moderately paced run. I was pretty certain that Lisa was moving considerably slower than her typical pace. I was thankful she'd shown mercy to me and Clarence, who had obviously missed our runs, too. We were both huffing and puffing five minutes into our workout.

"Have you been to the Outer Banks before?" I asked. "You seem to know where to go." If I kept my sentences short, I'd still be able to speak with Lisa. I wouldn't be reciting the Lincoln Douglas debates, but hopefully I could keep the conversation going.

"My family vacationed here when I was a kid," she said. "We rented houses in Kill Devil Hills, Kitty Hawk, Duck, and Corolla. My dad never liked staying in the same house twice, so we vacationed in many of these towns over the years."

"Are you excited to be back here?" I asked.

"Definitely," she said. "I also needed a break and time to think. Did Sebastian tell you about the FBI?"

I shook my head. Even short sentences were getting harder. Clarence's tongue was lolling along the side of his mouth. He stopped abruptly to use the bathroom, thank goodness. Both of us could use the short break to catch our breath.

Lisa kept chatting as I took care of Clarence's business. "The FBI has a special program for canines. Special agents are the handlers. I've applied to the program."

"Lisa, that's great news," I said. "Would Murphy go with you?"

"I think so," she said. "They have a preference for Labradors, and he'd fit well into the program, either sniffing for drugs or explosives."

Lisa indicated it was time for us to cross over Highway 12 so we could start our way back on the opposite side of the peninsula. We jogged onto a wooden boardwalk that ran alongside the marshy sound. Numerous businesses, from ice cream shops to fashionable apparel stores, dotted the boardwalk. The serene landscape of the sound was filled with birds and other wildlife—too bad I hadn't brought my phone. I would have loved to take a picture to capture the moment.

"Would that mean relocation?" I asked. There had to be a reason why Lisa chose to discuss this issue during our run.

"Most likely. After training, I would be stationed where the Bureau needed me and Murphy," she said.

I fell silent, mostly because we were now into the third mile of our run, and it was the farthest distance I'd moved at one time in a while. I also needed to ponder Lisa's revelation. Perhaps it was a good thing I hadn't had the energy to berate Sebastian last night about his behavior at the town hall meeting when we'd enjoyed a dinner of hot dogs and hamburgers poolside. Lisa's possible career change was probably weighing on his mind heavily.

Murphy's loud bark shocked me out of my deep thought. He and Lisa were several steps ahead of me and Clarence. It only took a second before Clarence joined in. Both dogs, who had behaved reasonably well during the jog thus far, were going berserk. We were next to an open-air bar, the quintessential waterside spot. Instead of tiki mugs, several dozen sparkling wine glasses were hung upside down over the bar. It was like someone had taken a swanky wine bar from Manhattan and plopped it down next to the Currituck Sound.

Clarence and Murphy's crazy behavior escalated quickly. Now they were pulling toward the edge of the boardwalk. Murphy had dragged Lisa to the side railing and Clarence wasn't far behind. I looked down to figure out what might be causing the fuss and that's when I saw the crimson stains on Clarence's white paws. A red, liquid substance covered the immediate area of the wooden boardwalk.

I raised my voice. "Lisa! There's something all over the ground. Look at Clarence's paws."

She glanced back to look at Clarence, but Murphy, who was at least seventy-five pounds of pure doggie muscle, dragged her in the other direction. "Murphy, what's wrong with you?" she scolded. As a police dog, Murphy typically was well behaved. However, much like Clarence, he was known to have his moments.

"Lisa, hold him back." I bent down to examine Clarence's paws. *Was that blood?* "There may have been an accident here."

My words came too late. Murphy stuck his head through the wooden railing slats and was barking his head off. Lisa peered over the wooden structure into the marshy waters below. She turned around and put her hand up as a warning.

"I don't know if it was accident or something else, but there's a dead body down there," she said.

I felt my face become flush, and it wasn't because of the jog. *How could this happen again?*

"Maybe someone had one too many at the wine bar and fell over the railing," I said.

Lisa shook her head. "I doubt it. This railing is too high. It was likely built to prevent that from happening. Unless someone was deliberately trying to climb over it, and I don't know why that would be the case."

She pulled out her cell phone from the arm band she wore when exercising. "None of these businesses along the water are open yet. I'm going to call 9-1-1."

Lisa moved away from the railing and stepped to the side of the boardwalk. Curious walkers stared at us as they strolled by, but no one had stopped to ask what the fuss was about.

I moved over to the spot where Lisa and Murphy had discovered the body. I knew I shouldn't look, but how could I not? *Curiosity killed the cat.* Wasn't there another part of that old proverb? *Satisfaction brought the cat back.* Of course, I wasn't a cat and I certainly didn't have nine lives.

When the police arrived, we'd probably be stuck here for a while. No harm in sneaking a peek before the authorities walled off the area. I peered down into the marsh. The body of a man was floating on top of the reeds and vegetation. He was several feet away from the railing and his face was partially obscured. But I did recognize the clothes he was wearing: light brown linen pants and a dark blue blazer. Mayor Ronan Godfrey was a dead duck.

Chapter Five

"Lisa, come over here!" I motioned for her to join me by the railing.

"Kit, you shouldn't be contaminating the crime scene. It's bad enough we stumbled through it once." She remained where she was.

"Okay, Ms. Police Officer," I grumbled as I walked over to join her. "But I know the dead guy."

Lisa narrowed her eyes. "You've been in the Outer Banks for fewer than twenty-four hours. How could you possibly know the victim?"

"It's Ronan Godfrey," I said. "He's the mayor."

Lisa eyes popped. "That's the mayor of Duck lying in the marsh?"

"Afraid so. He participated in the town hall meeting yesterday with my boss. I can't quite see his face, but I recognize the clothes he was wearing."

"Yikes. That'll make this investigation a top priority. Isn't he a millionaire?"

"Something like that. He dropped out of the tech world and relocated here. He was recently elected mayor and had been making some changes in town," I said. "In fact, I think this is the wine bar he opened."

We turned around to look at the open-air bar. A large sign at the entrance read "Sonoma Sunsets." Underneath, in smaller lettering, it said: "The Only Organic Wine Bar in the Outer Banks."

We walked over to the row of tall bar stools that spanned its length. I glanced down and realized there was more of the sticky red substance that Clarence had on his paws.

I pointed at the floor. "Lisa, look down here."

"Be careful, Kit. You don't want to mess up any evidence," she said.

"Take Clarence for a minute." I shoved the leash in her hand before she had a chance to object. We already knew about Ronan, and his fate was abundantly clear. What if someone else had been injured?

I carefully avoided any red substance as I made my way slowly around the bar. As I turned the corner, which led to the side of the bar where the staff worked, I saw the guilty culprit. A wine bottle had been smashed and its contents flowed from the point of impact.

"I found something!" I exclaimed.

"What is it?" Lisa didn't budge from her spot in the middle of the boardwalk.

"There's a broken wine bottle. I think the sticky red substance on Clarence's paws might be red wine." I bent down to get a closer look at the floor. The wine bottle had shattered into what seemed a million pieces. I didn't see anything else of significance, so I got up and walked back to Lisa and the dogs.

Lisa rubbed her chin. "Maybe there was a fight and Ronan somehow ended up dead."

"That sounds like you're saying it's a homicide," I said. "If it was an accident, someone would have reported it by now. Ronan wouldn't be lying in a marsh."

Lisa handed back Clarence's leash. "Let's wait for the police to arrive. They'll sort everything out."

I liked Lisa, especially since she'd provided much needed stability for my unpredictable brother. But we had precious few minutes before law enforcement arrived. If this was a murder, I wanted to take advantage of unadulterated access to the crime scene. As a law enforcement officer, Lisa didn't have the instincts of an amateur sleuth.

"Is the broken wine bottle connected to the fact Ronan is dead?" I asked. "Did someone hit him with it? Or was there was a struggle before Ronan ended up in the water?"

Lisa crinkled her forehead. "If this was foul play, something had to subdue Ronan before he ended up in the water." She motioned for me to return to the corner of the boardwalk. "It looks pretty shallow. Maybe one or two feet of water in this marshy part of the sound? It could cause drowning, but only if the person was unconscious. Otherwise, he would have been able to stand and walk or crawl out of the water."

"You can drown in shallow water, right?" I asked.

Lisa nodded. "About a quarter of all drowning deaths occur in shallow water, which means three feet or less. Many times, it's because someone loses footing in a swift current. In this case, I would guess the victim was incapacitated."

Lisa was turning out to be valuable. "Perhaps he was intoxicated," I said. "After all, he did own a wine bar."

Lisa looked at the railing and gave it a shake. "I don't think so. This structure is high and sturdy. You couldn't accidentally stumble over it. He probably went over unwillingly."

We were so engrossed in our conversation we hadn't heard anyone arrive on the boardwalk until a commanding woman's voice rang out from behind us. "Did someone call the police about a possible fatality?"

The two of us turned around to find a compact, dark-haired muscular woman in her thirties dressed in jeans and a polo shirt with the Kitty Hawk police insignia in the upper right corner.

Lisa stepped forward. "That would be me." She offered her hand. "Lisa Reddy. Law enforcement officer for the Capitol Hill police in Washington, D.C."

The Outer Banks officer winced slightly. Lisa might have missed it, but I was used to paying attention to body language when dealing with constituents and sometimes duplicitous lobbyists. I'd learned to monitor first impressions.

She accepted Lisa's hand and shook it lightly. "Carla Gomez. Detective for the Kitty Hawk police. We're a neighboring community here on the Outer Banks. I was called to the scene due to the serious nature of the crime."

Detective Gomez's occupied a wide stance, with her hips squarely facing both of us. Despite being vertically challenged, she must have read that women who occupy greater physical space exhibit a more commanding presence. If that was the case, Gomez certainly had achieved the desired goal. I got the impression crime didn't pay in Kitty Hawk.

"I can show you what we discovered by accident when we were jogging on the boardwalk," said Lisa. "In fact, it was my dog, Murphy, who alerted us to the body. He's a police canine."

Gomez's eyes grew wider. She was dealing with a team of police veterans and had to adjust her attitude accordingly. From the look on her face, she wasn't too happy about it.

Lisa recounted the entire story to Detective Gomez, including the fact that we had walked through the sticky substance spread throughout the area around the bar. Then Lisa turned to me. After an introduction, she explained that I might be able to identify the victim.

Gomez's cheeks blazed. "And why would that be the case? Aren't you both tourists from Washington?"

"I arrived yesterday with my boss, Congresswoman Maeve Dixon, for a town hall meeting at the Duck municipal building," I explained. "It was the last stop on her North Carolina listening tour. She *might* be running for Senate." I tried to emphasize the word "might." We'd already made news by finding a corpse. I certainly didn't want to make political headlines, too.

Gomez wrinkled her nose. "A politician? I would have guessed as much from D.C."

I ignored the snide remark. Washington and its so-called swamp inhabitants weren't going to win many popularity contests these days.

"We were hosted by the mayor of Duck. Perhaps you might know him? His name is, or was, Ronan Godfrey," I said.

Gomez snorted. "Tech guru turned millionaire who bought his way into local politics here. Everyone knows him."

"Then it won't be too difficult for you to identify the body," I said. "Because I'm almost certain he's the person lying in the marsh over there."

A flicker of worry passed over Gomez's face. She wasn't expecting that news. The detective walked over to the edge of the boardwalk and peered over.

"It looks like that could be Godfrey," she said. "How did you know it was him? You said you only met him once."

"His clothes," I said quickly. "I remembered what he wore to the town hall meeting yesterday."

Gomez's face twitched. "Fairly observant for a civilian."

Lisa interjected, "Oh, Kit isn't an ordinary civilian. She's helped with several murders on Capitol Hill."

Gomez turned back to face me. "Now, isn't that convenient? You're involved in murders in Washington and now we have one on our hands here in sleepy Duck. And the victim just so happens to be a politician."

"You misunderstood what I said," said Lisa, stepping forward. "Kit *solves* the murders."

As well-meaning as she was, Lisa wasn't doing me any favors. "What my friend is trying to say is that I've assisted law enforcement in the past with homicide investigations."

Gomez shrugged. "Whatever happens in the big city isn't my concern. However, I can tell you that in this neck of the woods, I'll be running the show." She placed both hands on her hips. "Do you understand? And that goes for police officers who are outside of their jurisdiction, too."

Lisa nodded. "We understand, Detective. Perhaps we should get out of your way."

"Stand over there." She pointed to an area of the boardwalk adjacent to the Sonoma Sunsets bar. "But don't leave. I may need to ask you more questions."

We retreated with the dogs to the spot Gomez had indicated. "She's a tough customer," I said.

"Not exactly the most collegial," agreed Lisa. "To be fair, I doubt they have many murders here. She's going to be under a lot of pressure to solve this one."

"How long do you think she'll keep us?" I glanced down at Clarence and Murphy, who were both panting. "The dogs need water."

"If you take Murphy's leash, I can run to Duck Donuts and get water for us. I know they're open early in the morning. It's only about a half mile that way." Lisa pointed away from the crime scene.

"Can you also let everyone at the house know we've been unexpectedly detained?" Doug would eventually wake up from his deep slumber and wonder why Clarence and I had not returned.

"Will do." Lisa gave me a two-fingered salute as she dashed off in the opposite direction.

Law enforcement and other officials were beginning to arrive. This section of the boardwalk was now cordoned off with yellow police tape. As more people came upon the scene, Detective Gomez's attention was diverted to other matters. I tried to come up with plausible theories about what happened to poor Ronan Godfrey last night. Now that I knew about the broken wine bottle near the bar, I could see that the wine and potentially blood stains trickled all the way over to the edge of the boardwalk. Lisa was right. The railing on the boardwalk was too high. He couldn't have accidentally stumbled over it or under it. How did he end up in the marshy edges of the sound?

I stepped back and surveyed the scene, and then it hit me. There was a dock only a few feet away from the boardwalk which projected at least twenty-five yards into the waters of the sound. I looked around for Detective Gomez. She was busy talking to a guy in a Dare County Coroner windbreaker. She was definitely occupied for the moment. Even though she'd told us to stay out of the way, I needed to figure out if my theory was right.

I bent down and whispered to Clarence and Murphy. "We're going to check something out, guys. Try to act inconspicuous." Both dogs panted and slobbered, which I assumed meant they understood the plan. I hoped Lisa had decided to sprint rather than jog and she'd be back with water soon.

We walked slowly over to the boardwalk and bypassed all those who were taking official crime scene photos and extracting the body from the marsh. Sure enough, the dock that ran perpendicular to the boardwalk wasn't secured with the same type of railing. Instead, there was just a rope that ran the length of the dock, which led to a boat launch and fishing pier further out into the sound. The water was likely too shallow at the edges of the sound to launch a recreational kayak, hence the necessity for a dock that extended into the depths of the sound.

If someone had gotten into an altercation with Ronan, perhaps hitting him with a wine bottle, then it would have been fairly easy to shove him underneath the rope and into the water below. We inched closer so I could inspect the area of the dock closest to the boardwalk. Sure enough, in the sunlight, I spotted the glistening of red. I bent down on my haunches to take a better look. The icky substance we'd seen elsewhere on the boardwalk was here, too.

"I think we figured it out," I said to Clarence and Murphy, who both responded with vigorous tail wags. Luckily, neither of them licked the evidence.

Then I heard a familiar voice behind me. "And what did you just figure out?"

I got up from the crouched position and turned around. Detective Gomez was glaring at me. To say the least, she did not look pleased.

"I wondered how Ronan ended up in the water," I explained. "The boardwalk railing is too high for an accident. Then I noticed this area of the dock doesn't have the same type of fencing around it."

I gestured towards the rope and paused. Gomez still looked annoyed, but I had her attention. "Go on, Ms. Marshall. I'm waiting."

"There are smears of the red substance right here." I pointed to the ground. "I think Ronan Godfrey was attacked with a wine bottle and then probably stumbled in this direction." I motioned to indicate the short distance between Sonoma Sunsets and where we were standing. "Then the killer finished off the job by pushing him underneath the rope and off the dock. He was probably unconscious. That's why he drowned in shallow water."

"Follow me," said Gomez. Clarence, Murphy, and I trailed

behind her to the area where I had been standing with Lisa.

"Didn't I tell you not to leave this spot?" asked the detective, her hands firmly on her hips.

"Yes, ma'am," I said weakly.

"And where is your friend? Did she not listen to direction, either?" she asked. "I expect better cooperation from a fellow police officer."

Thankfully, I spotted Lisa in the distance. She was headed in our direction with a plastic bowl and two bottles of water in her hands.

"She's coming back right now. The dogs needed water," I said.

Lisa jogged up to us. "Here's some water for us and the pups."

Gomez shook her head. "I'm not sure what arrangement you have in Washington with the police, Ms. Marshall. In my jurisdiction, you will do as you're told."

Lisa's eyebrows shot up, but she said nothing.

A uniformed police officer called out. "Detective Gomez, there's two men here to see you about the incident."

Gary Brewster and Tobias Potter, whom we'd met yesterday at the town hall meeting, were standing next to the yellow police tape.

"Great. The natives are already arriving," muttered Gomez. Then she looked directly at us. "Stay put. This time, I mean it."

Lisa waited until Detective Gomez had left us. After giving the dogs water in the plastic dish, she handed me the other bottle. "What did I miss?"

I explained how I'd come up with a theory about Ronan's death. Lisa frowned. "You need to let the local police handle this, Kit. You don't have a lot of political clout here."

I shrugged my shoulders. "Force of habit, I guess. We're on vacation so I suppose I should back off."

Our conversation was interrupted by raised voices in the direction where Gary Brewster and Tobias Potter had gathered. "Who are those guys? Do you know them?" she asked.

"I met them briefly yesterday at the town hall meeting. The older balding guy is Tobias Potter. He's on the town council and seems friendly with Ronan Godfrey's wife," I said.

"What about the other one?" asked Lisa.

"That's Gary Brewster. He knows Sebastian from his environmental causes. He's the reason why Sebastian came to the public meeting. When Gary found out he was in the Outer Banks, he asked him to attend."

Our discussion was interrupted by the loud voices of the two men. "Why can't you give us additional information?" demanded Tobias.

"For God's sake, I'm Ronan's business partner," said Gary.

Detective Gomez seemed unfazed. "We have procedures, gentlemen. No matter who is involved, I'm not deviating from them."

Tobias spotted me and Lisa. "Why are those two allowed within the police perimeter?"

I grabbed Lisa's hand. "We'd better go over there. I don't want Detective Gomez speaking for either of us."

As we joined them, Gomez gestured towards us. "I just explained you are both material witnesses to a suspicious death."

Tobias pointed at me. "I know her. She was at the town hall meeting yesterday with that congresswoman. And her brother was the one who caused a lot of trouble for Ronan."

"Tobias, calm down. Sebastian Marshall is an old friend of mine. I asked him to attend the meeting because I know he's interested in the issues that residents wanted to raise," said Gary.

It was too late. Detective Gomez was instantly interested. "Your brother was at this meeting yesterday? He's also from out of town?"

"Yes, but it was just a coincidence. Gary and Sebastian knew each other from their involvement in environmental causes," I said. "Otherwise, he wouldn't have had a reason to attend."

"What happened at this public meeting?" Gomez pulled out her notepad and was poised to write.

Before I could answer, Tobias spoke up. "The mayor got clobbered, at least politically speaking. It was a real mess. Lots of people were yelling, including her brother." He pointed at me again.

Gomez turned to me. "Is your brother still in town?"

"Yes, we're on vacation together. We've rented a beach house in Duck for the week," I said.

"Sebastian is my significant other," said Lisa. "That's how Kit and I know each other."

Gomez chewed on the end of her pen. "That's enough for now. Wait over there until I tell you otherwise."

We walked back to our original location. "If Ronan was murdered, it probably happened sometime last night, don't you think?"

"The medical examiner should be able to figure that out," she said. "But yes, I would assume that would be the case. There's a lot of people on this boardwalk when the restaurants and businesses are open. If someone tossed a body into the sound, someone would notice."

"Then we don't have anything to worry about." I sighed in deep relief. "If it happened in the middle of the night, you can serve as Sebastian's alibi."

Lisa shifted from one foot to the other. "That's going to be a problem."

"What do you mean, Lisa?" I asked in a shaky voice.

"I woke up in the middle of the night and Sebastian wasn't there," said Lisa. "I don't know where he went, but he wasn't with me."

Chapter Six

Before I could ask Lisa more questions, her phone buzzed. She glanced at it. "Everyone at the house is headed here now. They got my message about what happened."

"Tell them not to come to the boardwalk," I said. "There's too many people already at the scene of the crime." I motioned towards the growing crowd behind Gary and Tobias.

"Why don't I tell them to go to Duck Donuts?" asked Lisa. "I'm sure we can get Detective Gomez to release us soon if we provide her with our contact information."

"Good idea," I said. "We need to speak with Sebastian before the police ask more questions."

"I'll ask Gomez now if we can go," she said. "Right after she finishes speaking with that woman."

I looked across the way. "That's not just any woman. It's Thalia Godfrey, the victim's wife."

Lisa blinked rapidly. "Did you meet her yesterday, too?"

"She was at the town meeting. Do you notice anything about her?"

Lisa scrutinized the scene. "Seems sort of New Age to me, or maybe Boho chic. Loose flowing dress, long hair, big hoop earrings. Not exactly the person I'd expect as the spouse of a former tech entrepreneur, but maybe they met in California?"

"Anything else, Lisa?" I pressed.

"It's more about what's missing than what's there," she said.

"Which is?"

"There's no tears. In fact, she almost looks serene," said Lisa.

"Exactly. If you just found out your husband or significant other had died under suspicious circumstances, would you look that calm and collected?"

"Let's find out what she has to say," said Lisa. "You can offer your condolences, and I can get us sprung."

As we walked over with the dogs, Gomez spotted us coming. "I thought I told both of you to stay over there." She pointed in the direction from where we came.

"You did, but I saw Thalia and I wanted to offer my condolences." I extended my hand to her. "From both myself and Congresswoman Maeve Dixon, of course."

Thalia accepted my hand. "Thank you. Life is such a mysterious journey. We simply never know when it might end." She gazed wistfully into the distance.

Lisa bit her lip. "Do you have any idea who would want to hurt your husband?"

Detective Gomez crossed her arms. "You don't need to answer that question, Mrs. Godfrey. These two discovered . . ." She stuttered for a moment before continuing. "The body in the sound we presume to be Ronan Godfrey. Other than that, they have no bearing on this investigation."

Thalia waved off Gomez's comment. "Please, it's no matter to me. Of course, Ronan had his enemies. You saw that in full force at yesterday's meeting at the town hall building. But doing someone bodily harm is simply beyond my scope of comprehension."

Thalia closed her eyes and inhaled deeply three times while pressing her hands together in a prayerful pose. Then she looked at us. "I shall rely on my meditative yoga practice later today to restore my balance."

Lisa nodded politely at Thalia and then turned toward Carla Gomez. "Are we needed further at this time, Detective? We are willing to provide our contact information for additional questions, of course."

Gomez's face tightened. "Since neither of you will stay put, it might be better if I didn't have to deal with you when I'm trying to collect evidence." She whipped out her notepad. "Write down all your details here, including cell phone numbers, emails, your vacation home address, and your permanent address. We'll be in touch."

We did as we were told, and I handed the notepad back to her. "We'll be happy to cooperate with the police at any time."

"This goes without saying, but you need to check with me before you leave the Outer Banks. That goes for both of you." She pointed at us. "And that brother of yours. I'll need to speak to him later."

Dogs in tow, Lisa and I walked away without another word. We waited until we were far enough away from the crime scene to speak and not be overheard.

"Did you hear what she said about Sebastian?" I asked.

"I heard," said Lisa in a low voice.

"You can't vouch for his whereabouts last night?"

"I'm afraid not," said Lisa. "I woke up in the middle of the night. I'm not sure when, since I didn't check the time. But I was alone."

"Maybe he was in the bathroom," I said hopefully.

"I thought of that. But there was no light on. As you know, all the master bedrooms in our house have private bathrooms attached to the suites."

"He could have gotten up to get a snack." Despite being slender, Sebastian was always hungry.

"Maybe," said Lisa, albeit doubtfully. "I couldn't fall back asleep for a while, though. He didn't come back when I was awake."

"But he was there this morning," I said.

Lisa nodded.

"Did anything seem . . ." I paused to find the right word. "Unusual?"

"Nope. I meant to ask him where he'd gone after I got back today from our run."

"I think that's a good idea, Lisa. I want to hear his story before he has to tell it to Detective Gomez. She's not messing around."

"Definitely not," said Lisa. "I have a feeling there's not too many serious crimes in this area. In other words, it's her time to shine. She's going to make sure she does a thorough job, and that means interrogating all possible suspects."

We arrived at our destination to find that our entire vacation contingent had joined us. Doug, Meg, Trevor, and Sebastian sat at a table with faces so long, you would have thought they had just learned the truth about Santa Claus.

Immune to any semblance of glumness, Clarence and Murphy pulled on their leashes to join. Doug stood up and put his arm around me. "You discovered a dead body, *again*?"

"Not entirely true," I said. "Technically, Murphy spotted it and Clarence got some of the evidence on his paws. We noticed the dogs, not the body itself."

"That's pure semantics," said Trevor. "Is it true the mayor of this beach town is the victim, the infamous Ronan Godfrey?"

"I'm afraid so," I said.

The sweet smell of freshly made doughnuts made my stomach rumble. To make matters worse, I'd missed my morning coffee, which required an immediate remedy. Without java, I felt like my thoughts were forming slowly, like lazy clouds on a summer day. Fortified with sugar and caffeine, surely my little grey cells would kick into high gear.

Meg must have read my mind, or she knew me so well, she could tell when I needed sustenance. "Let's get in line for breakfast," she said. "Then we can discuss the murder."

We fell into a queue that snaked outside the actual store. The doughnuts were made to order, so hundreds of combinations were possible. I studied the menu intently. One problem at a time. First, I needed to figure out what flavor I wanted. Then, I could figure out how to deal with Sebastian and his whereabouts last night.

It was a hard call, but by the time I reached the front of the line, I knew what I wanted. "I'd like a doughnut with peanut butter glaze, graham cracker pieces, and a hot fudge drizzle."

Trevor was right behind me. "That is a disgusting combination," he said. "You might as well eat a chocolate peanut butter cup for breakfast."

I spun around. "No one asked your opinion."

Meg tugged on his sleeve. "Now, Trevor. Remember that Kit had a stressful morning."

Trevor wrinkled his nose. "I suppose so."

I got my order number and headed toward the doughnut pick up area across the way. Trevor soon joined me. "And what type did you order, may I ask?"

"Vanilla with rainbow sprinkles," he said in a defiant tone.

"Trevor, you can order that type of doughnut anywhere. The whole point of Duck Donuts is to eat something you can't get somewhere else," I said.

"I'm perfectly satisfied with my choice. Ordinarily, I would not eat a doughnut for breakfast. It's unhealthy and a poor choice of carbohydrates," he said.

Trevor was right, of course. However, discovering a dead body came with a free "eat whatever you want" pass for the remainder of the day. At least that was my philosophy.

We found an empty table and sat down. Doug had opted for the maple glaze with chopped bacon, Meg went for vanilla icing, Oreo crumbles, and chocolate drizzle, Lisa picked strawberry frosting with chopped peanuts, and Sebastian chose lemon with coconut and marshmallow. Each of us gripped a large cup of coffee.

Meg was the first to take a bite. "Nothing like a freshly made doughnut," she proclaimed as vanilla liquid confection dribbled down the edge of her mouth.

Mine tasted like a warm piece of Reese Peanut Butter cake. Pure heaven. I sighed, half with pleasure and half with sadness. "This would be the perfect way to start our vacation if we hadn't found Ronan Godfrey dead this morning," I said.

Doug grabbed my hand and squeezed it. "Tell us what happened."

I recounted this morning's events to everyone. Besides my voice, the only sound was the persistent chewing of doughnuts and large gulps of hot coffee.

After the story was over, Trevor rubbed his temples. "I really don't know how you become embroiled in these situations." He looked at Meg and me. "You should take a pass on this one. It's different when you're in Washington, D.C. and your boss wants you to investigate."

Lisa squirmed in her chair. "It's not quite that simple."

Doug ran his fingers through his thick hair, which was unrulier than ever due to the salty ocean air. "I can't believe I'm saying this, but for once, I agree with Trevor. It's unfortunate that the mayor of Duck was killed, most likely murdered. But I don't see why it's our concern. Shouldn't we let the police figure out this one?"

I finished the last bite of peanut butter chocolate deliciousness. After swallowing, I opened my mouth to explain. "You're absolutely right, Doug," I said. Then I took a deep breath. "As Lisa says, there's a catch."

Lisa pushed the rest of her doughnut away and faced Sebastian, who was sitting next to her. "The problem is that you apparently made a spectacle of yourself at that town meeting yesterday. Several townspeople remember you as someone who had it in for the victim."

Sebastian, who was wearing an "Earth Day is Every Day" t-shirt, shrugged. "I didn't do anything out of the ordinary. In fact, I'd say that I held back during the meeting. I was only called in at the last minute as a reinforcement." He grinned.

I motioned for everyone to lean closer. In a hushed voice, I said, "The real problem isn't your protesting. It's the fact that the mayor was likely killed last night." I took a deep breath. "And Lisa can't provide you with an alibi."

Meg blinked rapidly. "What are you saying, Kit? Is Sebastian a suspect?"

"That's exactly what I'm saying." Then I turned to Sebastian. "Where were you last night? Lisa said she woke up and you were gone."

Sebastian pushed back from the table. "This is ridiculous. I didn't even know the mayor. But I have known Gary Brewster for years. He's been active in a variety of environmental causes. I got the sense he wanted to make sure Godfrey received a clear message during that town hall meeting."

"It seems that someone sent him a *deadly* message," said Trevor.

Doug cleared his throat. "Sebastian, where were you last night?"

"I went for a walk along the beach. It was a full moon out, so there was plenty of light for a stroll," said Sebastian. "I couldn't sleep."

"Did anyone see you?" I asked hopefully.

"It was two o'clock in the morning, so I think the answer is no," said Sebastian. "I certainly didn't see anyone."

"How long were you gone from the house?" asked Meg.

"I think about an hour," said Sebastian. "I'm not exactly sure."

"Determining an exact time of death is going to be tricky since the body was submerged in water," I said, almost absently.

"And how do you know this? Have you obtained a doctorate in forensic science over the summer?" asked Trevor.

"I'm not sure where I saw it," I said. "Or maybe I read it. But it has to do with the temperature of the body and the temperature of the water. I don't think the police will have a precise time for Godfrey's death."

"That's not ideal, since Sebastian can't say exactly how long he was gone from the house," said Lisa.

"Let's just say it won't dispel any clouds of suspicion," I said.

Sebastian uncrossed his legs and leaned forward. "What should I do, Kit?"

"Tell the police the truth when the detective asks you questions," I said. "There's not much else you can do at this point."

Meg licked the last crumbs of doughnut from her lips. "Are we going to investigate? It sounds like Sebastian needs our help."

I glanced over at Doug. His face was expressionless. He definitely wanted this vacation to be a relaxing week. "Murder" and "relaxation" didn't exactly go hand-in-hand; but I couldn't leave my little brother hanging, especially with an eager detective looking for a convenient tourist as a scapegoat for the murder.

"I think we'd better make a few inquiries," I said.

Doug nodded slightly in my direction. He understood that I'd want to keep Sebastian out of trouble.

Meg's eyes glowed. "How exciting! I wasn't sure if this place had enough action for me." She looked around skeptically. "Solving a murder will liven things up."

I'd explained to Meg several times that Duck was a family beach. We weren't reprising the party scene at Dewey or Ocean City. I'm sure Ronan Godfrey was not pleased he'd become Meg's main antidote for vacation ennui.

"I feel much better that you're looking into it," said Sebastian. "But you need to be careful. Someone must really have it out for Ronan Godfrey."

"Let's walk back to the beach house and we can figure out what we need to do next," I suggested.

During our stroll, I asked to borrow Lisa's phone and called my boss. To my surprise, Maeve Dixon was uncharacteristically calm after she heard the news about Ronan's death.

"That's unfortunate," she said. "Keep an eye on the investigation and let's hope it's solved without a lot of fanfare."

Congresswoman Dixon was always keen on controlling the media message related to her political career. She must have really needed the time with her family to think about her political future. The brief conversation ended after I promised that I'd let her know if an arrest was made or other startling details were revealed.

We returned to our vacation house as the sun emerged from behind the clouds. Within minutes, the temperature had risen at least ten degrees, reminding us all that even though we had a murder to solve, we were only steps away from the Atlantic Ocean.

Meg flopped down on the oversized sofa inside the palatial living room on the third floor. "I'm happy to plan our next steps for solving the murder, but I'd rather do it poolside."

"Excellent idea," I said. "Let's meet outside in ten minutes."

Trevor spoke. "I'm not much for sunbathing. I think I'm going to check out options for fishing."

"Fishing?" asked Doug skeptically. "Since when are you interested in fishing?"

"Since right now," said Trevor. "I've got a few things on my mind. Fishing seems like a peaceful activity. I'm going to try my hand at it." He peered over his wire-rimmed glasses at Doug. "Care to join, Dr. Hollingsworth?"

"I'll take a pass for now, Trevor. Kit needs me to brainstorm the case with her," Doug replied.

I suppressed a chuckle. For a long time, Doug hadn't supported my amateur sleuthing. He thought it was too dangerous and took me away from my official work duties. However, about a year ago, he'd decided to join the excitement and discovered he liked trying to solve the mysteries we encountered. It was considerably more fun having Doug as a part of our merry band of sleuths. He was also wicked smart, which never hurt when matching wits with diabolical criminals.

Everyone else agreed to meet outside by the pool. I dashed inside our bedroom and put on the new black one-piece swimsuit I'd purchased on the road with my boss. It was touted as the "most flattering" swimsuit in North Carolina. I certainly hoped so. My standard work attire was a black pantsuit. This swimsuit was the closest I could get to my normal clothes. After applying sunblock, I grabbed my beach towel, sunglasses, and flip-flops and headed downstairs to our outdoor oasis.

Meg was already setting up her lounge chair when I arrived. She wore a red checkered tankini, large Jackie O style sunglasses, and a floppy straw hat.

"Do you need suntan lotion?" I asked, pointing to her hat.

"I've already put sunblock on," Meg said. "But that won't do anything to protect my hair. It will be bleached white if I don't cover it." She affectionately touched her blonde bob.

Leave it to Meg to think about her hair above all else.

"What's up with Trevor and fishing?" I asked. "He said there was something on his mind."

Meg waved her hand dismissively. "He's looking for his next career opportunity. He's been a Senate staffer, a powerful lobbyist, a bestselling author, and now a senior leader in the administration of Congress. He's thinking about what he should pursue next."

Everyone seemed to be pondering their life goals. I had no doubt Sebastian had decided to go for a walk on the beach in the middle of the night because he was concerned about Lisa's application to join the FBI. Given the peck of trouble he'd gotten himself in, I wished his relationship troubles had been better timed.

While we were chatting, the rest of the gang, sans Trevor, joined us. Sebastian sat down on a lounge chair and sighed. "I'm getting too soft. Backyard pools are a big waste of energy. Here I am vacationing at a house with one."

I pursed my lips. "You've got bigger problems than the environmental dangers of swimming pools. You need to get prepared for a tough interrogation from Detective Gomez. Lisa can tell you. She is not messing around."

Lisa nodded. "She seems tenacious. I don't think she'll rest until she finds the killer."

"I'm not sure where you should start, Kit," said Doug. "You're usually able to work from a ready-made group of suspects. This is completely new territory for you."

"I've done it before," I said, thinking of the time I solved a double murder at the swanky Continental Club to clear Doug's father of suspicion. "Let's start with who we know. Sebastian, do you think you can ask your friend to drop by the house?"

"You mean Gary Brewster?" he asked.

"Yes. He was at the scene of the crime this morning. Gary was Ronan's partner in the wine bar business. He must have known the mayor pretty well. Let's get some information from him."

Sebastian nodded and grabbed his phone. "I'm texting him now."

"Who else do we know that could be helpful?" I asked.

"Ronan's wife seemed like she might be willing to tell us more," suggested Lisa.

I snapped my fingers. "Great idea. At the meeting yesterday, Thalia invited us to her daily yoga session on the lawn in front of the town hall."

"I'm always game for a good downward dog, but do you think she'll still have the session today?" asked Meg.

"I think she will. She mentioned something about needing to focus on her meditative practice. I have a feeling Thalia isn't the typical grieving widow," I said.

"It's settled, then. We'll join her class and see if she'll talk to us about who might have wanted to kill her husband. Right now, it's time for a dip." Meg took off her hat and jumped into the pool.

"I think I'll join you," said Lisa. "It's already blistering hot."

"Sebastian, any luck with Gary?" I asked.

He nodded. "He's leaving the boardwalk now and said he'll swing by. His house isn't far from here. I gave him the address."

Doug's nose was buried in a book. With Meg and Lisa splashing away in the pool, this would be a good opportunity to find out what was bothering my brother. I got up and sat down next to Sebastian on his lounge chair and lowered my voice. "Why were you walking the beach in the middle of the night? Does it have to do with Lisa's job situation?"

His forehead crinkled. "This is an incredible opportunity for her. If she gets into the program, I'm not sure where she'll end up."

I patted Sebastian's hand. "I'm sure it's difficult not knowing what's next for her."

"I couldn't sleep so I got up to take a walk," he said. "And now, I've made everything worse."

"Don't worry. You might not have an ironclad alibi, but the detective is going to need more than that to make an arrest," I said.

"Arrest?" Sebastian's mouth gaped open. "Do you think I could be arrested?"

I took a deep breath. "Sebastian, there's no need to get upset. Let's talk to Gary and see what he has to say."

As if on cue, a man's voice called out from behind us. "Did I hear my name?"

We turned around. Gary was standing on the other side of the fence surrounding the pool.

"I knocked on the front door, and when no one answered, I figured you were outside," said Gary.

Sebastian got up and opened the gate. "Come in," he said, shaking his hand. "I appreciate you stopping by." While Sebastian did a quick round of introductions, Lisa and Meg inched over to the edge of the pool.

"Any news to report about Ronan's death?" I motioned for Gary to take a seat poolside.

"It's a homicide," said Gary. "When they pulled him out of the water, the medical examiner identified a severe wound on the side of his head."

"What do the police think happened?" I asked.

"Detective Gomez from Kitty Hawk wasn't too forthcoming," said Gary. "But Tobias and I picked up several snippets of conversation. It looks like Ronan was hit on the head with a wine bottle and then pushed into the water."

"I wonder if that means the murderer was a man," said Doug.

"Why do you think that?" I asked.

"Dragging the body," said Doug. "Ronan Godfrey wasn't a big guy, but it would take a lot of strength to move him."

"They're using the wine and blood splatter to figure that out," said Gary. "It might be that Ronan fell down near where he went into the water."

"If that's the case, then we can't rule out a woman," said Lisa. "Pushing him underneath that kayak launch rope and into the marsh wouldn't have been too difficult."

I walked over and put my arm around Doug. "Good thinking, though."

"Do they know when the murder happened?" asked Meg.

Gary shook his head. "That's going to be complicated, from what I gather. There will have to be some careful calculations concerning his body temperature and the temperature of the water," he said. "I eavesdropped when Gomez was talking to the medical examiner."

I'd been right about the lack of clarity concerning the time of death. The timing wouldn't help exonerate Sebastian, at least for now.

"It had to happen after the bar closed," said Lisa. "When's that?"

"Probably around eleven. I was there last night and so was Ronan," said Gary.

"When did Ronan leave?" I asked.

"He was there when I left at ten. He usually stayed until closing with Tobias. He's our manager. You might have met him at the town hall meeting," said Gary.

"Maybe someone saw something," said Doug hopefully. "A witness could still come forward."

Gary shrugged. "Could be, but I doubt it. Once Sonoma Sunsets closes, the boardwalk gets deserted really fast. It's not like the Jersey shore where people enjoy the nightlife into the wee hours of the morning. Our wine bar is pretty much it."

"That's how I remember it when my family vacationed here," said Lisa.

I stood up and raised my hands. "Let's think about this for a moment. The killer waited until the bar closed, right?"

No one objected to my premise, so I kept going. "Maybe there's a disagreement or maybe it's premeditated. We don't know. The killer grabs a bottle of wine and hits Ronan over the head. Then shoves his body into the marsh."

"How did the killer get a bottle of wine?" asked Meg.

"The bar is open-air," said Gary. "We keep the bottles locked up in the back, but there's plenty in the front of the bar. We've never had any issue with theft, so I can't say for sure that Tobias makes sure every last bottle is stowed away each night before he leaves."

"So, we're not sure if access to the murder weapon was an issue," said Sebastian.

"Hard to say. Also, Ronan had a few glasses of wine last night, so he may have been tipsy," said Gary.

I perked up. "Who would have known that?"

"Anyone who was at the bar," said Gary. "I'd have to think about who was there, but we often get a lot of locals on Saturday night. Tourists have just started their vacations. They're busy unpacking and getting settled in their rented houses, so they typically don't venture out on Saturdays."

"Anyone out of the ordinary at the bar?" asked Lisa. "Maybe someone who might have picked a fight with Ronan?"

"Nope, not that I can remember. It was like any other busy evening. Lots of people hanging around, ordering drinks and bites to eat. You know, we're the only organic wine bar in the Outer Banks," said Gary, with a hint of pride in his voice.

Gary was our connection to the townspeople of Duck. If an

arch nemesis from another life hadn't appeared to antagonize Ronan, it was likely a local resident who killed him.

"I think we should be completely honest with you, Gary." I paused a moment before continuing. "Sebastian will be a suspect for this murder until the real killer is caught."

Gary inhaled sharply. "Because of the town hall meeting yesterday?"

Sebastian cleared his throat. "That didn't help. But I also don't have an alibi for last night. I took a late-night walk when I couldn't sleep." Sebastian added, "Alone."

Gary rubbed his temples. "And Detective Gomez is determined to solve this quickly, so you're a convenient scapegoat."

"Something like that," I said. "We know Sebastian didn't do it, which means finding the real killer is the only way forward. Can you help us brainstorm possible suspects?"

Gary put his arm affectionately around Sebastian's shoulders. "For this guy, I'd do anything. We're kindred spirits."

Finally, Sebastian's protesting had accomplished something else other than getting me in trouble with my boss. Gary appeared willing to help us navigate the complex waters of the Outer Banks, no pun intended.

"Before you talk about suspects, can you tell us more about Ronan Godfrey?" asked Doug. "Everyone knows he earned millions at a young age and left the tech industry. Why did he end up in Duck, North Carolina?"

Doug had matured into such a promising amateur sleuth. I felt a swell of pride.

"I don't think Ronan ever explained why he ended up here. He said he loved the beach and wanted out of the rat race in Silicon Valley. I got the sense he and Thalia bumped around for a while in a variety of locations, but they eventually settled here a few years ago."

"When did he become mayor?" asked Meg.

"A little over a year ago. Ronan felt as though the town wasn't living up to its full potential. As much as he wanted to leave the stressful world of business, he couldn't really shake the entrepreneurial approach. He ran for mayor on the promise that he would make Duck the premier resort town of the Outer Banks." He took a breath before continuing. "Sort of a like a Nantucket of the south."

"Some people didn't like this?" asked Lisa.

"Everyone liked that he promised home values would increase. But then he started to suggest other changes in the town that weren't so popular, particularly with our year-round residents," said Gary.

"Like what?" asked Meg. "He opened a wine bar. That sounds popular to me."

"The idea of Sonoma Sunsets might have been popular, although what actually happened was not," said Gary.

"You mean the lady who owned the pizza place?" I asked.

Gary tipped the rim of his baseball hat in my direction. "Not much gets by you. That would be Jean Rizzo. She owned a run-of-the-mill, takeout-pizza place right on the sound. The business had been in her family for years. Ronan convinced the owner of the property to sell it to him. Then Ronan terminated her lease and opened up Sonoma Sunsets."

Meg's mouth dropped. "While he was the mayor?"

Gary grimaced. "I'm afraid so."

"But aren't you Ronan's partner in the business?" asked Sebastian.

"Kicking out Jean wasn't my idea. Ronan told me she wanted to leave and find a location that would be cheaper rent. She did find a place on the other side of the highway that was lower cost. Ronan stretched the truth," said Gary.

"So, Jean Rizzo is a suspect. She certainly has motive," I said. "By any chance, was she at the bar last night?"

Gary nodded. "She was. After the pizza place closes up, she often comes by for a drink. Ronan always lets her have a glass of wine for free. I think he offered it as a way to keep her discontent limited to a dull roar."

"What other changes was the mayor planning to make in Duck?" asked Lisa.

"There were a number of ideas he was tossing around related to the businesses in the heart of Duck. Nothing firm yet." Gary snapped his fingers. "But he did start to question whether Duck should keep its policy about allowing dogs on the beach at all times."

"That's one of the reasons why we decided to vacation here," said Doug. As if on cue, Clarence and Murphy both opened their eyes, despite the fact they were taking a snooze in the shaded poolside.

"Dogs can enjoy the beach unleashed in Duck year-round," said Gary. "Ronan thought it would conflict with his image of attracting more affluent visitors. Bitsy and Biff might not like the Johnson's golden retriever slobbering all over them when they decide to take a romantic stroll on the beach." Gary chuckled.

"I bet that went over like a lead balloon with the people who have lived here or owned houses for a while," said Meg.

"A number of people didn't like it, as you might imagine. The person who was most disturbed was Lacy Madison. She owns the Duck Dogs store in town," explained Gary.

"I assume it sells pet merchandise," said Doug.

"Yes, and even more than that, Lacy hosts Yappy Hours a couple times a week for people who are visiting with dogs. She works alongside the rescue community," said Gary. "I might add, she's also a big supporter of the horses in Corolla."

"Lacy was at the town hall yesterday," I said, mostly to make sure everyone kept note of her name as a potential suspect. Then I shifted gears. "Tell us more about the horses. We didn't get a chance to learn more yesterday because the meeting ended so . . ." I searched for the right word. "Abruptly."

Gary smiled. "The horses are the reason I came to live in the Outer Banks. They are Colonial Spanish Mustangs that live beyond the paved road at the far northern end of the island. They came here in the sixteenth century on Spanish ships," he said.

"That's pretty amazing," said Sebastian. "You run the organization that helps protect them?"

Gary nodded. "I've got a lot of help. We monitor the herd and provide rescue assistance when necessary. We also advocate for the healthy continuation of the herd."

"That's the focus of the legislation we talked about yesterday," I said.

"It is. The herd has gotten too small, and now it's suffering from a lack of genetic diversity. We need to bring some horses from neighboring islands to strengthen it. But the bill hasn't passed Congress." Gary dropped his head and frowned.

"That doesn't seem terribly controversial," said Doug.

"The U.S. Fish and Wildlife Agency opposes it, because they argue the horses compete with native species for resources." Gary rubbed the back of his neck.

"Don't worry," I said. "When we get back to Washington, we'll try to do something about it."

Gary's expression brightened considerably. "Thank you. I really appreciate it." He looked at his watch. "I should be going. Without Ronan, I'll need to spend more time with Sonoma Sunsets, although I suppose we'll be closed for the next couple of days."

"Before you go, is there anyone else who might have had a motive for killing Godfrey?" I asked. "You mentioned Jean Rizzo and Lacy Madison. Did you miss someone?" I didn't say that Thalia Godfrey was also on my list of suspects. No point in sharing that information with Gary, who might feel the need to tell Thalia.

Gary shifted in his chair. "I suppose you'd have to put Tobias Potter on that list. It pains me to say it. Tobias is our manager at Sonoma Sunsets, and I've known him for as long as I've lived in the Outer Banks."

"What's his story?" asked Meg. "He spent a lot of time talking to the mayor's wife yesterday."

An expert flirt and a frequent recipient of attention from the opposite sex, I could always count on Meg to notice signs of romantic interest.

Gary drew back in his chair. "Tobias has lived his whole life in the Outer Banks. He's served on the town board of Duck for decades, as I understand it."

I knew where this was headed. "He waited for his turn to become the mayor."

Gary chuckled. "You know politics. He thought he'd serve as

the next mayor, but then Ronan announced he was running. Tobias didn't even throw his hat into the ring. With Ronan's considerable resources, it would have been futile."

"And his relationship with the mayor's wife," said Meg. She wasn't giving up on that angle.

Gary blinked rapidly, shifting nervously again in his seat. "I don't know anything about that. I think they're friends. You'd have to ask Thalia or Tobias."

Such question will be high on our list.

Sebastian stood and extended a hand to Gary. "Thank you for spending time with us. I know you must have a million things to handle today."

Gary got up and shook Sebastian's hand. "Anything for an old friend." He exited the pool area and then turned around. "By the way, I wouldn't waste too much time on Ronan's murder. He might have just been in the wrong place at the wrong time. You don't want to miss out on your vacation. I'm sure the Kitty Hawk police will figure this out."

After Gary was out of earshot, Meg spoke first. "He doesn't know us very well. We solve murders in the middle of political campaigns, major thefts of priceless items, and even flower shows." She paused for a second. "Should I go on?"

"You've made your point," I said, smiling. "A little sand and sun shouldn't prevent us from finding the killer."

As they say, don't underestimate the power of underestimation.

Chapter Seven

MEG GOT OUT OF THE POOL and grabbed her beach towel to dry off. "Isn't it time for yoga? You don't want to miss Thalia."

Lisa glanced at Sebastian. "Do you mind if I stay here?" she asked.

"Not a problem." I knew Lisa probably wanted to spend time alone with my brother. "Doug, are you coming?"

He placed his book to the side. "Sure, although I'm not a very accomplished yogi."

Meg punched him lightly on the arm. "That doesn't matter, silly. We're going to investigate, not for the exercise."

Doug and Meg struggled with their relationship, and I could tell that Doug was pondering a smart-aleck reply. Instead, in an even voice, he said, "You're absolutely right, Meg."

"It's settled, then. Let's meet outside the house as soon as you're ready," I said.

Ten minutes later, Doug and I waited for Meg to join us. I was just about to text her when she emerged from the house wearing a light blue outfit, including matching yoga tights.

"Were you planning on attending yoga classes during vacation?" I asked. I'd thrown on a pair of pink running shorts and a t-shirt I found in the bottom of my suitcase.

"I always pack for a variety of experiences," said Meg. "You should know that about me, Kit."

"You're right, Meg." I gave her a shoulder hug. "Maybe it's because we haven't spent enough time together the past couple of months."

She linked her arm in mine. "We can fix that this week." She glanced at Doug, who had put on a headband to keep his bushy hair in check. "You look like Richard Simmons if he was a professor," said Meg.

Doug adjusted his glasses. "I'll take that as a compliment."

We spent the rest of the walk catching up about mutual acquaintances, gossip, and political shenanigans. As expected, Thalia Godfrey was sitting on the front lawn of the town hall, seemingly deep in meditation.

Doug whispered, "I don't think we should bother her."

"Definitely not," I said. "Let's talk to her after the class."

Meg motioned to a stack of yoga mats sitting to the side. After picking up mats, we selected spots in the third row of participants.

"There's a lot of people here, despite the murder," said Meg.

"Tourists like us," I said. "If they haven't ventured to the boardwalk today, they probably don't know anything about it."

All of a sudden, Thalia's eyes opened. She spread her arms wide. "Today, my friends, I've experienced a significant disturbance of the life force that surrounds me. Some may wonder why I didn't cancel this session." She paused and looked directly at me. "However, I can think of no better affirmation than to celebrate our bodies through exercise and meditation."

After a series of chants, in which we were encouraged to repeat after her, Thalia popped up. She immediately issued a command. "Downward-facing dog!" It was more like an order than a suggestion. I quickly bent down, sticking my rear in the air with my arms extended in front of me. Doug's hair was flopping over his face, making him look like an upside-down version of "It" from the Adams Family.

"Chaturanga!" From what I could tell, this pose was a sadistic version of a pushup. Instead of moving up and down, the goal was to hold the lowest possible position for what seemed like an interminable amount of time. Meg's face turned beet red, a striking contrast to her light blue fancy yoga attire.

"Jump those feet together!" Then a second later. "Now, stand up for chair pose so we can engage those thighs."

Meg turned her head. "I thought this was meditative yoga. I didn't sign up for the yoga version of Army boot camp."

Doug panted. "I should have stayed by the pool with my book."

"Is something wrong?" asked Thalia, who was staring right at us.

I shook my head vigorously because I wasn't sure I had enough air in my lungs to speak.

"Yoga practice is silent. We must respect its spiritual sanctity." She shot us a yoga look that would kill. Apparently, Thalia wasn't quite as easygoing as I first thought.

The next twenty minutes proceeded much like the first five with Thalia barking out commands while Meg, Doug, and I struggled to comply. No one else seemed in as much agony as we were, although we weren't exactly practiced yogis, as Doug had presciently pointed out.

Finally, Thalia announced we had entered the "relaxation" portion of the class. We stretched out on our mats as she wove her way through the rows, providing soothing thoughts and observations. After a couple chants to conclude the practice, Thalia folded her hands and wished us "Namaste." I couldn't remember the last time I was so happy to hear the word.

I whispered to Meg and Doug. "Let's catch her now. We don't want to have endured this torture for nothing!"

We scrambled to the front, where Thalia was rolling up her mat. I approached her gingerly. "Thalia, can we ask you a few questions?"

She swung her long brown hair around and recognized me. "You're the woman from the town hall who discovered Ronan's body."

"Yes, my name is Kit Marshall. We spoke briefly this morning at the boardwalk shortly after you arrived. This is my friend Meg Peters and my husband Doug Hollingsworth."

Thalia bowed slightly. "Thank you for participating in my yoga practice. Did you have a restorative experience?"

"You could say that," I said. *If you meant restorative like restoring my belief in sitting on the couch and not exercising.*

"We'd like to ask you a few questions about your husband," said Meg.

Thalia stared at the sky. "Ronan is at peace now. The practice today helped clear my head and restore a healthful balance in my soul."

"That sounds very positive," I said. "Have you had any time to think about who would have wanted to kill Ronan? As we understand it, his death is now considered a murder."

Thalia pursed her lips. "I don't like thinking about violence. It's against my nature." She sighed. "But I suppose the killer should be brought to justice."

"Any idea who that might be?" asked Doug. His hair had now flopped down over his headband. He looked pretty cute as a historian-turned-athlete.

"I simply cannot speculate who would commit such an act," said Thalia.

"Is there someone he had a conflict with recently?" asked Meg. I shot her an appreciative glance. Nice redirect.

"For a variety of reasons, he had been spending a considerable amount of time with the woman who owns the Duck Dogs store. Her name is Lacy Madison," said Thalia.

"And they were fighting?" asked Doug.

"Ronan didn't tell me much about conflict. There was that business about restricting dog access to the beach." Thalia wrinkled her forehead. "I told Ronan that idea didn't have legs. Too many dog lovers in this town. Nonetheless, he persisted with it. Lacy didn't like it, for obvious reasons. Her store depends upon Duck continuing to be a dog-friendly vacation spot."

"That's helpful," I said. "Anyone else?"

"I can't think of anything." Thalia looked at her watch. "I'm afraid I must go. My friends are expecting me."

"That sounds like a kind gesture," I said. "Who are you meeting?"

"Tobias Potter and Jean Rizzo," she said.

"Wasn't Tobias your husband's political rival?" asked Doug. "Tobias wanted to become mayor, as we understand it, but Ronan ran and won instead."

Thalia waved her hand. "That was water under the bridge. Besides, it has no bearing on *my* relationship with Tobias."

"Really?" asked Meg. "How so?"

Thalia picked up her yoga mat. "I didn't let my husband's relationships, business or political, infringe upon my social calendar. I really must go now."

"Thank you for speaking with us," I said. "Again, we're sorry for your loss."

Thalia scurried away in the direction of the town hall parking lot without another word. After she was out of earshot, the three of us huddled together. "Well, what did you make of that?" I asked.

"Obviously, we need to talk to Lacy. If Ronan was threatening to limit dog access to the beaches in Duck, it would adversely affect her business," said Meg. "She has a clear motive for wanting him out of the picture."

"Isn't it odd that the day her husband dies, Thalia decides to seek comfort from his political rival and the woman whose business he damaged?" asked Doug.

"I found that very strange," I said. "Once again, there wasn't much remorse."

"I wonder if we need to add Thalia to the suspect list," said Meg.

"Definitely," I said. "She's probably going to inherit a lot of money now that Ronan is dead."

"And her relationship with that Tobias guy is suspect," said Meg. "I know it when there's romantic interest, and I sensed it yesterday after that town meeting when they were talking."

"Maybe Thalia teamed up with Tobias to get rid of Ronan," said Doug excitedly. "She could have hit him on the head with the wine bottle and Tobias could have pushed him into the water."

"That's certainly plausible," I said. "We'll have to start checking alibis. It seems like everyone knew that Ronan liked to hang out late at Sonoma Sunsets. It wouldn't have been difficult to wait until everyone left for an opportunity to kill him."

My iPhone buzzed and I swiped it open to read the text message. It was from Sebastian.

Detective Gomez is headed here soon to interview me...

The symbol at the end of his message was the text emoticon for "worry" or "anxiety." I knew it because it was commonly used at work in the congressional office.

I typed back a reply.

We're headed back now.

"Let's go, gang. Exercise time is over," I said. "The detective is headed to speak with Sebastian, and I don't want to miss it."

We hustled back to the house. Despite our fast walking, we hadn't beat the detective. Her Kitty Hawk PD car was parked in the driveway when we arrived.

"I hope Sebastian keeps his mouth shut," I muttered.

Doug put his arm around me. "Kit, your brother is a smart guy. Besides, he didn't do anything wrong. If the detective is as ambitious as you describe her, she's not going to want to arrest the wrong person for the murder."

Doug was right. I couldn't help but worry about it, though.

We walked up the flights of stairs and found Detective Gomez, a uniformed police officer, Sebastian, and Lisa seated in the spacious living room.

Gomez glanced in our direction when we walked in. "I guess the gang's all here," she said.

Sebastian leaned back in the armchair. "Detective Gomez arrived a few minutes ago. She asked me about my whereabouts last night."

Gomez referred to her notebook. "No alibi for the time of the murder."

"Someone might have seen Sebastian walking on the beach." I tried to keep the desperation out of my voice.

"We'll make those inquiries when it's necessary," said Gomez.

I gulped. I didn't like the phrase "when necessary." Did she mean when they arrested Sebastian?

There was an uncomfortable silence in the room as Detective Gomez flipped through the pages in her notebook. Finally, Doug spoke. "Are there any further questions for Sebastian?"

Gomez fixed a steely gaze on Doug. "As a matter of fact, I do have a few more questions for Mr. Marshall." She shifted in her chair to face Sebastian. "How many times have you been arrested before?" Sebastian's face turned red. He stammered, "I don't know."

"You've been arrested so many times you've lost count?" countered Gomez.

Sebastian's brow furrowed. "No, I mean, I have to think about it." He paused for several seconds. "Maybe ten times?"

Lisa squirmed on the couch. She knew about Sebastian's protesting, but I doubted she knew he'd gone to jail on numerous occasions.

"The correct answer is twelve," said Detective Gomez. "That's quite an arrest record, Mr. Marshall."

"My brother is passionate when it comes to politics and the environment. Resisting arrest or disturbing the peace is hardly a precursor to murder." I didn't bother to hide the defensive tone.

"So passionate that he might have been motivated to kill Ronan Godfrey," said Gomez.

"With all due respect, Detective, my wife is correct. Getting arrested at a protest is hardly a pretense for homicide," said Doug.

"Maybe, maybe not," said Gomez. "It does show a high level of commitment to these causes."

"You think Sebastian would kill someone after only meeting him one time?" I asked.

Gomez shook her head. "I don't believe he planned on doing it. But I do think your brother went for a walk, like he said. However, instead of walking along the beach, he crossed the road and decided to stroll along the boardwalk. That's where he ran into Ronan Godfrey," said Gomez. She took a breath before continuing.

"But . . ." I protested. Gomez silenced me with her finger.

"Let me finish. We know that Ronan had enjoyed a few drinks that night at his bar. Perhaps Mr. Marshall exchanged terse words with Godfrey. Who knows? Maybe Godfrey even pushed him." She looked at Sebastian pointedly. "Before you know it, Mr. Marshall has a bottle of wine in his hand. He hits him over the head and disposes of the body over the side."

For the second time, we sat in silence. I tried to control the anxiety that threatened to overtake me. The police had already created an elaborate storyline to pin the murder on Sebastian. Instead of panicking, I focused on the scenario that Gomez outlined. Was there a hole in her theory?

All of a sudden, it came to me. I snapped my fingers. "There's a problem with your hypothesis."

Gomez shifted to face me. "Please enlighten us, Ms. Marshall."

"The entire boardwalk has protective railings," I said. "It's only along the kayak docking area where there's rope instead of the wooden railings. How would Sebastian know about that? He's never been to the town of Duck before. Right, Sebastian?"

My brother eagerly nodded. "Never."

"Rather than an out of town visitor, I think your killer was a local," I said. "Someone who knew the kayak launch didn't have a railing."

Gomez rubbed her chin. "He could have seen the kayak launch earlier. If he approached the bar from the opposite direction, he would have walked right past it."

"But in your scenario, the crime wasn't premeditated," Meg protested. I shot her a grateful glance.

"He still might have observed it." Gomez a trace of defensiveness entered Gomez's voice. "Who knows? Maybe he thought about going on a kayak tour the next day. Then he comes across Ronan, kills him, and realizes he can toss the body into the water by the launch."

Lisa stood and faced Gomez directly. "I'm not a lawyer, but I am a police officer. I know you don't have enough to charge Sebastian. He's cooperated voluntarily. Now I think it's time for this interview to end."

Gomez glanced to the uniformed cop, who nodded in assent. "We'll leave you for now." She stood up. "I'll repeat what I said earlier. No one leaves the Outer Banks without clearing it through me. I expect I'll have more questions as my investigation develops."

Gomez and the cop headed for the stairs. I followed them down to the front door. I wanted to make sure they immediately left the property, but I also hoped Gomez might answer a few questions of my own.

Before they left, I asked, "Detective, can you answer a question or two?"

She spun around. "It depends on your questions, Ms. Marshall."

Touché. Gomez was a firecracker. I wasn't going to get anything by her. I'd better make this count.

"Do you know what the cause of death was?" I asked.

Gomez pursed her lips together in a tight line. "Why do you need to know?"

"I've been wondering why the killer bashed Ronan Godfrey over the head with the wine bottle and then pushed him into the marsh. If the blow killed him, then why dispose of the body in that way? In the shallow water of the sound, he wasn't going to move very far."

"How do you know about the shallow waters?" she countered.

"I searched online. The Currituck Sound has an average depth of only five feet. Much less near the shore, of course," I said. "Locals would know this fact. There had to be another reason why the murderer decided to dump the body in the water."

"You're assuming the perp is a local. I'm not ready to make that assumption, Ms. Marshall." She stared pointedly. I got the drift. Sebastian was still a top suspect, in her mind.

"I'm proceeding on the notion that the killer is from this area," I said. "Because I know my brother didn't do it."

"You have that luxury, Ms. Marshall. I do not." Gomez crossed her arms. "Is your interrogation over now?"

"You never answered my question." I crossed my arms. Two could play this game. The uniformed police officer twitched.

"As a matter of fact, the autopsy report indicates that Ronan Godfrey did *not* drown," she said.

"He was dead before he went into the water," I said.

"It appears so, Ms. Marshall. Not a difficult determination for a medical examiner to make. Given your previous investigations, I gather you understand this."

"Thank you for this information, Detective. This reinforces my earlier question. Why would a person add the extra step of throwing the body into the water if Godfrey was already dead?"

The uniformed police officer spoke for the first time. "Excuse me, ma'am and Detective Gomez. Perhaps the assailant didn't know the victim was dead. So, he or she wanted to make sure of it."

I nodded my head. "It's not a bad theory. But if you were going to go to the trouble of moving the body to the kayak launch, wouldn't you take twenty seconds to confirm that Ronan Godfrey was still alive?"

Both Detective Gomez and her colleague were silent for several seconds. "I'll give you that, Ms. Marshall. I still don't know where you're going with this."

"The murderer hits Godfrey over the head with the wine bottle. For some unknown reason, he or she wants his body submerged in the water. The problems is solved by using the kayak launch," I said. "I'd say this crime wasn't necessarily premeditated, but it was committed by someone who knew the Duck boardwalk quite well."

Detective Gomez's face was placid. "Anything else, Ms. Marshall? We have a busy schedule today, as you might imagine."

"Alibis," I said. "Have you started to collect them?"

"We're interrogating suspects as we go," said Gomez.

"I'd like to know where Thalia Godfrey was at the time of the murder. I assume you consider her a person of interest," I said.

"Ms. Marshall, you know we always examine the spouse's whereabouts," said Gomez. "I'm not sure I need to share that information with you, however."

I sighed. There was an easy way to do this, or a hard way. I suppose we'd have to go the latter route.

"I understand, Detective." I reached past her and opened the door. "Best of luck in finding the *true* identity of the killer."

Gomez said nothing as she walked out the door. After she and her colleague had exited the porch, she turned around. "Remember, Ms. Marshall. This isn't Washington, D.C. We don't like politicians, and we especially don't like it when they meddle in our business."

Chapter Eight

I HAULED MYSELF BACK UP the two flights of stairs. Everyone was sitting inside the living room, not saying much.

"Whose funeral is it?" I asked, in a joking voice. No one laughed. I broke the silence again. "Come on, people. This is our vacation. You heard Detective Gomez. They don't have anything substantial on Sebastian."

My brother ran his fingers through his dishwater blond locks. "Then why do I feel as though I'd better find the best criminal defense attorney in North Carolina?"

"That's ridiculous," I said. "Lisa, what do you think? You're a police officer."

Lisa pursed her lips together tightly. "I wouldn't say there's *nothing* to be worried about. However, Kit is right. The police need more evidence to arrest Sebastian. Unless something else shows up, he should be fine."

"See?" I said triumphantly. "Let's end the doom and gloom, shall we?"

"Greetings, everyone!" A booming male voice broke the tension inside the room. We all turned as Trevor entered.

"You're back from fishing?" asked Meg. "I texted you multiple times, and you didn't respond." Her mouth turned downward in a pout.

"I'm sorry, sweetheart." Trevor affectionately touched Meg's shoulder. "I was so engrossed by what I was doing, I lost track of the time!"

I hadn't heard Trevor express this much enthusiasm since he'd scored a six-figure book deal for his tell-all missive about our nation's capital.

Doug shot Trevor a skeptical glance. "Fishing was that exciting, Trevor?"

"It was precisely the opposite, Dr. Hollingsworth," said Trevor. "It was *relaxing*."

Meg, Doug, and I stared at Trevor with open mouths. Trevor had never been relaxed a day in his life.

"That's really something, Trevor," I said. "We've had a busy day here with the murder." We caught him up on the details, including our yoga excursion and Detective Gomez's visit.

After listening, he asked, "What's your next move?"

"I think we'd better try to speak with Lacy at the Duck Dogs store," I said. "It's time to enlist Clarence."

Our chubby beagle had been taking a nap. When he heard his name, his ears perked up immediately.

"Clarence seems ready to report for duty," said Doug. "Do you mind if I stay here? I'd really like to continue reading my book." Doug gazed longingly at the latest historical tome he'd been devouring poolside.

"Of course not. After all, we are on vacation, and you should enjoy yourself," I said.

"Speaking of enjoying myself, I plan on taking a nap," said Meg. "Yoga was exhausting. No one should exercise that hard on vacation."

"Since I missed the earlier activities and Meg will be resting, I'm happy to accompany you," said Trevor. "I'll need to take a quick shower to remove the fishy smell from my clothes. Please excuse me." Trevor disappeared in a flash before I could speak. Our quirky friend wasn't known for his love of canines, but I suppose I could put his eagle eye to good use.

"I'd like to help," said Sebastian in a quiet voice.

"I'm sure you would, but I think it's best you're not seen poking around," I said. "We don't want to arouse any more suspicion than necessary."

"Come on," said Lisa. "Let's go for a walk on the beach with Murphy." Sebastian's face brightened at Lisa's suggestion, and they took off for their stroll.

I got Clarence situated with his harness and leash and waited for Trevor downstairs. A few minutes later, he appeared, wearing a stylish collared polo shirt and crisply pressed linen shorts. I still had on my yoga attire, which had become quite rumpled.

Trevor peered at my clothes. "Do you want to change, Kit? After all, we are interrogating a suspect."

"Yes, but we don't want her to know that we are interrogating her," I said. "I should look like a tourist."

"Very well," said Trevor. "I suppose this beach is more suited for casual attire."

It was good to know that despite Trevor's newfound discovery of fishing, he hadn't completely shed the Type A personality we'd all grown to love.

After we settled into our walk, Trevor said, "Let's discuss our approach."

"Good idea," I said. "Lacy Madison owns the dog store in town. Understandably, she was strongly opposed to Ronan's proposal to limit dog access on Duck beaches." I took a breath. "Thalia also told us that Ronan had been spending a lot of time with Lacy recently. It sounded suspicious."

"As I recall from your description, this woman is considerably younger than our victim and reasonably attractive. Correct?" asked Trevor.

"That's right. It could be possible they were romantically involved. Perhaps Lacy was trying to persuade him to abandon his efforts about dog access to the beaches."

"Could be," said Trevor. "If Ronan was attracted to Lacy, then she might have thought she could influence him."

"Let's pretend we're customers," I said. "That's why I brought Clarence. We can figure out a way to strike up conversation with Lacy. She might recognize me from the town hall yesterday, but I don't think that will matter."

"We can see if she admits to spending considerable time recently with the victim," said Trevor.

"We also need to find out if she has an alibi. I hope that Sebastian isn't the only suspect without one."

We turned onto Duck Road and headed toward the main shopping area in town, called Scarborough Faire. Lisa had told us that's where we'd find the dog store.

"Trevor, can I ask you a question unrelated to the murder?"

"I suppose," said Trevor. "Although I'm utilizing my brain power right now on the task at hand."

I groaned inwardly. Trevor had a laser-like focus that made it sometimes difficult to interact with him on a personal basis. We'd grown to embrace it or work around it, whatever the situation demanded. I hadn't thought his relationship with Meg would last, but it turned out that the old adage "opposites attract" had considerable appeal.

"What's the attraction to fishing all of a sudden?" I asked. "It seems so . . ." I couldn't find the right word.

"Uncharacteristic," said Trevor, without hesitation. "You are certainly correct."

I nodded. "Is something bothering you? I know I've been out of pocket for a few weeks and I haven't kept with everyone as much as I should."

Being on the campaign trail was notorious for alienating people from their friends and family. Working on a political campaign was like serving on an extended jury; it was all-encompassing, tightly knit, and sequestered.

"I'm thinking about the next step in my career," said Trevor. "I find it difficult, if not impossible, to concentrate with others around. Therefore, I selected the most solitary beach activity that exists, which is fishing."

"So, you really have no interest in it?" I asked. "It's just an excuse to be alone?"

"It was, but now that I've done it, I find that I enjoy the activity itself," said Trevor. "I've rented fishing gear for the entire week."

I wanted to ask Trevor why he was thinking about leaving his current job, but we'd arrived at the Scarborough Faire shopping area. It was spread out over several buildings and two floors. Luckily, we spotted a directory near the entrance. We strolled over to figure out where Lacy's store was located within the outdoor complex.

After finding the location on the map, we walked up a flight of stairs and down a long walkway, past a gourmet popcorn store, a women's clothing boutique, a vintage jeweler, and a wine shop. Finally, we saw the sign for the Duck Dogs store.

"That's it," I said, pointing ahead of us.

"I hope you have a good idea for a cover so that you can engage her in conversation." Trevor held open the door for Clarence and me to enter.

"I have a plan," I muttered under my breath.

We walked inside and scanned our surroundings. One side had dog-related souvenirs, such as t-shirts, coffee mugs, signs, and other mementos. The other side of the store contained items specifically for dogs, like leashes, bowls, treats, and toys. Lacy was behind the register, waiting on a customer. At least we'd get a chance to speak with her.

"I'll follow your lead," said Trevor under his breath. "I'm out of my element here. Dogs are not my specialty."

Clarence spotted the rawhides and pulled in that direction. I got him under control and waited until Lacy had finished with the person she was helping.

"Lacy, my name is Kit Marshall. We were at the town hall together yesterday. I work for Congresswoman Dixon," I said. "This is my friend Trevor and my dog Clarence."

Lacy's face brightened when I mentioned Clarence. She emerged from behind the cash register and stooped down. "Hello, Clarence. I hope you're enjoying Duck and all it has to offer for dogs." She put her hand out for Clarence to inspect and sniff. Once he rubbed her hand with his snout, she petted his head and scratched his ears. Clarence immediately sat down and waited patiently for whatever affection he could solicit.

She'd given me the perfect opening. "Well, that's what I wanted to talk to you about," I said. "I'm afraid Clarence is not maximizing his time in Duck."

As if on cue, Clarence put on his saddest puppy-dog look. It fit right into my story. The real reason for his pleading eyes was that he spotted treats across the way. After all, Clarence had grown up in Washington, D.C. He knew how to manipulate emotions for his benefit.

Lacy fell for it. Hook, line, and sinker. "Oh, no. What's wrong, Clarence?"

"He doesn't seem to like the water. I bought him a life vest so he could swim in the ocean, or at least splash around. But he won't even go near it," I said.

Lacy stood up and scrutinized Clarence. "What kind of dog is he?

"He's a mixed breed. Mostly beagle, according to the doggie DNA test I ordered on the internet," I said.

"I'm afraid that explains it," said Lacy. "Beagles aren't the best swimmers. They don't typically like water. If you wanted to teach him to swim, you would have needed to do it as a puppy."

Well, that was one mystery solved. "Thanks for that information. I didn't know that about beagles. I guess Snoopy didn't hang out in the pool." I laughed, and Trevor rolled his eyes.

"Guess not," she said. "Can I help you with anything else?"

That was a perfect opening. "Terrible news about your mayor, Ronan Godfrey," I said. "Did you know him well?"

Lacy winced at the question. "Everyone in town knew Ronan."

"We heard he was trying to change a lot of things in Duck," said Trevor.

"Politicians tend to do that." Lacy's voice dripped with sarcasm. "It's in their nature."

"Ronan really wasn't a politician, though. He was a rich computer whiz who'd come to Duck in search of the perfect beach town," I said. "At least that's what we heard."

Lacy snickered. "I guess that's one way to put it. Ronan might have been a techie, but he'd become a full-blown politician in the past couple of months."

"I take it you didn't agree with him," said Trevor.

Lacy pursed her lips and didn't say anything.

"Don't feel like you're the only one," I said. "From what I gather, a lot of people weren't interested in what he was trying to promote. The town hall meeting was evidence of that."

Lacy's forehead wrinkled. "Since you were at the meeting, you know he wanted to revisit the policy of allowing dogs on the beach." She quivered in anger. "My entire business model is built on the fact that Duck is one of the most popular beaches in the country for dogs. I have razor-thin margins at this store. I can't even afford to hire another person to help me out on a regular basis. And to think he was going forward with it when . . ." She stopped herself before continuing.

"When what?" I asked.

She stammered before answering. "When I asked him not to do it," she said finally.

"Did you feel like you had a lot of influence over him?" I asked. "His wife Thalia mentioned you'd been spending a considerable amount of time with him lately."

"She would say that." Lacy's eyes sparkled with annoyance. "Thalia talks more than she should."

"Were you at the bar last night?" asked Trevor. "The one that Ronan owned?"

"Everyone goes to Sonoma Sunsets on Saturday night," she said defensively. "Why does that matter?"

"Did you hear anything suspicious, like someone threatening the mayor? Maybe he got into a disagreement with a customer?" I asked.

"Not that I remember. It was a typical summer evening. Everyone had a few drinks," she said. "Even though most of the business owners were angry when Ronan tossed Jean out of that space to make way for his fancy organic bar, the ambiance is nice. I went home after last call."

"You live locally?" asked Trevor.

"Within walking distance of my store," she said. "My mother

passed away a few years ago and I inherited the family house. It's located on the sound side of the island, where the prices are less exorbitant."

"After the evening at Sonoma Sunsets, you walked home." It was more of a statement than a question. "Do you live with anyone? A roommate or a partner?" I noticed she didn't wear a wedding ring.

"Yes, no, and no," she said in a matter of fact tone. "I live with a dog. His name is Jimmy, and I'm sure he'd be willing to vouch for me."

"Jimmy aside, that means you don't have an alibi for the time of the murder," said Trevor. While it was a statement of fact, it sounded more like an accusation.

"I suppose not, but there's no reason for me to need one. I didn't murder Ronan Godfrey," Lacy said. "If you understood . . ." Her voice trailed off, and she didn't finish the sentence.

"Who might have wanted to kill him?" I asked.

Lacy thought for a moment. A customer interrupted our conversation and asked for help finding the right dog food for her pup. Lacy left us for the far corner of the store.

"What do you think?" I whispered to Trevor.

"She avoided your questions about spending a lot of time with the victim," said Trevor. "I think she's hiding something."

Trevor glanced in Lacy's direction. She was deeply ensconced in discussing the multitude of nutritional options for the customer's dog. He motioned for me to step behind the counter.

Without a word, I handed Clarence's leash to Trevor and slowly stepped into Lacy's work area so I could snoop. There was a framed picture of a cute yellow lab, which I presumed was Jimmy. Besides strewn sticky notes and invoices, I didn't see too much of importance. But then I spotted a loose photo, taped to the inside wall of a cubbyhole underneath the countertop. I couldn't quite make out who was pictured in the photo because there was no light where it was placed.

"Make sure she doesn't come back here for another minute," I whispered to Trevor.

Trevor took his charge seriously. As I hunched down to

investigate, I heard Trevor announce, "Clarence needs a new harness. The one he's wearing is worn and it could break. What would fit him? Clarence, please sit so you can get measured."

Clarence had no fewer than three harnesses, but another one couldn't hurt. The photograph had been obscured by paperwork and other items. I grabbed my phone to shine a light on it so I could see what it was without removing it. I suppressed a gasp when I made out the two people in the snapshot. With their arms around each other, Lacy and Ronan Godfrey smiled back at me.

Chapter Nine

I WAS TEMPTED TO FILCH THE PHOTOGRAPH so we'd have evidence to show Detective Gomez. But then Lacy would know about it, and I didn't want to spook her. At the very least, I could let the police know about it, and Gomez could discover it herself.

"This one seems to fit," Trevor said loudly, letting me know he couldn't keep Lacy occupied much longer.

I remained hunched down and scooted my way around the counter. Then I stood up and found myself face to face with Lacy. "Why were you bent over on the ground?"

I could see Trevor motioning to me behind her, but for the life of me, I couldn't make out what he was trying to say. I wasn't very good at charades.

"Um... I lost something," I stammered. I also wasn't very good at lying on the fly.

"What did you lose?" asked Lacy pointedly.

"My phone," I said lamely. "But I found it." I waved it at her with my left hand.

Lacy narrowed her eyes but didn't say anything. Trevor spoke up, "I think we'll take this harness, won't we, Kit?"

"Yes, of course." I was grateful for Trevor's distraction. I pulled out my wallet and placed my credit card on the counter. "I can't believe I didn't bring Clarence's back-up harness with me to the beach."

Lacy rang up the purchase. As she handed me the item, she said, "You might consider looking closer at Thalia Godfrey and Jean Rizzo."

"You think one of them killed Ronan Godfrey?" asked Trevor.

"That's what we were talking about before we were interrupted, right?" She paused. "Thalia and Jean spend a lot of time together, and both of them had reasons for killing Ronan."

"Didn't you spend a lot of time with Ronan?" I asked. She'd ignored my earlier question about this.

Lacy bristled. "We'd gotten to know each other better," she said. "Nothing out of the ordinary. I'm a business owner in a small beach town. It makes sense that I should know the mayor."

I couldn't disagree with her reasoning. "Did Thalia and Ronan have an unhappy marriage?"

Lacy swallowed hard. "It was more like they went their separate ways. Thalia is into that New Age stuff. Ronan might have left Silicon Valley, but he couldn't pry himself away from business or making money. It was in his blood."

"Why did he move here in the first place?" asked Trevor. "I've read several stories published about him, yet none of them say why he relocated to the Outer Banks."

"I don't know," said Lacy quickly. A woman entered the store with a large Boxer. Clarence wagged his tail in excitement.

Lacy motioned toward the new customer. "I'd better get back to my job. Excuse me."

After Clarence greeted his new doggie acquaintance, we left the store and began the walk back to our beach house. "Did you find something underneath the counter?" asked Trevor. "I tried to stall her as long as I could."

"You did a great job," I said. "And, as a matter of fact, I did find something underneath the counter." I told Trevor about the chummy snapshot of Lacy and Ronan.

"She obviously wanted to keep it private," said Trevor. "But she also wanted it in a place she would see it every day."

"With such a small operation, Lacy might not have another regular employee. If that's the case, only she works behind the counter. No one else would see it," I said. "It definitely signals they were involved in some sort of secret relationship. Don't you think?"

Trevor adjusted his glasses. "I would have to concur with that assessment, Ms. Marshall."

We arrived back at the house to find it empty. "I guess everyone headed to the beach for fun in the sun while we were sleuthing."

Trevor wrinkled his nose. "I've had more than enough sun for the day. I think I'll retire to my room for a brief rest."

I thought about taking a nap, but I wasn't really tired. The walk back from the store and the yoga class earlier in the day had invigorated me. Instead, I grabbed a mystery novel I'd been dying to read (pun intended) and headed outside to the pool. I hadn't gotten through the first chapter when I heard noises from the house.

"We're back!" Doug opened the sliding glass door from the second-floor deck.

"How was the beach?" I asked.

"We didn't go to the beach. We got dinner!"

Sebastian emerged onto the balcony, carrying a large silver pot. "Lisa had a good idea. We went to a place in town called Cravings and bought everything for a seafood boil tonight."

My eyes opened wide. "That's very ambitious. I thought we'd eat hot dogs and hamburgers again."

"It's a lot easier to prepare than it sounds. You tell them how many people you want to feed, and they give you everything you need. Including the pot to cook it in," said Doug.

"We got the Yankee pot, which includes lobster tails and clams," said Sebastian.

"That sounds like a splurge." My mouth was watering. There had been no time for a proper lunch today and the Duck doughnut I inhaled at breakfast seemed like an eternity ago.

"I hope it's not my last meal as a free man." Sebastian's lips pursed together in a worried line.

"Don't be ridiculous, Sebastian," said Doug. "No respected police officer is going to arrest you based purely on circumstance."

I'd left the pool and joined Sebastian and Doug on the balcony.

"Doug is right. You need to give us some time to unearth other suspects. For example, we discovered an important clue when we visited Lacy Madison at her dog store this afternoon." I told Doug and Sebastian about the hidden photograph I found underneath the counter.

"She must have had an affair with Ronan Godfrey," said Doug. "But he was keeping it under wraps, so she kept the photo out of sight."

"That also gives Thalia a clear motive for murder, especially if she suspected Ronan was messing around," said Sebastian.

"It becomes even more relevant if she thought Ronan might end their marriage because of it," I said. "She and her husband might not have been that close, but I doubt Thalia wanted to risk losing her affluent lifestyle."

Lisa emerged from the kitchen and joined us on the balcony. "The seafood pot will be ready in thirty minutes. In the meantime, I'll set out cheese and crackers as an appetizer."

After we thanked her, I lowered my voice and turned toward Sebastian. "Are you sure she has to join the FBI? She's a keeper."

Sebastian's face clouded over again. "Don't remind me. I couldn't sleep last night worrying about it and that's why I'm in this mess with the murder."

"Hopefully you can use the time on vacation to talk to Lisa about it," I said. "Most relationship problems can be solved if both people want to make it better."

Sebastian gave me a hug. "Thanks, big sister."

After Lisa came outside with a cheese plate that could have sufficed for dinner, Sebastian ran downstairs to let Trevor and Meg know that the seafood boil would be ready soon. Lisa was also pouring a chilled white wine, and I doubted Meg wanted to miss out on a pre-dinner libation.

Doug stuffed a hunk of cheddar into his mouth, washing it down with a sip of wine. "Are you feeling better about the case?"

I held up my hands like a scale and tilted them from side to side. "Maybe. There was definitely something suspicious between Lacy and Ronan. Likewise, Thalia doesn't seem too broken up about her husband's death. But it's all circumstantial."

Meg and Trevor trailed Sebastian up the steps and sat down outside. Meg's eyes lit up when she saw the cheese plate.

"Is that Asiago?" Meg popped a piece into her mouth. "Heaven," she pronounced. "What were you talking about?"

"What else?" asked Lisa, smiling. "Murder, of course!"

"Trevor told me what happened at the doggie store," said Meg. "What's our next move?"

"Good question." I thoughtfully sipped my wine.

"It was a beautiful, clear day," said Lisa. "That means the sunset will be spectacular tonight."

It was nice of Lisa to comment on the weather, but my mind was more focused on figuring out who killed Ronan Godfrey, so my brother didn't have to spend his entire vacation under police investigation.

"What's your point?" asked Trevor. With Trevor around, I never had to worry about asking the tough questions.

Lisa folded her arms across her chest. "My point is that when there's a beautiful sunset, people often gather on the boardwalk by the sound to watch it. It might be a good opportunity to interrogate a few suspects."

"What a great idea," said Sebastian enthusiastically. "We can walk over after dinner."

Lisa appeared with the big silver pot, which now smelled heavenly. After transferring the seafood to a large serving bowl, we dug in. Instead of talking about murder, Doug engaged Trevor in a spirited discussion about his next book. Doug had already written about U.S. presidents, Supreme Court justices, and even a former Speaker of the House. He was looking for a new challenge and hadn't yet found it.

"What about an American inventor, like Alexander Graham Bell?" asked Trevor.

Doug wrinkled his nose. "Would I need to understand science? That's not my strong suit."

"What about a captain of industry, like Andrew Mellon?" suggested Trevor.

"Business is boring to me," said Doug.

Now Trevor was getting exasperated. He rolled his eyes. "A literary figure? Mark Twain, for example?"

Doug sighed. "No, that doesn't seem right."

"You clearly want to write a book on another political figure, so why don't you just do it?" said Trevor.

Doug grumbled, but didn't say anything. I knew he was having a hard time figuring this out, which made him uneasy. If he wasn't working on a book, Doug became restless. It was probably why he was so fascinated with trying to help me figure out who killed Ronan Godfrey. A historian without a book topic was like a man without a country. I hoped Doug would come up with something innovative soon.

After dinner was finished and everything was tidy, we decided to leave in twenty minutes for the sunset at the boardwalk. All of us, including Clarence and Murphy, walked to the end of our street and across Duck Road. Sure enough, a crowd of people had already assembled on the wooden pier. A band was playing outside Aqua, an upscale restaurant situated directly on the sound. A group of tables lined the sound with perfect views of the sunset. They were all filled, so we would have to find a place amongst the numerous outdoor Adirondack chairs and tables adjacent to the restaurant. While Lisa and I remained outside with Clarence and Murphy, everyone else went inside to purchase a drink from the bar.

Lisa scanned the crowd.

"Do you notice anyone who we might want to interrogate?" I asked.

She shook her head slowly. "Not right now," she said. "It looks like mostly a tourist crowd."

The rest of the gang appeared with glasses of wine, pints of beer, and a seltzer water with lime for Trevor. "I need to be fresh for my fishing expedition tomorrow," he explained.

Meg handed me a glass of Prosecco. "I think I saw that lady from the pizza shop inside the bar," she said. "The one who was at the town hall meeting yesterday."

"Jean Rizzo," I said. "We definitely need to talk to her." I glanced at Clarence. "Maybe Doug should watch Clarence so I can go inside."

Lisa glanced at her watch. "I wouldn't worry about it," she said. "Sunset will happen in about ten minutes. She'll come outside for it."

Sure enough, everyone who had been inside the bar and restaurant began filing outside. Now the outdoor area was packed with onlookers. Sebastian pointed off in the distance. "It's getting closer."

Lisa had been right about the beauty of the sunset that evening. Shades of red, orange, golden yellow, and blue blended together to create an impressive tapestry in the sky. Everyone grabbed their phones and started snapping as the sun dropped closer to the horizon.

"Definitely the best part about the Outer Banks," said Lisa. "Sunrise in the mornings over the ocean and sunsets in the evening over the sound. It's one of the advantages of a barrier island. You get the benefits of both east and west."

For the next couple of minutes, everyone faced the sound and watched as the sun edged closer to the waterline. Finally, it disappeared behind the sound completely. The pastiche of colors continued to decorate the sky even as twilight enveloped us.

Doug gave me a squeeze and a quick peck on the cheek. "Aren't you happy we decided to vacation at the beach this year?"

"Yes, but I'd be happier if my brother wasn't a suspect in a murder investigation," I answered. After scanning the crowd, I spotted Jean Rizzo. "That's her," I said. "I'd better go speak with her."

"I'm coming with you." Doug trailed behind me and Clarence.

Jean's curly, auburn hair was swept back into a ponytail, and she wore an old t-shirt and casual shorts. I guessed she'd come directly from work. She was engaged in what was apparently an animated conversation with a man in a baseball hat I didn't know. Her hands waved wildly, even though she had a glass of red wine in her hand. As we approached, Jean stumbled a few steps to her left. If I wasn't careful, I'd be wearing that wine soon.

I approached her gingerly and waited for a break in the conversation. "Jean, my name is Kit Marshall. I attended the town meeting yesterday with my boss, Congresswoman Maeve Dixon." I extended my hand.

Jean turned to face me, her eyes slightly unfocused. She placed her wine glass on a small table. At least I didn't have to worry about her spilling it all over me. "Did you like the Outer Banks so much you decided to stick around?" The words slurred at the end of her question.

"We had a vacation planned in Duck," I said. "Unfortunately, when I was on a jog this morning with a friend, my dog and I discovered Ronan's body."

Jean glanced down at Clarence. "What a perceptive pooch. We should give him an award from the town." She giggled as she swayed back and forth.

Doug whispered in my ear. "I think she's had too many drinks, Kit. Maybe we should postpone our chat for another time?"

I put my hand up to indicate that Doug should desist. Who knows when we would have the chance to talk to Jean again? A sleuth had to make the most of these opportunities when they presented themselves, no matter the difficulties. Besides, what was the popular saying in World War II? *Loose lips sink ships.*

"You didn't like Mayor Godfrey very much, did you?" I asked.

Jean nudged the man she'd been speaking with before we interrupted. "This one is a regular Nancy Drew, isn't she?" The baseball hat man laughed uncomfortably and then made an excuse to leave the conversation.

"Now you've really done it," said Jean. "I was explaining to that guy about why he should try my pizza during his vacation."

"I understand your restaurant used to be on the boardwalk, before Ronan opened his organic wine bar," said Doug.

Jean nodded, her head bobbing up and down a little too rapidly. Clarence growled softly. It wasn't an aggressive growl, but more of an alert. Clarence could tell when people were acting strangely, and he'd decided Jean's behavior qualified as out of the ordinary.

I decided to ignore it and keep going. "Where is it located now?"

Jean waved her hand in the direction of Duck Road. "It's across the street and down a few blocks. Not a bad location, but certainly not anything like being on the water."

"Your business has decreased, I suppose." It was more of a statement than a question.

"It has, but I'm looking into other options," said Jean, smiling. "Things are looking more promising."

I was about to ask her where she was at the time of the murder when Tobias Potter suddenly appeared. "What's going on here?" he asked.

"Just a friendly conversation with Jean," I said.

Tobias's eyes narrowed. "I heard the police think your brother might have killed Ronan."

Jean's smile widened. "Wasn't he the one who caused all that trouble at the town meeting?"

"He didn't cause any trouble," I said swiftly. "He attended because he's an old friend of Gary Brewster's."

"Well, if he killed Ronan, he did us all a favor." Jean's laugh sounded like something between a giggle and a cackle.

"That's enough," said Tobias. "It's about time you head home, Jean. Remember what we talked about earlier today."

Was he referring to the fact that he, Thalia Godfrey, and Jean had hung out together after the yoga session? Were the three of them in cahoots? Did they meet earlier today to get their stories straight?

Jean seemed to ignore Tobias. Instead, she muttered something about finishing her wine before leaving. She made an unsteady motion to try to grab her glass but lost her balance in the process and stumbled. Clarence was already on high alert due to her previous behavior.

I saw what happened next in slow motion. When she wavered, Clarence jumped to his feet and swung his tail around, knocking her wine off the table and onto the ground. Oblivious to what he'd done, Clarence sat down next to me and gave my leg a lick.

"Now look what your mutt has done," said Jean, her nostrils flared. "Isn't it enough he stuck his nose once where it didn't belong?"

Clarence's ears flattened against his head. He didn't like raised voices and sensed hostility. I reached down to pat him on the top of his head, so he'd know he wasn't in trouble.

Tobias grabbed Jean's arm. "Now I'm going to insist you return home," he said. "Come on. I'll walk with you."

Jean walked away with Tobias guiding her. When she was about to exit the restaurant parking lot, she turned around to look back. Her flinty eyes stared directly at me. If looks could kill, Jean Rizzo would have murdered me in cold blood.

Chapter Ten

THE NEXT MORNING, I WOKE AT THE CRACK OF DAWN. Old habits die hard. I'd been on the road with Maeve Dixon for weeks, and our days had started when the sun came up. A military veteran, my boss believed in the "early to bed, early to rise" adage. Her idea of a late morning event was a breakfast starting at eight o'clock. My circadian rhythms might never recover. On the other hand, Doug had no problem adjusting to vacation life. He was snoring loudly with no signs of waking anytime soon.

Clarence must have decided it was simply too exciting to stay in bed while visiting the beach. He jumped off the bed and stared at me with his big, brown eyes. When I didn't move, he picked up his paw and hit my hand dangling next to the bed. Finally, when that didn't work, he started licking my hand. He was just about to move to my face when I gave in.

"You win," I grumbled. "We can go for a walk."

Clarence knew a handful of words in the English language, including "pepperoni," "breakfast," "treat," and certainly "walk." His butt wiggled in delight when he heard the magic word.

I threw on shorts, a t-shirt, and sandals. We'd gone for a jog yesterday and it hadn't turned out so well. Today we would aim lower, like a walk on the beach. Perhaps Clarence's ocean phobia could be overcome if he experienced it with fewer people around to distract him.

When I opened our bedroom door, I was surprised to see Meg sitting on the living room couch. "Good morning," I said. "You're awake early." In all my years of friendship with Meg, I'd never known my best friend to forego sleep, at least willingly.

Meg tugged at her oversized pajama top. "Trevor got up at a ridiculously early hour for a morning fishing trip on the sound."

"And you couldn't go back to sleep?" I asked. Meg usually slept like a baby, so I was surprised she hadn't simply turned over when Trevor left.

She clenched her jaw as she answered. "No."

Something is wrong in paradise. I'd been preparing myself for this. Since I'd been out of town, I had missed any developing drama. Obviously, I needed the download. It was almost as important as solving the mystery of who killed Ronan Godfrey.

"Would you like to accompany us for a walk on the beach?" I asked. "You're already awake. Might as well burn a few calories." The last inducement was a farce. Meg had a superpower, which was her ability to eat and drink whatever she wanted without any obvious consequences. She was a svelte size six, and I doubt she'd ever waver from it.

Meg remained silent for several moments, apparently considering whether it would be better to wallow in her despair or join us for some early morning exercise.

"Ok-a-y," she said, drawing out the word. "Give me a few minutes to change."

Clarence watched as she walked past us and headed downstairs. He sat down, looking at me expectantly. *Time for the walk, lady?*

I hooked Clarence's harness to his leash and headed downstairs. We only had to wait a mere twelve minutes before Meg emerged, wearing grey jogging shorts with a matching sporty top. She'd even added a purple headband as a complimentary accessory.

Our street was completely silent. If there were early risers around us, they weren't venturing outside. It was Monday morning, the first official day of vacation. Weekends didn't count. What really mattered was that first morning when the alarm clock didn't go off, forcing a race-against-the-clock routine to exercise, shower, dress, and make sure everything and everyone was ready for the day. It might have been the crack of dawn, but we were up willingly. Instead of rushing through the normal morning rituals, we were walking to the beach. Murder or no murder, at least we had that going for us.

"Is Clarence going to be okay with walking on the beach?" asked Meg.

"I thought I'd see if he liked it any better without a lot of people around." I gestured with my right hand. "I brought the retractable leash just in case. He can walk near the dunes away from the water if he's still afraid."

We walked in silence until we reached our destination. Clarence took one look at the gently crashing waves and abruptly pulled in the opposite direction.

I sighed. "I suppose it was worth a try." I allowed the leash to expand so Clarence could walk as far away as possible from the water. He seemed satisfied with this arrangement, his tail wagging as he sniffed the sand and dug for elusive, disappearing crabs.

"It's very hard to change someone's nature," said Meg, almost suddenly. "Or something's nature."

I tilted my head to the side. What a curious comment. "You're right," I said slowly. "Although people do change. Dogs, too." I paused for a long moment before speaking again. "Would you like to talk about what's bothering you?"

"Why do you think something is bothering me?" countered Meg as she flipped her blonde bob held back from the ocean breeze by the purple headband.

"The best friend I know doesn't wake up this early unless there's a good reason. She also doesn't make comments about unchanging natures and the like." I giggled to ease the tension.

Meg turned towards me. "You know me too well, Kit. I can't hide anything from you."

"Why would you want to hide something from me?" I asked in a soft voice. "I know I've been traveling for several weeks, but there's always the phone. Or even video chat."

Her blue eyes had welled up in tears. We stopped walking, and I put my arm around her. "It can't be that bad, Meg."

She wiped away the stray tears and forced a smile. "It's not, really."

"Does it have to do with Trevor?" I asked.

She shook her head. "The problem isn't with Trevor."

We started walking again. "Then who? Or what?"

Meg avoided my stare. "Kit, it's me. There's something wrong with me." She pointed to herself.

A wave of panic shot through my body. Was Meg sick? I studied her face carefully. She didn't look any different. I'd been away for close to a month. Wouldn't I have noticed a change in her appearance?

"What do you mean?" I asked. "What's wrong with you?"

"It's like what I said before. Nature doesn't change," she said. "I'm a commitment-phobe. And I always will be."

Relief washed through me. This was Meg being Meg. Melodramatic as always. There was nothing wrong with her, at least nothing seriously wrong.

"You're upset because Trevor is pushing you to commit to the relationship?" I guessed.

Meg nodded. "That's my suspicion. I think that's why he's so focused on considering the next step in his career. His job working for the Chief Administrative Officer is a good one and he really likes it."

Trevor worked in the House of Representatives in an advisory role. It was a senior position and seemed to suit him well.

"Go on," I said. "What's the problem, then?"

"It doesn't pay a ton," she said. "I think he feels pressure to make more money."

"To get married?" I asked.

Meg's face turned red. "I suppose."

Months ago, Trevor had indicated he wanted a permanent, committed relationship. Meg had been dating another guy but had decided to end it so she and Trevor could become exclusive.

"And I'm guessing you're not ready?" I asked.

"Kit, you know me. I've had a lot of boyfriends and now it's just

Trevor. I don't know if I'm made out for . . ." She trailed off.

I finished the sentence for her. "Monogamy?"

"Yes," she said irritably. "When you say it, it sounds so stodgy." She added, "Almost like an *illness*."

I laughed, this time not to break the tension but because Meg cracked me up. We were very different people, yet I loved her like a sister.

"Listen, Meg," I said. "You need to tell Trevor how you feel. You don't want him to make a major career change and then find out you need more time to figure things out."

We turned around so we could head back in the direction of our house. Clarence seemed happy enough, as long as I allowed him to stay as far away from the ocean as possible.

Meg picked up our serious conversation. "I've tried to talk to him about it. Once Trevor gets his mind fixed on something, it can be hard to persuade him otherwise."

"You should use this week on vacation to explain it to him," I said. "Tell him you need more time."

"Most women are excited about finding a guy who wants to marry them," said Meg, lowering her voice to almost a whisper. "It's harder for me. It doesn't come naturally."

There was that word again. *Nature*. Perhaps Meg had a point. Were some people naturally inclined to resist commitment? Just as others were naturally inclined to hate spinach or fear the ocean? If that was the case, what could be done about it?

I thought carefully before responding. "Don't put so much pressure on yourself, Meg. You shouldn't label yourself."

We'd exited the beach and walked along the sidewalk of the street. Meg smiled. "Thanks, Kit. It's always good to talk to you."

"And we didn't talk about the murder for even a moment," I said. "But, don't worry. There will be plenty of opportunity for it later today, I'm sure."

When we arrived at the house, Doug had awoken from his slumber and was sitting in the living room. He seemed to be staring into space when Clarence and I presented ourselves.

"What are you doing?" I asked.

He turned his head quickly. "You startled me."

"Sorry. We just came back from an early morning walk on the beach," I said.

"I was trying to decide if I should make coffee or if we should walk to that cozy bookstore in town for it," said Doug.

I laughed. "That's a good vacation problem. Clarence has already had his walk. I'm up for the bookstore."

Doug jumped up. "I'll be ready in five minutes." He practically ran into our bedroom and shut the door.

"That's the fastest I've seen Doug move in years," said Meg.

I nodded. "And all I had to say was the magic word." I paused for a beat. "*Bookstore.*"

"I wish some of Doug's clarity would rub off on me," grumbled Meg.

I put my arm around her and gave her an affectionate squeeze. "Don't despair. Think of the bright side. You have an incredibly successful and smart man who adores you. How bad can it be?"

Meg blinked several times. "I suppose. The question is whether I want him to be the last man who *adores* me."

I couldn't argue with that sentiment. Marriage and romantic commitment had numerous advantages. However, it did put a significant crimp on your dating life.

Doug emerged from our bedroom, dressed in his swimming trunks, flip-flops, and a Georgetown University t-shirt. "I figure I'll head to the beach after our trip to the bookstore."

"Great idea. After all, where else will you read all the great books you're going to buy?" I asked.

I made sure Clarence was settled with fresh water and his breakfast. Moments later, we were walking arm in arm in the opposite direction I'd gone with Meg.

"How long of a walk to the bookstore?" I hadn't noticed it yesterday during our quick tour around the town.

"Fifteen minutes or so," said Doug. "You might have seen it already, but you probably didn't know it was a bookstore. It's called Duck's Cottage, and it used to be a hunting lodge. I read about it online."

When exploring a new location, some men researched sports bar options or perhaps the best place to get a juicy burger or authentic barbecue. Doug was a recovering academic, which meant he immediately figured out which bookstore in town looked the most promising.

"Why don't you tell me about it?" I squeezed his arm as we walked.

"Apparently, this cottage was the only hunting lodge in Duck. It was built in the early nineteen-hundreds by a bunch of guys from New York City who liked to hunt waterfowl in this part of the Outer Banks," he said. "It was privately owned until 2001 and then it became a bookstore and coffee shop."

"I bet the ducks were happy with the change in business model," I said.

"What time do ducks wake up?" asked Doug.

"Is this some sort of riddle?" I giggled.

"No, silly. At the quack of dawn." Doug slapped his leg with his right arm.

After a big guffaw, I squeezed Doug's arm again. "Thank you for the corny joke. I needed to laugh."

"You did, Kit," he said. "I know you're concerned about your brother and this murder business, but please remember that you're on vacation. Try to enjoy yourself."

We had come upon a wooden lodge alongside the main road. I could smell the freshly brewing coffee from outside. That morning aroma couldn't be beat.

"I do plan on enjoying myself," I insisted. "The faster I can clear Sebastian, the more fun in the sun I can enjoy."

Doug sighed, but said nothing further. He'd raced up the stairs of the porch and held open the cottage door for me.

"Enjoy your happy place," I whispered. "I'll order coffee for us."

The store wasn't very big. The coffee bar was directly to the left; books were straight ahead and on the right. I got in line and studied the menu, which presented a wide array of espresso options. Normally, Doug and I went for basic lattes or cappuccinos. However, Duck's Cottage had an array of carefully curated coffee concoctions.

We simply couldn't go with the unadulterated versions.

When it was my turn, I stepped up and placed my order. "A Mucky Duck and Ruddy Duck, please." After I paid for our drinks and a souvenir bag, emblazoned with the "*Peace. Love. Books. Coffee.*" logo, I stood to the side of the counter to wait for our drinks. I heard a familiar voice next to me. "Ms. Marshall?"

I looked to my left and was surprised to see Tobias Potter.

"Good morning, Tobias," I said. "Did Jean get home last night without incident?"

His lips formed a tight, thin line. "She did. Sorry about her behavior last night at sunset. She's been under a lot of stress lately."

"It must be difficult to move your business from a prime location like the waterfront," I said. "I'm sure it has been jarring for her to adjust."

"It's certainly not ideal," said Tobias.

The barista handed Tobias his drink, and he was about to leave the store. I had to act swiftly if I wanted to continue the conversation.

"Would you like to join me outside on the porch?" I asked. "My husband will be examining the books here for a while. I'd appreciate the company."

Tobias didn't hesitate. "Sure. I have a few minutes before I have to get back. I'll grab a table and meet you outside."

When our drinks were ready, I walked over to Doug and lowered my voice. "Tobias Potter is outside, and he's agreed to chat with me." I presented the two coffee cups to Doug. "Do you want the Mucky Ducky or the Ruddy Duck?"

"I'd rather be ruddy than mucky any day," said Doug seriously.

I smiled and shoved one of the drinks in Doug's hand. "Come outside when you're finished looking around."

Tobias had secured one of the tables on the porch. He'd removed his ever-present baseball hat and was sipping his hot coffee. I slid into the seat across from him and lifted my cup to meet his. "Cheers," I said. "Let's toast to finding Mayor Godfrey's killer."

Tobias frowned. "Isn't your brother a suspect?"

I licked the froth off my upper lip before responding. "The

police have questioned him. But Sebastian didn't kill Ronan. He only met him earlier in the day at the town hall meeting."

Tobias shook his head slowly. "In these parts, outsiders often take the rap. You might want to keep that in mind."

"I'm quite aware of the . . ." I searched to find the right word. "Geographic insularity of our surroundings. There's still not one shred of evidence to tie Sebastian to the crime."

"Well, Ms. Marshall, if not your brother, then whodunit? I believe you've had experience in these types of matters."

I narrowed my eyes. "How did you know that?"

He leaned back in his chair. "There's a little thing called the internet. Perhaps you've heard of it. We might not be quite as fancy as the big city, but we can still get information when we want it."

"Fair point," I said tersely. I wasn't quite sure how much I should open up to Tobias Potter. He was close with Jean Rizzo and Thalia Godfrey, two prime suspects. For all I knew, Tobias might have bumped off Ronan.

Tobias took a long sip of his coffee and stared at me. He was waiting for me to divulge whom I suspected, but I was headed in another direction with my questions. "You must have known Mayor Godfrey well. You worked at Sonoma Sunsets and serve on the town council, right?"

The creases on Tobias's face deepened as he smiled. Years of living at the beach had weathered his appearance, yet he wore it well. It was hard to guess if he was in his fifties or sixties. Was his relationship with Thalia more than just friendship, as Meg suspected? Even though he was at least fifteen years older than her, I could see the appeal, especially if her marriage to Ronan was on the fritz. Tobias seemed like a caring guy. He might have been more than willing to provide Thalia with the warmth that Ronan could or would not.

"When Ronan was elected mayor, I tried to help him in the initial months," said Tobias. "It became clear he wanted to approach things in his own way. I backed off." He paused to take another sip of coffee.

"And Sonoma Sunsets?" I prodded.

"I didn't help him acquire the spot on the water. I've known Jean Rizzo for a long time. I knew moving her restaurant could potentially hurt her business."

"But then you somehow ended up working there?" I asked.

Tobias nodded. "Ronan got Gary Brewster to sign on as a partner first."

I cleared my throat. "Surely Ronan didn't need Gary's money. He had plenty from the fortune he made earlier in his career."

"It wasn't the money Ronan was after. It was Gary's connections to the environmental community," said Tobias. "Ronan loved the idea of opening the first organic wine bar in the Outer Banks. But he didn't know anything about organic products or farming. Gary had those connections, or at least he knew how to make them."

I took another chug of my Mucky Duck and savored the sweet blend of chocolate, caramel, and espresso. I could almost feel the caffeine coursing through my veins and traveling to my brain. The little grey cells, as Hercule Poirot called them, had been activated.

"And in addition to the Corolla horses, Gary had always wanted the opportunity to do something significant in the environmental community," I said. "It was a win for both of them."

Tobias nodded. "Mutually beneficial, you could say. Gary suggested that I could become a manager at the wine bar. I'm retired, but the extra income is helpful."

"Were you working the night that Ronan Godfrey was murdered?" I asked. Doug would finish up his book shopping soon, and I wanted to make sure I got what I needed from Tobias.

"Sure was," said Tobias.

Apparently, now it was his turn to be reticent. If I needed to pull details out of him, so be it.

"Anything out of the ordinary that night?" I asked. "Like an angry customer or something unexpected?"

"Nope. That's what I told the police, too. Everyone had a few drinks, but that's typical for a Saturday night."

"As the manager, is it your job to make sure everything is locked up?" I asked. "How late did you stay?"

"I think I was the last one there." Tobias rubbed his chin. "We try to put everything away overnight, but we deal with a lot of bottles of wine. I can't say there wasn't a bottle or two behind the bar, especially if they'd been opened."

That confirmed what we heard earlier. Anyone could have walked behind the bar, snagged a bottle, and bashed Ronan over the head.

"Do you remember Ronan saying he was going home?" I asked.

"I think so. He had two or three glasses of wine, but he was walking home to his big beach house. Typical behavior for him."

"When did the other regulars leave?" I asked.

"All about the same time," he said. "Everyone took off after they finished up."

"You were there alone for a while?" I asked.

"Probably thirty minutes. It doesn't take too long to clean up." Tobias stared at me. He knew what I was going to ask next before I even said it, so he beat me to the punch. "I can guess what you're thinking. Ronan could have returned to the bar, and I could have killed him."

I leaned back in my chair. "I didn't say anything of the sort."

"You didn't have to say it," said Tobias. "But that's not what happened. I never saw Ronan again after he left the bar that night."

"If it wasn't you, do you know who might have killed Ronan Godfrey?" I asked.

He answered quickly. "An outsider." Then he realized the import of his words, since Sebastian would fit the bill. "If it wasn't your brother, then someone else who came to the Outer Banks to settle a score with Ronan."

The problem was that no one had seen anyone like that lurking around town before Ronan's death. If someone like that had shown up, Ronan hadn't shared it with anyone.

I thought about the hidden photograph of Lacy and Ronan I'd discovered underneath the counter at the doggie store. "I heard Ronan had been spending a lot of time with Lacy Madison lately. Was something going on between them?"

Doug appeared at our table, holding a tote bag filled with books. Tobias stood. "Looks like your husband has done his share in supporting the local economy." He motioned for Doug to take his seat. "I really need to get going."

Before I could press him to answer my questions about Lacy and Ronan, he sped off the porch and hustled in the direction of the boardwalk, disappearing into the crowd of tourists who were strolling along the sound for a morning walk.

"Bad timing," I muttered.

"What did you say?" he asked.

"Never mind." It was no use blaming Doug. After all, it wasn't his fault. I had a feeling Tobias didn't want to touch the topic of Lacy and Ronan's relationship with a ten-foot pole. "Did you find a lot of books?"

Doug's face brightened. "Absolutely. I got a mixture of history, biography, and fiction. I even bought you a mystery set in the Outer Banks."

I smiled and thanked Doug for the book. Before I could enjoy reading it, I had my own beach mystery to solve.

Chapter Eleven

Doug and I finished our espresso drinks and decided it was time to head back to the house. As we strolled along the walking path, Doug inquired about my next move. I answered with my own question.

"Are you hungry for a pizza lunch?" I asked.

Doug rubbed his belly. "I'm always up for pizza. Somehow, I don't think we're going to have much time to sample the extraordinary seaside cuisine of the Outer Banks until we apprehend the killer."

"Nope, but there's no reason why we can't enjoy a slice or two while I interrogate Jean Rizzo," I said. "Let's hope she's sobered up from last night and can give us some answers."

We were just about ready to turn down our street when I spotted a familiar face jogging towards us. I put my hand on Doug's arm and gestured down the path. "Detective Gomez is headed our way."

Carla Gomez was dressed in jogging shorts and a Kitty Hawk PD tank top. She was moving at a fast clip, but when she recognized us, she slowed down.

"Taking a break from the case for morning exercise?" I asked in a friendly voice.

She wiped a stream of sweat off her forehead. "It's the only chance I have to get my PT in today." Despite my light-hearted tone, Gomez didn't crack a smile.

"How are you progressing on the investigation?" asked Doug. "Caught the guilty party yet?"

Gomez motioned down the street. "This is where your beach house is located, right?"

I nodded, gulping hard. Why was she asking that?

"I need to pay your brother another visit this morning. Is he around?" she asked.

"I think so. He was sleeping when we left the house this morning to get coffee," I said.

"As soon as I clean up from my exercise, I'll come by. Please don't go anywhere before that." Even though she'd used the word "please," the way she said it implied more of a command than a request.

"Can I ask what this is about?" I knew it was futile, but I had to try so I could prepare Sebastian.

She shook her head. "I'd rather speak to your brother directly. You can remain in the room when I talk to him if you like. He's not under arrest." She paused for a beat. "Yet, that is."

Doug pulled me toward our street. "We'll see you soon, Detective," he said.

We walked out of earshot before I unloaded. "What could she possibly have discovered that points a finger at Sebastian?"

My brother might be a hippie protester who previously got himself in trouble with the law for his ideological beliefs. That did not make him a killer. In fact, Sebastian literally wouldn't hurt a fly. When he found an insect inside the house, he scooped it up with a paper towel and placed it outside so "it could continue to live a full life." Those were his words, not mine.

Doug shook his head. "I don't know, Kit. We'll have to wait to hear what she says." He put his arm around me. "We know Sebastian didn't do anything wrong. It just means we need to try harder to find the actual murderer."

That was the understatement of the year. Talk about a botched vacation. I didn't want to return to North Carolina to visit my one and only sibling in prison.

Doug must have sensed I was upset. When we reached our house, he said, "Why don't you go upstairs and relax for a few minutes? I'll tell Sebastian what happened and make sure he's ready for Detective Gomez."

I mustered a smile. "Sounds like a good plan, Doug."

I trudged up the two floors to our bedroom and walked inside. Clarence was sleeping on our bed, snoring like a champion. I jumped next to him and gave him a squeeze. He woke up with a start, but when he saw who it was, he gave me a big lick on the nose—exactly what I needed to get through this unexpected wrinkle. I took a few deep breaths and decided it was best to face the music.

Sebastian, Doug, Lisa, and Meg were sitting around the sectional living room sofa with faces that looked like a wet weekend. I had to break the tension.

"So solemn. Who died?" I forced a smile. "Besides Ronan Godfrey, that is."

Unfortunately, my attempt at levity was unsuccessful. No one mustered even an iota of cheerfulness.

Doug jumped up. "Who wants coffee? I'll make some." He dashed off to the kitchen to start a fresh pot.

"No matter what Detective Gomez says, don't get rattled," said Lisa. "Remember, you don't have to answer her questions."

Sebastian ran his hand through his sandy hair. "I have nothing to hide. I didn't kill Ronan Godfrey."

"Try not to sound exasperated," I said gently. "It seems desperate."

Sebastian rolled his eyes but kept his mouth shut, which I interpreted as a positive sign he understood what Lisa and I were trying to say.

Doug returned with mugs of hot coffee. Even though we'd had an espresso already this morning, I welcomed the extra caffeine. We all needed to remain alert and observant.

Ten minutes later, a knock at the door broke the silence.

"That's her," said Sebastian. "It's not like we're expecting any other visitors on vacation."

"I'll get it," I said. "Stay put and don't look so nervous, for goodness's sake."

I opened the door, and Detective Gomez didn't wait for me to ask her inside. She stepped forward as she spoke. "Is your brother home?"

"He's upstairs," I said, pointing up. Gomez was joined by a uniformed police officer, who didn't bother to introduce himself. He simply followed her up the stairs, leaving me trailing behind.

She strode into the living room and looked around. After clearing her throat, she said, "I'm here to speak to Sebastian Marshall." She turned toward my brother. "Do you want everyone to listen while I ask you questions about the murder of Ronan Godfrey?"

"It makes no difference to me," said Sebastian evenly. "Everyone here knows I didn't kill anyone."

Gomez pulled out her notebook and flipped through a few pages. "Is it still your contention that you went for a walk on the beach the night in question?"

Sebastian nodded. "That's what happened. I woke up and couldn't fall back asleep, so I went for a walk."

"And you didn't walk over to the boardwalk, near Sonoma Sunsets or any of the businesses situated on the sound?" asked Gomez.

Sebastian shook his head back and forth. "No. It was a clear night and there was plenty of moonlight. I walked on the beach, listening to the ocean. Then I returned to our vacation house."

Gomez pursed her lips. She motioned toward the uniformed police officer, who pulled out a plastic baggie from his pocket before handing it to her.

Gomez turned the baggie over so she could examine its contents. There appeared to be a small piece of paper or card inside. She walked over to Sebastian and handed it to him.

"Look familiar?" She squinted at him.

Sebastian didn't hesitate. "That's my business card." He rubbed the back of his neck with his other hand. "More of a contact card. It's what I use when I'm doing my volunteer environmental advocacy work."

"You mean protesting, which has gotten you arrested several times?" Gomez stated it more as a fact than a question, but Sebastian responded anyways.

"When I go to . . ." He paused for a moment as he considered his words. "A participatory event, if I meet interesting people with similar beliefs, I give them my card."

"May I?" I motioned toward the evidence bag.

"Of course," said Detective Gomez. "Be my guest."

Inside the plastic baggie was a single business card. There was a small emblem of the Earth with a peace symbol superimposed on top of it. To the right of the graphic was the text:

SEBASTIAN MARSHALL
ENVIRONMENTAL JUSTICE EQUALIZER
NO CAUSE TOO SMALL TO SAVE THE PLANET

I didn't know whether to laugh or cry. No doubt, this was my brother's "business" card. I doubted the self-anointed title of "Environmental Justice Equalizer" had impressed Detective Gomez. I could be wrong, but she probably wasn't a vigilante sympathizer.

Gomez pointed to the baggie, now in my hand. "Do you know how I came to possess your business card, Mr. Marshall?"

Sebastian swallowed hard. "I have no idea."

"Our crime scene technicians found it on the ground behind the bar, not far away from where the homicide took place," she said. "However, you contend you weren't anywhere near the boardwalk on the night in question." She threw her shoulders back and assumed a commanding posture. "This evidence puts you at the scene of the murder."

"Not necessarily, Detective," said Meg. "Someone else might have dropped the card."

"Was there anyone else who might have come into possession of your card?" asked Detective Gomez.

Sebastian shook his head. "I don't know. Gary introduced me to several people after the town hall meeting broke up." He paused for a moment. "I can't remember if I gave anyone my card. I always keep them in my pocket."

Gomez didn't say anything as she continued to write in her small notebook. Finally, she looked up. "Right now, from my perspective, Mr. Marshall's business card at the scene of the crime suggests to me that he isn't telling the truth and he ended up at the boardwalk that night. The way I see it, Ronan Godfrey decided he needed to return to the bar that night. Maybe he forgot something or maybe he wanted to have one last drink by himself. Mr. Marshall went out for a nighttime walk and they happened to run into each other. Perhaps the mayor becomes enraged because of the way the town hall meeting turned out. After all, he was embarrassed in front of a number of residents, who will vote in the next election. Godfrey might have blamed Mr. Marshall for meddling in town business."

She paused to take a breath before continuing. "There might have been a fight. Things could have gotten heated. Who knows? Maybe Godfrey even pushed Mr. Marshall or took a swing at him. There was an open bottle on the bar. Mr. Marshall grabbed it and hit Godfrey over the head." She pointed her pen at Sebastian. "If it happened the way I described it, Mr. Marshall, we could talk to the District Attorney about self-defense as a factor."

Sebastian's nostrils flared. "*It did not happen that way* . . . I didn't kill Ronan Godfrey, either by accident or on purpose. I wasn't anywhere near the boardwalk that night."

Normally soft-spoken Sebastian had been pushed too far. When the detective's gaze was elsewhere, I motioned discretely with my hand for him to tone it down. There was no sense in angering her. We'd already blown her theory out of the water, or at least cast reasonable doubt on it.

Gomez wrote a few more things in her notebook and then flipped it closed. She instructed the uniformed police officer to take the evidence baggie from me, which he did.

"Before you leave, Detective," I said. "Can you tell us if you've come across any other physical evidence at the crime scene?"

Gomez sighed. "Listen, Ms. Marshall. I hear from my superiors that you're politically connected, and your current boss might become our next United States Senator. Quite frankly, it means nothing to me." She put her hand on her hip. "But you can't get too far away from politics, even in the Outer Banks."

Normally, I would never accept favors because of my job. Since the detective had just admitted she liked my brother for the murder, I wasn't going to let any advantage slide. "No, you cannot, Detective. I would appreciate any information you can share. After all, everyone wants the guilty party brought to justice, right?"

She opened her notebook up and consulted several pages. "We're working on processing the scene right now. It's a forensics mess. The wine from the broken bottle, apparently a Cabernet Sauvignon, got mixed up with the evidence from the murder, as you know from the mess on your dog's paws. We're contacting the vineyard where the wine was produced to see if anyone there can help our chemists at the lab."

"You don't think there will be any fingerprints on the murder weapon?" I asked.

She shook her head. "We'll see what we can do, but the bottle shattered into a lot of pieces. Fragments might have ended up in the water below. It's going to be next to impossible to get anything from it."

So much for finding a smoking gun that could clear Sebastian. It didn't sound like there was a whole lot of physical evidence that could help find the identity of the killer. Unfortunately, the one piece of evidence that did show up pointed straight to Sebastian. Even though he may have given out his cards earlier in the day, the fact that one of them showed up at the murder scene didn't help us clear him from suspicion. Just the opposite, it kept Detective Gomez's desire to pin the crime on an outsider alive.

"Even if you could obtain prints from the bottle, it might not help identify the killer," said Lisa. "Who knows how many people handled that bottle of wine before it was used to kill Ronan Godfrey?"

"I agree with that assessment of the forensics," said Gomez. Even the toughest-minded detective had to give props to a fellow law enforcement officer.

"If we come across anything important, we'll let you know about it," I said. After all, it was imperative to remind Detective Gomez we wanted the killer caught.

"Please let us do the investigating," she said. "This isn't Capitol Hill, Ms. Marshall. Politics or not, I believe you're outside of your jurisdiction."

She motioned for her colleague that it was time to leave. As she headed down the stairs, she called out a final command, "Don't leave the Outer Banks without notifying me!"

"Doesn't she know how much it costs to rent these houses in August?" muttered Meg. "It's not like we're going to ditch our vacation voluntarily."

"That was a warning for me," said Sebastian glumly. "She wanted to make sure I won't skip town to avoid a murder charge."

"No one is getting charged for homicide or any other major felony," I said, using my I'm-in-charge-and-don't-mess-with-me voice.

"I like your confidence," said Lisa. "What's our next move?"

"I need to talk with Jean Rizzo. She'd had too many drinks last night when we saw her at sunset. I couldn't get anything useful out of her," I said.

"Maybe I could join you," said Lisa tentatively. "I don't think Jean knows who I am, so maybe she wouldn't be threatened by me."

I could tell Lisa wanted to assist with Sebastian's defense. "Of course. You were very helpful with Detective Gomez."

Doug cleared his throat. "I was looking forward to a pizza lunch."

Meg said, "Pizza would be perfect!"

"Then it's settled," I said. "Let's plan on leaving here at noon. Sebastian, we'll bring you a slice or two home. I think it's best you steer clear of our interrogations."

Sebastian's shoulders slumped forward. "I understand. I'm going for a swim in the ocean to clear my head."

We had some time before lunch, and the sun was already blazing. "Let's hit the pool," said Doug to me. "You need to relax after a stressful morning."

As always, Doug was right. I couldn't settle into the mystery novel he'd bought me at the bookstore this morning, but I did flip through the women's magazine Meg lent me. Within thirty minutes,

I read about what Reese Witherspoon liked to for breakfast, why one-shoulder bathing suits were uniformly flattering, and how I could maximize my preferred viewing list on Netflix. All in all, I learned more than I bargained for. More importantly, my body and mind took a break from murder.

After a dip in the pool and more than enough ultraviolet light exposure, we struck out on our walk to Jean's pizza shop. "At least we're getting exercise while investigating," I said, trying to keep everyone's mood upbeat.

"That's one of the best parts of vacationing in Duck," said Lisa. "You can walk everywhere. The beach, restaurants, and shops are all nearby."

"Do we know if this pizza is any good?" asked Meg. My best friend could get a little ornery about her food and wine selections.

"No idea," I admitted. "But it doesn't matter because we're going there to find out more about Jean Rizzo and whether she killed Ronan Godfrey."

"To Meg's point, we're also going there to eat pizza," said Doug.

"Yes, we will be eating pizza for lunch," I said. "However, the main objective is to speak with Jean Rizzo."

"There's no reason we can't do both, Kit," said Meg.

I rolled my eyes. I'd given up. Thankfully, we arrived at Jean's shop and walked inside. The cool air conditioning was a welcome respite from the heat and humidity outside. The beach breeze tempered the hot weather, but there was no escaping the ninety degree plus temperatures.

The restaurant had about ten tables, a countertop to place orders, and a cooler for drinks. The place was bustling with customers. I only spotted one free table.

"Meg, can you and Doug grab that table before someone else snags it?" I asked. "Lisa and I will try to find Jean."

Meg and Doug hustled over to the empty table. "Don't forget that I like pepperoni!" she called over her shoulder. How could I possibly forget?

Lisa and I walked toward the college student working the counter, who snapped her gum as we approached. She appeared as excited as one of Doug's history students during one of his infamous early morning lectures.

"Ready to order?" she asked, her pen poised to write on her trusty notepad.

"We're here for lunch, but we'd like to speak with Jean Rizzo. I believe she's the owner of the establishment," I said.

Her sparkling blue eyes narrowed. "Why do you want to speak to Jean? Are you her friends or something?"

Lisa started to say, "Not exactly" but I cut her off before she finished.

"Sort of," I said. "I had a drink with Jean last night, but she left unexpectedly before we could finish our conversation." That was a sanitized version of the truth, but not a total lie, either.

That seemed to soften up our friend behind the counter. "I think she's in her office. Let me check."

A minute later, Jean Rizzo emerged. Her posture stiffened when she recognized me.

"Oh, it's you. The woman with the dog that can't stop wagging its tail," she said.

"I brought my husband and friends here for lunch," I said. "I thought we could chat for a few minutes, if you have the time."

She seemed to consider my offer for a long moment before answering. "You can order first, and I'll join you while you wait for the pizza."

"Sounds like a plan," I said. After Lisa placed our order, we joined Doug and Meg at the table.

"Any luck?" asked Doug.

"Jean is headed our way now," I said.

"Is she eating lunch with us?" asked Meg. "I hope you ordered enough pizza."

I shook my head in disbelief and ignored Meg's question and comment. Jean came over to the table and sat down. She'd met Doug and Meg at the town hall meeting, but didn't know Lisa, who introduced herself as a "D.C. friend" but astutely avoided any reference to Sebastian.

"As I explained last night, Lisa and I discovered the body of

Ronan Godfrey yesterday morning," I said. "Do you know who might have wanted Ronan dead?"

The counter girl put pitchers of water on our table. Jean helped herself to a glass and took a sip before she answered. "Not to be funny, but our esteemed mayor wasn't exactly the most popular duck in Duck."

"We gathered that already," said Doug. "You had a long-standing feud with him over the relocation of your restaurant, right?"

Jean sighed. "Everyone knows that. Even though Duck is one of the most popular vacation spots in the Outer Banks, Ronan got it into his head that it could be more exclusive. You know, a higher income crowd. If that happened, rental rates for the vacation houses would go up. A certain group of property owners liked hearing that. Higher rental income means an increase of home values."

"And that's why he decided to open Sonoma Sunsets?" asked Lisa.

"Partly. I think Ronan also desperately wanted a business so he could connect himself to the town in a more meaningful way," said Lisa. "Most people grew up in the Outer Banks. Ronan moved here a few years ago with no ties to the area. Voters didn't fully understand why he wanted to be mayor."

"He forced you out of the waterfront location, though," said Meg. "Not very nice."

"It was ugly," said Jean. "My family has owned this business for a long time. It's my turn to run it, and I don't want it go under." She looked around the busy restaurant. "But we're making do in the new location."

"Were you at the wine bar the night Ronan was killed?" I asked.

Jean nodded. "You probably heard that Ronan said I could drink for free at his place. It was his version of a peace offering. It's the place the locals gather on Saturday nights, so I usually join in."

"How late did you stay?" asked Meg.

"Not very late, as I recall. Tobias said they didn't have the wine I usually drank, a Cabernet Sauvignon. I had some other wine and didn't care for it." She wrinkled her nose. "You know that all the wines there are organic? Most of the time, they're pretty good. Every once in a while, there's something funky about the taste."

"Then you went home?" asked Doug.

"I walked home," said Jean. "The house where I live has been in my family for a long time. It's not one of the huge, new construction vacation homes. But it's still only a short walk to town and the beach."

"Nothing out of the ordinary that night?" I asked. "Did you happen to see Ronan talk to anyone unusual? Perhaps a stranger you didn't recognize?" I still thought it was possible someone from Ronan's past could have showed up in the Outer Banks and killed him. He must have made considerable enemies on his way up the tech ladder.

Jean thought for a moment. "Not that I can remember. I saw him huddled with Tobias and Gary at different times. That was normal. As I'm sure you've already figured out, Gary was his business partner and Tobias helped him with the day-to-day management of the bar."

"Were they on amicable terms with Ronan?" asked Lisa. It was a good question, and I shot her a look of gratitude.

"It appeared so. Ronan handled the business operations, as far as I could tell. Gary was a part of it because of the focus on organic wines. He's our resident expert environmentalist in Duck," she said.

"And Tobias?" I asked. "Didn't he want to be the next mayor?"

"I'm sure Tobias felt as though he was entitled to that position. His family has lived in the Outer Banks for many years. But he seems to have gotten over it," she said.

"Sort of unusual to go to work for the guy who took your dream job away from you," said Meg.

"Tobias mentioned to me that the money was good. Let me enlighten you about the economy of a beach town." Jean waved her hands around. "We have this type of business for three or four months a year. We have to make enough during the high season to last the entire twelve months. That means employment is seasonal. When Ronan opened Sonoma Sunsets, he pledged to keep it open almost the entire year. I think Tobias appreciated the extra cash."

Two hot pizzas arrived at our table, along with the enticing aroma of tomato sauce, garlic, and oregano. It was New York style pizza, with hand-tossed thin crust, wide slices, and a thick sauce. We'd ordered one with pepperoni and the other with veggies, since Lisa and Sebastian didn't eat meat.

Jean stood up. "Enjoy your lunch. Thanks for stopping by my restaurant."

Before I could stop her, Jean had scurried behind the counter and disappeared. I still wanted to ask her about Thalia Godfrey. It seemed as though those two were close friends, and she might have been able to provide some insights about Thalia's relationship with Ronan.

We helped ourselves to slices and fell silent as we chomped away. Finally, after we'd all had a chance to enjoy a few bites, Doug leaned closer. "What did you think?"

"Interesting about Tobias," I said. "It seems as though he might have some financial pressure on him. If that's the case, there could be a motive we haven't uncovered yet. Maybe Tobias got into a fight or disagreement with Ronan about money."

Lisa spoke next. "Jean Rizzo is still a prime suspect. I wouldn't let her friendly demeanor today dissuade you from thinking she did it."

Meg finished off her first slice and grabbed another. Wonders never cease. How she managed to stuff her face and remain skinny should be considered the eighth wonder of the world. Before she bit into it, she asked, "Why do you think so? She seemed totally fine today. She probably had too much to drink last night. You can't equate a few too many glasses of wine with murder." She giggled. "If so, we'd all be in prison."

Lisa motioned for us to come closer so she wouldn't have to speak too loudly. "She lied to us. And I don't trust people who lie."

We stared at each other. "How do you know that, Lisa?" asked Doug.

"She said that on the night of Ronan's murder, she didn't stay at the bar for very long because they weren't serving her favorite wine, a Cabernet Sauvignon," said Lisa.

We all nodded. "And she wasn't telling the truth?" said Meg.

"Nope," said Lisa. "We know there was at least one bottle of that wine available that night. Because it was used to kill Ronan Godfrey."

I snapped my fingers together. "You're right, Lisa. Detective Gomez mentioned that during her interrogation of Sebastian this morning."

"So, you're saying that perhaps Jean Rizzo did stay at the bar longer than what she described?" asked Doug.

"I don't know why she fibbed," said Lisa. "But in my experience, suspects connected to a crime tend to lie when they have something to hide."

Munching on my pepperoni slice, I had to agree with Lisa. It seemed like everyone in the small town of Duck had something to hide, but the question was who was lying to cover up involvement in murder?

Chapter Twelve

SEBASTIAN TEXTED TO FIND OUT if we were able to talk to Jean and, perhaps of more immediate importance, whether we were bringing pizza for him. After responding in the affirmative for both, we started to walk back to the beach house.

My phone buzzed again. It was another message from Sebastian.

Are you up for a field trip this afternoon?

Doug and Meg had both stuffed themselves with Jean's pizza. I'd indulged in an extra slice, as well. I sure hoped she wasn't the murderer. If she was, maybe she'd give us her pizza recipe before she went away to prison.

"Are you interested in going somewhere when we get back? Sebastian has an idea for hitting the road," I asked.

"I don't think I could go swimming for a few hours." Doug rubbed his stomach. "Don't you sink if you've eaten too much?"

"I believe so," I said. "Perhaps a few hours out of the sun would be beneficial."

Meg shrugged her shoulders. "I've got SPF fifty sunblock on. There's no chance I'm getting burned. But I'm up for exploring the Outer Banks. What's Sebastian's idea?"

I texted him back to ask for more details. My phone pinged a minute later.

Tell you when you get here.

I explained that Sebastian preferred to hold us in suspense.

Lisa chuckled. "That sounds like Sebastian. He never wants to reveal his cards."

Lisa's description of my brother was accurate. Sebastian's occasional caginess never bothered me much before. But now, as he faced a possible murder charge, I really hoped he'd leveled with us about the night in question.

We were back at the house soon enough. After climbing the stairs to the second floor, I plopped down a pizza box on the granite kitchen countertop.

"Sebastian!" I called out. "Your lunch has arrived."

In ten seconds flat, he appeared from the floor below with both Clarence and Murphy in tow. Rubbing his temples, he said, "After I went for a swim, the dogs and I took a quick nap downstairs. We're famished."

My lanky brother seemed to always be hungry, and the canines were no exception. They smelled the leftover pizza and started circling like sharks. Sebastian helped himself to a slice and quickly polished it off. Clarence and Murphy split the crust and then licked their lips like they'd just died and went to doggie heaven.

"Now that you've had something to eat, do you want to tell us about this secretive excursion you want us to go on?" I asked. The pizza smelled awfully good. Although I'd tried to restrain myself at Jean's, I decided to help myself to another slice. If we were headed on an adventure with Sebastian, who knew when might get a chance to eat next? You could never be too careful with rationing when it came to food, coffee, or wine. That's why the grocery store, Starbucks, and the liquor store were always overrun when a snowstorm threatened.

Sebastian had grabbed another slice, so his mouth was full. He put up his finger to indicate he had to stop chewing before answering. At least my parents had raised us correctly. Pizza was the priority, then conversation.

"Gary Brewster invited us to see the wild horses in Corolla today," he said, after swallowing. "I think you know that he runs the foundation that helps support them. Since the wine bar is closed until further notice, he went out to his office in Corolla for the day."

Doug snuck up behind me and gave me a squeeze. "I'd love to see the wild horses. The herd is thinning from what I hear."

Sebastian nodded. "That's why Gary got involved. His foundation protects them, so they don't disappear completely."

I texted Meg about Sebastian's idea, and she replied that she was in. To my surprise, Lisa declined the offer.

"I'll stay here with Clarence and Murphy," she said. I noticed she had dark circles under her eyes.

"Do you feel okay?' I asked.

"I didn't sleep well last night," she said. "There's a lot in flux these days."

That was an understatement. Between Sebastian's status as a murder suspect and her potential job with the FBI, it had become a stressful time.

Sebastian put his arm around Lisa. "It's my fault. I can't believe I got caught up in this mess, especially on our vacation."

Lisa rubbed her forehead. "A nap might help."

"I hope the dogs behave for you," I said. "We'll take them out for a walk before we leave."

Twenty minutes later, with the dogs exercised and everyone situated, the four of us climbed into our Prius and pointed the car due north on Highway 12 with Doug at the helm.

"It's about twenty miles to the wild horse foundation that Gary leads," said Sebastian. "After we meet him at the office, he'll take us to see the horses."

"I can't help but think there's something funny going on between Thalia, Jean, and Tobias," I said. "But I don't have the first idea what it is."

Doug kept his eyes on the road. There were a lot of pedestrians and cyclists on the roadside trails. "Perhaps Gary will know something," he said.

"We should ask him about your business card," said Meg. "Someone might have been showing it around and might have dropped it by accident near the bar."

"If that's the case, we can tell the detective and it could help clear Sebastian," I said. "Or at least remove the suspicion that he was on the boardwalk the night of the murder." I turned around in the car and looked at my brother. "By the way, you can't remember who might have gotten one of your business cards at the town hall meeting?"

Sebastian shook his head. "I really can't say. Gary was introducing me to a lot of people. I can't remember their names. I didn't get any cards, though. I checked my pockets."

"Not to change the subject, but we can't forget Lacy when we talk to Gary," said Doug. "There's more than meets the eye between her and the victim. Why else would she have a photo of him at her place of business?"

Meg pointed her finger in a Sherlockian gesture. "Furthermore, why would she feel the need to have to hide it?"

"Obviously, it's because she had a secret relationship with Ronan. She wanted to be reminded of him but knew it was improper. So, she placed the photograph in a place only she would see as the proprietor of the store," I said.

Doug gripped the wheel as we entered the town of Corolla. Once again, there were numerous beachgoers crisscrossing Highway 12. In Corolla, the beachfront homes seemed enormous. That meant even more tourists, both on foot and bicycle.

"There's only one problem with that theory," said Doug. "If Lacy was having an affair with Ronan, then why was he threatening to restrict dog access to the beaches in Duck? Wouldn't he want to help his mistress?"

Meg shook her head vigorously. "You're not thinking like a murderer, Doug. In fact, that makes perfect sense. From what we've heard from others, Ronan seems like a pretty ruthless guy. He did what he wanted and got what he wanted." Her voice became animated. "Even if he was sleeping with Lacy, he didn't care."

Meg had a point, and it got me thinking. "And that enraged Lacy," I said.

"Exactly!" exclaimed Meg. "I'd say that's a perfect motive for murder."

"It definitely has potential," said Doug. "Sebastian, can you tell me the address again?"

Sebastian repeated the exact location of Gary's office. "I think it's on the right side of the highway."

Sure enough, just ahead we spotted a roadside sign that read "Corolla Wild Horse Foundation." Doug turned the Prius into the strip mall and parked in the lot. We piled out of the Prius and headed towards the modest storefront that served as the headquarters for Gary's organization.

Sebastian led the way and opened the glass door. The small office space was decorated with large, colorful posters of the majestic horses. The slogan "Save the Horses, Save the Planet" was plastered on signs and other paraphernalia strewn around the cramped space. Despite the unlocked door, the place was empty.

Meg pointed to a call bell on the countertop. I shrugged my shoulders. Meg took that as a license to act and dinged the bell twice. Sebastian called out, "Gary? Are you here?"

A moment later, a door opened in the rear of the office suite, and Gary emerged. He smiled broadly when he recognized us.

"Welcome to the Corolla Wild Horse Foundation!" he exclaimed. "Sebastian said he might bring friends and family for the tour. I'm glad he didn't disappoint."

Sebastian reintroduced all of us, although we'd met briefly before.

"I heard the Kitty Hawk police are bringing heat on Sebastian for Ronan's murder," said Gary.

I explained that Detective Gomez had found one of Sebastian's business cards at the scene of the crime. "You were at the bar that night. Did you notice anyone with Sebastian's card? Perhaps the person was showing it to someone and accidentally misplaced it."

"That could explain why the detective found the card behind the bar. Let me think about it." Gary rubbed his chin. "It was a busy night. I was taking inventory of the wine we had in stock and was hustling around. I don't remember seeing anyone with Sebastian's card." He must have seen the disappointment on my face. "Someone else might have seen it, though. Like I said, I was occupied with other things."

Sebastian put his arm around me. "My sister would talk about murder all day long if I let her," he said jokingly. "But we didn't drive all the way out here for that. Tell us about the wild horses of Corolla."

Gary motioned for us to take a seat at a table. "It's better for you to see the horses, but before we do that, I'll give you a short history lesson."

I glanced over at Doug, whose eyes were twinkling. Gary had just said the magic words: history lesson. Doug was going to eat this up like a slice of Jean Rizzo's pepperoni pizza. If Sebastian had cut short my murder talk, at least Doug would be happy.

"Are the horses native to the Outer Banks?" asked Meg.

"That's a good place to start," said Gary. "The Corolla horses have lived along the beaches of the Outer Banks for five hundred years. No one is exactly sure the circumstances of their origin, but we do know that many Spanish trading ships were shipwrecked along the coast of the Outer Banks. If there were horses on board, they could have certainly made it to land."

"That's a fairly dramatic story," said Meg. "Is it really true?"

"Actually, the truth is we don't know," said Gary. "The other explanation is that there was a Spanish explorer in this area named Lucas Vasquez de Allyon. He definitely brought mustangs with him. As the story goes, he ran afoul with the Native American Indian population and had to leave swiftly, leaving his horses and other livestock behind when he fled."

"The horses have continuously lived on the Outer Banks for the past five hundred years?" asked Doug. "If so, that's quite impressive."

"Yes, the horses you'll see today are the descendants of the Spanish mustangs. We've had their DNA analyzed," said Gary. "My undergraduate degree in biology does come in handy every once in a while."

"Gary leads a team that engages in extensive herd management," said Sebastian. "They use the best principles of conservation and ecology to protect the horses. His biology background does help. He's not exaggerating."

Gary beamed. "I promise you. I didn't pay him to say that," he said, chuckling. "But he's right. The foundation raises money to monitor the horses, observe them, and provide veterinarian care when necessary."

"It seems like a very noble cause," said Doug. "And the history is fascinating."

Meg waved her hand. "That's like the pot calling the kettle black." She turned to Gary. "Doug is our resident historian. He's obsessed with anything over a hundred years old."

"I'm actually an early American historian." Doug straightened in his chair. "So, it's more like over *two* hundred years old."

Gary raised a single eyebrow. "I can tell this is going to be an interesting tour." He stood and slapped his legs. "Should we head out to the Jeep to see the horses? I can fill you in on more details as soon as we're underway."

"Can I use the restroom before we go?" asked Meg. "I assume there won't be an opportunity for a pit stop once we're underway."

Gary smiled. "That is correct. We'll be on the beaches north of Corolla, called our four-by-four area. There are no businesses or restaurants in that stretch of beach, only private residences. I can explain when we're in the Jeep."

"In that case, I'd better join you, Meg," I said.

Gary motioned towards the door he'd emerged from earlier. "There's a bathroom back there across from my office."

We scurried back. "Can I go first, Kit?" asked Meg.

I hesitated. Meg took a long time in the bathroom, mostly because she always reapplied her makeup and made sure her hair and outfit were just right. We were headed out on an open-air Jeep tour. Surely Meg wouldn't care about her appearance too much given the circumstances.

"Sure," I said. "Go ahead."

Meg went inside the bathroom and closed the door. My eyes drifted across the hallway to Gary's office. It was adorned with an assortment of environmental posters, not unlike what Sebastian might choose as decorations. His desk was predictably messy. I spotted two bottles of wine sitting on the edge. Curious enough, the cork had been removed. Had Gary been drinking in his office? If so, I didn't want him driving us in a Jeep, pursuing wild horses across a sandy beach.

I walked into his office and picked up the bottle. One bottle was a Cabernet Sauvignon and the other was a Merlot. There was a small amount of wine in each bottle. I looked around but didn't see any used wine glasses. On his desk was a catalog labeled "U.S.A. Organic Wines." I picked it up and leafed through it. Certain pages were dog-eared, and descriptions were circled and annotated, some with a star and others with a question mark. Gary must have been researching which wines to order for Sonoma Sunsets. It was amazing the number of organic options grown in the United States. The industry must have exploded in recent years.

A male voice broke my concentration. "Find something you like?"

My head jerked up. Gary was standing at the entrance of his office, staring at me.

I dropped the wine catalog. "Sorry. I . . .um . . ." I stammered for what seemed like forever but was probably only thirty seconds. Gary didn't make it easy on me. He simply glared at me.

Finally, I was able to put together a coherent sentence. I shouldn't be so flustered. "I saw you had a few open wine bottles on your desk. I was curious to see if they were empty or not." I forced a laugh in a feeble attempt to lighten the situation.

Meg emerged from the bathroom and interjected herself. "What's going on here? Kit, don't you want to use the restroom?"

Gary finally spoke. "She wandered into my office while she was waiting." He sucked in his breath. "I suppose."

Meg giggled and touched Gary's arm. "Oh, don't worry about Kit. She's a natural snoop. Can't keep her hands to herself, if you know what I mean." She tugged at Gary in the opposite direction. In her flirtiest voice, she said, "Of course, I could say the same thing for myself."

Gary followed Meg like an infatuated puppy. I could always count on Meg for an effective diversion when it involved the opposite sex. Before they went through the door to the front of the office, she turned around to look at me. Even though I was no ventriloquist, I could certainly read her lips.

"You owe me."

My best friend was certainly right.

Chapter Thirteen

B<small>Y THE TIME</small> I <small>LEFT THE BUILDING</small>, everyone was already waiting inside the Jeep. I climbed inside and squeezed in the backseat next to Doug. Gary turned around. "Are you ready to go?"

"Of course," I said. "Sorry for the delay."

"Just wanted to make sure you'd seen everything at this location," he said.

I didn't respond. Meg had gotten me out of a tight jam but obviously hadn't made Gary forget he'd caught me snooping.

Doug narrowed his eyes after Gary's remark. I reached for my phone and texted him.

I'll tell you later what happened.

Doug's phone pinged. He looked at his phone and then back at me. "Did you text me?"

I winced. Despite being super smart, sometimes my husband was downright clueless.

"No, you must be mistaken." I grabbed his phone and gave him a knowing glance. "It was your mother. Right, Doug?"

Finally, he must have gotten my drift. "Oh, I see. Yes, it was my mother. Sorry."

After reading my message, Doug gave me a "thumbs up" sign. It was good that Doug had found a home in academia and research. He would have failed the CIA field recruit test.

Gary spoke up. "The wild horses used to roam in this part of

Corolla. That was before all of this development."

"When did that happen?" asked Sebastian.

"Before 1985, there was no paved road between Duck and Corolla. After the road was constructed, houses and businesses followed. With the increased population and traffic, accidents started to happen. Over twenty horses were killed in the decade after the road was built," said Gary.

Sebastian shook his head. "What a shame. Needless sprawl crowds out wildlife."

"It's a blessing and curse. There's now a vibrant economy that didn't exist previously," said Gary. "The remaining horses were relocated to the northern edge of the island, which is known now as the four-by-four area. You need a four-wheel drive because there are no paved roads."

We approached a fence with a ramp, indicating the end of Highway 12. "Once we enter this part of the Outer Banks, we may encounter the horses. You can't get out of the vehicle to approach them," said Gary. "We'll stay at least fifty feet away from them at all times."

To my surprise, Gary drove directly on the beach, right down the middle. It must have surprised Meg, too. "Are we allowed to drive on the beach like this?" she asked.

Gary nodded. "Absolutely. Vehicles stay in this area of the beach. There's no other way to get around this part of the island."

After a few miles, Gary slowed down and pointed to a large single-family house. "There's two horses over there, feeding on marsh grass."

Sure enough, we spotted them. They were small and compact, chestnut in color with dark manes. "Do people try to interact with them?" asked Sebastian.

"Of course," said Gary. "That's why we put up signs everywhere to let people know." He pointed in the direction of the horses. A large sign read: "DO NOT FEED THE HORSES. REMAIN FIFTY FEET AWAY AT ALL TIMES."

"What happens if tourists renting the houses ignore your warnings?" asked Meg.

Gary shook his head. "It's not good. Horses that become dependent upon humans can't remain a part of the herd. Feeding them apples or corn can kill them. Their digestion is only suited to the beach grass they're grazing on right now. Their restricted diet is why they remain smaller in stature as horses."

Gary pointed out several more horses as we drove further along the beach and during our return back to Corolla and the highway. "Can you tell me more about the legislation you'd like Congress to pass concerning the horses?" I asked. If Maeve Dixon became the next senator from North Carolina, she'd have to make this a priority on her agenda.

"As I mentioned before, we need more genetic diversity to add to the breeding," said Gary. "There's my biology degree at work again. We'd like to introduce horses from the Cape Lookout herd to assist."

"And the Fish and Wildlife Service opposes this?" I recalled our conversation from the day of the town hall meeting.

"Yes, because these horses are technically not native species to the Outer Banks. Remember the history I shared with you. The Spanish brought them here and left them, either by accident or on purpose," said Gary.

"Five hundred years should count for something," said Doug. "I'm not an ecologist, but those horses predate human habitation in this part of the island, correct?"

"You're right," said Gary. "We'd also like to grow the herd. Right now, it's too small." Gary sighed. "The Fish and Wildlife Service consider them nuisance animals. It's a constant battle."

"If I remember correctly, Ronan Godfrey strongly supported the wild horses of Corolla," I said.

"He was supportive," said Gary. "But Ronan was no true environmentalist. He knew that the horses meant a lot to me, so he offered to help. As the mayor, he interacted with politicians and government officials at times, and he would lend support if he could. Duck doesn't have any wild horses, but plenty of the tourists staying in Duck travel north to Corolla to see them. It's a major attraction for vacationers. Plenty of tour companies operate from this location."

"I'll see what Representative Dixon can do to help," I said. In my job as a chief of staff, sometimes I had to stretch the truth and promise to do things I knew my boss couldn't get done. This time, I truly meant what I said. I hoped Maeve Dixon would be able to make a difference for the horses.

Meg picked up on the mention of Ronan. "If the mayor wasn't really an environmentalist, then why did he own the only organic wine bar in the Outer Banks?"

"That's how Ronan got me to invest with him in Sonoma Sunsets," said Gary. "I know several organic wine producers in California, so I had the connections to get us started."

"Speaking of connections, has Detective Gomez contacted you about the vineyard who produced the wine which ended up on the floor after the bottle shattered?" I asked. "She'd like help with processing the crime scene, which was pretty messy."

"No, she didn't," said Gary. "I haven't heard from the police again about Ronan's death."

"Any other ideas about who might have killed Ronan?" asked Meg. "We need a break to clear Sebastian once and for all."

Sebastian smiled. "It was great to see the horses. Meg is right, though. The detective seems to have it in for me."

"It's too bad you don't have an alibi for the time you were walking along the beach," said Gary.

"I know," said Sebastian glumly. "That's keeping me at the top of the suspect list."

We were pulling back into the parking lot of the Corolla Wild Horse Foundation, but I had one more question for Gary. "By the way, do you know if Ronan was carrying on a relationship with Lacy Madison?"

Gary parked the Jeep and turned around to look at me. "You mean an affair?"

"Perhaps," I said.

"Why would you think that?" asked Gary.

I didn't want to divulge that I'd found that hidden photo of Ronan and Lacy underneath the counter in her store. If I admitted I'd found that, it would be another instance of snooping, and then Gary might really think I had a problem. Well, I *did* have a problem, but that was beside the point.

"I went to see Lacy at her store," I said. "I just got the feeling it was more than a casual relationship." That wasn't really a lie, right?

"I never knew Ronan to have an extramarital affair," said Gary. "But he did spend time with Lacy. I always thought it was because she was lobbying him to preserve the dog ordinances in Duck. He was also supportive of other business owners, and Lacy is young to own her own shop in town."

"We had lunch at Jean Rizzo's restaurant today," said Doug. "Kit tried to speak to her outside Aqua last night during the sunset, but she'd had too much to drink."

Gary shrugged his shoulders. "Sounds par for the course. If you're interested, everyone will be at Sunset Grille tonight. They run specials on Monday evenings. If you haven't been there, you should check it out. Their pier extends into the sound, so it's ideal for the sunset. Hence the name." He chuckled.

"Appreciate the tip. We might do that," I said.

We got out of the Jeep and Sebastian gave Gary a man hug, which is defined as a hug between two males that's something between a handshake and an embrace. It lasts for no more than a second and usually ends with a slap on the back. This one fit the bill perfectly.

"Thanks, Gary," said Sebastian. "I really needed the diversion today after the police stopped by this morning. Seeing the horses in nature was perfect."

"Anytime," said Gary. "Maybe we'll see you later tonight." He tipped his hat at us and headed towards his office.

We climbed inside the Prius and drove south on the highway back to Duck. Meg reached forward from the backseat and tapped me on the shoulder.

"You're welcome, Kit," she said.

I rolled my eyes. "Thank you, Meg. It wasn't like I could say anything when we were on the horse tour."

"What are you two talking about?" asked Doug. "Does this have to do with the text from you?"

"Gary caught me snooping in his office," I said. "I really didn't mean to do it. There were a couple of open wine bottles, and I was curious about whether he'd been drinking. I didn't want him driving us all over a sandy beach if he'd just thrown back a few."

"That seems like a lame excuse, Kit," said Sebastian.

"Whatever," I said flippantly. "Meg was in the bathroom and his office was wide open. So I walked inside to take a look."

"And did you find anything?" asked Doug.

I shook my head. "No. Just a catalog of organic wines. Gary must pick which ones they serve at Sonoma Sunsets."

"He probably wants to keep an eye on their stock. There's been controversy in that industry lately," said Sebastian.

"What do you mean?" asked Meg.

"What products are considered organic or what isn't," said Sebastian. "I don't know many details, but it's very common with agriculture in the United States. Everyone wants the organic label, yet sometimes producers don't want to follow the guidelines."

"Not to change the subject, but something really bothers me about this murder. I still don't understand why Ronan's body was dumped into the water," I said. "The blow from the wine bottle killed him. The person responsible could have checked to see if he was breathing. We already know there was no one else on the boardwalk to witness the crime."

"It is strange," said Meg. "Almost like the killer wanted to murder Ronan twice."

"It was probably to make sure he was dead," said Doug. "Why else would someone go to the extra trouble?"

I appreciated Doug's logical mind. However, something didn't make sense to me. It was one of those nagging feelings I got when contemplating the more intricate components of the mysteries we confronted. Nothing else came to my mind right now, so it was best to file the suspicion away and try to figure it out later when more pieces of the puzzle surfaced.

We pulled into the driveway of our beach house and piled out of the car. It was late in the afternoon, yet the sun still blazed. "I think I'll head to the beach for a swim," I announced.

Doug volunteered to take Clarence for a walk so he could

think more about the subject of his next book. Sebastian wanted to find Lisa to catch up, and Meg opted for a dip in the pool. Twenty minutes later, I had on my trusty black swimsuit, a beach wrap, and enough sunblock to prevent a burn at the equator.

At the entrance to the beach, I stood on the wooden boardwalk built on top of the dunes and looked back and forth in both directions. Off in the distance to the right, I spotted a familiar figure attached to a fishing pole.

"Hello, Trevor," I said. "Catch anything today?"

Trevor's head jerked back in surprise. "You startled me, Kit. Really, you should announce yourself instead of sneaking up on people."

"This isn't a library. It's a public beach," I said.

Trevor wrinkled his nose. "Point taken. However, I was deep in thought, and you disturbed me."

"I thought you were going on a fishing trip on the sound this morning," I said.

"I came out here after I was done." He motioned to the red Igloo cooler behind him. "I even caught a few fish. The guys on the boat cleaned them up for me. We can eat them tonight."

I peeked inside the cooler. Packed in ice, there were three small fish filets that were slightly larger than guppies.

"Trevor, I'm impressed." I crossed my fingers behind my back. "You're really getting the hang of this."

"I never had a hobby. Fishing is so . . ." He searched for the right word. "Contemplative."

"And you have a lot to contemplate these days, I gather?" I asked gently.

"You've talked with Meg," he said.

"She doesn't want you to make a change in your career that you might regret down the road," I said. "Do you really want to leave your current job?"

Trevor shrugged his shoulders and kept his eyes on the ocean in front of us.

I decided not to press him on the matter. My experience with Trevor was that he talked when he was ready. Instead, I changed the subject and told him about Detective Gomez finding Sebastian's business card at the crime scene.

"Obviously, someone dropped Sebastian's card there, on purpose or by accident," said Trevor. "Unfortunately, it's physical evidence that ties him to the murder."

I nodded and told him about our lunch with Jean Rizzo.

"Why would she lie about her favorite wine not being available?" asked Trevor. "You need to think about the reason for her prevarication."

Leave it to Trevor to throw out a SAT vocabulary word in the middle of normal conversation.

"Perhaps she wanted us to think she had a reason for going home early that night," I said.

Trevor waited for a group of beachgoers to pass by before tossing out his line again. "You also need to track down the mystery behind Lacy Madison," he said. "If she was carrying on an affair with Ronan, then maybe she killed him. Or it gives motive for Ronan's wife to want him dead."

Trevor was right. A secretive relationship with Ronan was almost certainly a critical part of the mystery. I glanced at my watch. It was close to five o'clock.

"Are you coming back to the house with your fish?" I motioned to his cooler.

Trevor stuck out his chest. "Yes, and I hope we can eat them tonight for dinner. I think they would taste best grilled."

"I'm going to try to speak to Lacy before we have to leave for the Sunset Grille," I said. The dip in the ocean would have to wait. It was foolish to think I could relax and enjoy vacation until Sebastian had been cleared of any suspicion of wrongdoing.

I had already started to hustle back to the beach access point when Trevor called out. "I thought we were going to eat my fish for dinner tonight!"

I waved to acknowledge that I'd heard him but didn't have the heart to tell him what he'd caught would be eaten by Clarence and Murphy in three swift gulps. Sometimes, it was best to let friends enjoy their bliss.

Chapter Fourteen

I THOUGHT ABOUT MY CONVERSATION with Trevor on the short walk back to the house. His difficulties with Meg would have to sort themselves out. Commitment was either in Meg's blood or it wasn't. I couldn't change her, and neither could Trevor. Only time would tell how things would work out between my two friends.

Notwithstanding his romantic difficulties, Trevor was always helpful when trying to noodle my way through a vexing mystery. This one certainly qualified. With other murders, the suspects all had legitimate alibis. With this one, no one had a credible one. Each suspect could have killed Ronan, but without any concrete physical evidence, it was impossible to point the finger.

I reverted back to the "big three" of crime: motive, means, and opportunity. With an open-air bar, there was no question of who had access to the wine bottle that killed Ronan. Although it took a degree of strength to drag his body underneath the railing of the boardwalk so it would fall into the marshy water below, it might not have been a big distance between where he fell down and where he went into the marshy water below. Thalia, Lacy, or Jean could have done it. Who knows? Maybe two of them were in cahoots together. That would have made it much easier to shove Ronan's body in the desired direction. Furthermore, without corroborating alibis, all suspects had the opportunity to commit the murder. Even Sebastian had to be included in this category; his decision to take a stroll by the ocean to cure his insomnia guaranteed he also *could* be the culprit.

The only variable that might tip the scales in one direction or the other was motive. Nothing was clear yet. Did Jean Rizzo kill Ronan because he'd taken her coveted sound side restaurant spot? Had Tobias decided to eliminate his political opponent once and for all? With divorce as a messy option, perhaps Thalia believed murder would be more beneficial? And what about Lacy? Had her cozy, yet secretive, relationship with Ronan driven her to murder?

None of these motives were concrete. I had the sense that once I figured out *why* Ronan Godfrey was killed, I would easily figure out *who* did it.

That got back to Trevor's comments. He'd thought it odd that Jean Rizzo had lied about her favorite wine being out of stock at the bar on Saturday night. I'd have to follow up on that detail. He'd also mentioned the curious photo I'd seen of Lacy Madison and Ronan underneath her cash register. It was hidden for an unknown reason. In my experience, secrets and murder made strange bedfellows.

When I arrived at the house, I pondered my next steps. Everyone had apparently decided to take a siesta after our excursion to Corolla. The house was as quiet as the main reading room inside the Library of Congress. The only movement was from Clarence, who I could always count on for company. He came over and gave my hand a few licks. Truth be told, I wasn't quite sure the beach vacation was meeting Clarence's expectations. He'd discovered a dead body, gotten yelled at by an intoxicated pizzeria owner, and rejected the idea of frolicking in the ocean.

As I rubbed his ears, he wiggled his butt with delight. "What would you like to do on vacation, Clarence?"

"Woof," said Clarence. It was a friendly little bark, an excited response to the attention I was bestowing on him.

He scampered next to the couch and shoved his nose underneath a small pile of dirty beach towels that had been tossed on the ground. I'd have to get after my friends. This wasn't a vacation frat house. People needed to clean up after themselves.

Clarence unearthed the harness we'd bought at the Duck Dogs

store. He picked it up with his teeth and brought it over to me, wagging his tail like a metronome going out of style. Suddenly, I had an idea. I glanced at my iPhone. It was almost five o'clock, but sunset wouldn't be for another couple of hours. I had plenty of time.

"Nice work, buddy!" I patted Clarence on the head and took the harness from his mouth. "Let's go for a walk."

I didn't want to wake anyone from their naps, so I texted Doug to let him know I would return in an hour or so. If Clarence and I hurried, we would make it in time.

Twenty minutes later, I was sucking wind and Clarence was panting, but we'd arrived at the Duck Dogs store. Just as I remembered, the chalkboard outside indicated that the infamous doggie "Yappy Hour" was taking place until six.

The sign directed all canine attendees to the wooded area behind the shopping complex. We walked around the corner and sure enough, there was a substantial gathering of dogs and owners hanging out in the shade.

I sensed hesitancy in Clarence as we walked toward the cluster of canines and humans, who were either respectively engaged in friendly sniffing or chatting. Clarence had adapted better than we anticipated to Murphy's inclusion in our lives, save one or two unfortunate incidents involving food. Nonetheless, he still remained skittish around dogs he didn't know. Perhaps it was from the time he spent in a shelter before we adopted him from a local rescue program. I bent down and gently patted his head. "You'll be fine, Clarence. These dogs are friendly." Clarence licked me on the nose to signal an affirmative response.

We ambled up next to a pleasant-looking golden Labrador mix. The owner was an older gentleman wearing a blue baseball hat with the capital letters "OBX" on it. Smiling at me, he said, "This is Honey. She's five years old."

"Nice to meet you. My name is Kit, and this is Clarence. He's a beagle mutt."

The man nodded. "I can see that." Clarence, who was governed by his nose and stomach, was presently sniffing Honey and the grass around her.

"Are you here for vacation?" I asked.

"We used to come here a week in the summer when the kids were growing up. Then my wife and I decided to retire here. We bought one of the few houses that aren't mega-mansions."

"That sounds lovely." My mind quickly pivoted. "You've lived here a few years, then?"

Honey wanted to play and jumped up and down, trying to get Clarence to engage. Instead, he sat down and whimpered. Honey didn't give up. She pawed at Clarence in desperation. Finally, Clarence conceded and gave her a few licks.

"Three years and counting," he said. "Summer is nice for the beach, but my favorite season is fall. No offense, but the tourists go away, and the weather is just as nice." He motioned toward the crowd of people and dogs. "Events like this are awfully crowded this time of year. It's all vacationers."

"You must have known Ronan Godfrey then," I said. "He was killed a few days ago over on the boardwalk."

"Terrible tragedy. We don't have that kind of violence in the Outer Banks, and certainly not in Duck," he said.

"Did you know him well?" I asked. "It's a small town."

"Everyone knew Ronan. I wasn't friends with him, and I didn't appreciate his efforts to change Duck into some high-end resort for the rich and famous."

"Isn't it strange that a tech millionaire would settle in a sleepy ocean town like this?" I asked.

"I suppose so, but Ronan had a history with this place. He came here as a kid, as I understand it. That's pretty common. Vacationers turn into residents," he said.

Honey made another fast move on Clarence. This time, he uttered a low growl. My time was running out.

"Sorry about that," I said. "He gets a little antsy with other dogs. I didn't know Ronan had a connection to Duck earlier in his life."

"No reason why you would." The man took a step backwards before continuing the conversation. "Why do you care about our mayor so much if you're only here on vacation?"

While a perfectly appropriate question, it was a good excuse to end the conversation. "No reason. Just curious," I said. "I'd better get my dog some water. Thanks for the chat."

Before he could ask me any more pointed questions, I snapped on Clarence's leash and led him over to the row of water bowls. While he was drinking, I surveyed the scene and spotted Lacy Madison at the edge of the crowd. She was standing next to a picnic table, pouring wine for the human attendees.

After Clarence finished lapping up the water (it took him a while because he was a very sloppy drinker), we walked over to speak with Lacy.

"Hello," I said in my friendliest voice. "We decided to stop by for your famous Yappy Hour." I pointed to Clarence. "He's wearing the harness we bought at your store yesterday."

Lacy smiled. "Glad we could help. We don't want any lost dogs in Duck during the height of visitor season." She raised the bottle of wine in her hand. "Care for a drink?"

I studied the bottle. It was a Cabernet Sauvignon, and it was pointedly labeled as organic. I noticed she had several bottles of the same wine on the table—coincidence? I didn't believe in them when it came to murder.

"Sure, thank you," I said. "Can I ask where you got these bottles of wine?"

"Gary Brewster gave them to me," she said. "They were from Sonoma Sunsets. I guess they weren't going to sell this particular vintage at the bar anymore."

I remembered the wine catalog I'd spotted on Gary's desk at the Corolla Horse Foundation. Gary must have wanted to change the wine offerings at the bar.

"I don't want to spoil your party," I said. "But I think Ronan Godfrey was hit over the head by a bottle of wine of that vintage."

Lacy recoiled instantly. "What are you saying? Do you think I killed Ronan?"

She'd misunderstood what I meant, although now that she'd said it, the fact that Lacy had access to this particular type of wine did place her even higher on the suspect list—not to mention that she'd become immediately defensive for no credible reason.

"No, that's not what I was saying. It just seemed like a strange coincidence. Maybe more macabre than strange," I said.

"I had no idea this type of wine was used to kill him," she said. "Why would I know?"

Good answer. Either it was true, or Lacy was trying to outsmart me. "Certainly," I said. "The only reason I know that detail is that the detective in charge mentioned she needed to contact the vineyard that produces that wine for help with processing the crime scene."

Lacy shuddered. "I don't like to think about it. Can't we talk about something more pleasant?"

"I'm sorry for being so insensitive," I said. "I know that you and Ronan had recently become close. Talking about his death must be very disturbing for you."

Lacy stammered in her reply. "It's upsetting. I mean, we all knew Ronan." She added. "For better or worse."

It was time for me to come clean with her. I took a sip of my wine to give me some courage. If it got too heated, I could always use Clarence as an excuse to bolt, although at this moment in time, he was contentedly sniffing underneath the picnic table.

I lowered my voice and moved closer to her; no need to draw attention to others attending the Yappy Hour. "Lacy, I saw the photo." I looked at her pointedly. "Of you and Ronan Godfrey."

Her eyes narrowed. "Underneath my counter in the store?"

"Yes. When I was looking for my phone." No need to tell her I was snooping on purpose. Gary already had caught me in the act. If I wasn't careful, the entire town of Duck was going to be on its guard when I walked into a room.

Lacy shook her head. "You're making assumptions you shouldn't be making."

I backed up a step after Lacy's accusation. "I didn't assume anything. I'm simply telling you what I saw. Most people don't keep photographs hidden if everything is on the up and up."

"It's not like that at all," Lacy hissed. She waved her hand in a circular motion. "If you haven't noticed, I've got a lot of customers here today. Do you mind?"

I got the hint. We'd been asked to move along. Obviously, I'd hit a nerve. But I still wasn't any closer to finding out the nature of Lacy and Ronan's clandestine relationship. As soon as the last drink was served, Lacy would remove the photograph from underneath her counter. Any evidence of a past liaison between her and Ronan would disappear.

I had planned to purchase something at the store at the end of the Yappy Hour but given the fact that Lacy had effectively asked us to leave, I concluded that I was absolved from making yet another obligatory purchase.

I bent down to scratch Clarence on the belly. "You were a good doggie sleuth." His eyes opened wide, and he licked my face before I could get away. We headed back to the walking path along Highway 12, and I thought more about what I'd learned, which wasn't as much as I'd hoped. While some high-end property owners might have welcomed it, not many residents liked Ronan's ideas for making Duck more exclusive. Lacy had gotten defensive and antsy when the talk turned to Ronan's murder. She was also serving wine from his bar, which seemed a bit unusual but could have a simple explanation. Perhaps Gary was in the business of providing extra bottles to Lacy for Yappy Hour. It seemed like something one animal lover might do for another.

A final tidbit was that Ronan had spent time in Duck earlier in his life. I didn't see how that connected to anything relevant about his murder, but no one else I'd spoken with had mentioned it. Buying a big house in a resort town filled with childhood memories made more sense than randomly picking a place without a previous connection. At least one mystery was solved, although I didn't know if it got me any closer to figuring out the identity of the killer.

I needed more face time with the suspects. Someone who had been at the bar on Saturday night had likely left with everyone else, circled back, and bashed Ronan over the head with a wine bottle. I knew Lacy had the type of wine that had been used as the murder weapon in her possession. Did that place her at the top of my list of suspects? Perhaps the Yappy Hour was a convenient way to get rid of the evidence. That might have been the reason she got so upset when I recognized the particular vintage and brand.

We walked inside the house and I called out. "Hello! We're back!"

No one answered. I checked the bedrooms on the first floor and then headed upstairs to the living room and master suite. The house was completely empty. I looked at my phone. Had I missed a text inviting me to the beach or an early evening excursion? There were no new messages to read. Perhaps I missed an email? I refreshed my inbox—nada.

Clarence looked around with a puzzled expression on his canine visage. I could practically read his mind. *Have we been ghosted?* I was positive Clarence understood and was experiencing the same feeling of abandonment as me. After all, Murphy was nowhere to be found, either.

I sat down on our bed and sighed. This was depressing. My friends had left me, probably for some fancy party on the beach. Then, in an instant, a feeling of terror bolted through me. Had Detective Gomez arrested Sebastian? Had she come to the house, apprehended him, and everyone had followed him to the police station? I stared at my phone. If that was the case, surely someone would have called or texted me.

Clarence's ears perked up. With beagle hearing, he had a serious advantage over my mere human senses. He got up and trotted out of the bedroom, headed for the sliding glass door that opened to the balcony. After I followed him, he sat next to the door and pawed the glass. He wanted me to let him onto the balcony, so I removed the wooden security stick and slid the door open. He sprinted outside and issued several staccato barks. Clarence had several different types of vocalizations. There were warning barks, impatient barks, and territorial barks. These vocalizations were barks of excitement.

Then, I heard what Clarence had likely heard in the bedroom. Voices were coming from below. I walked out on the balcony and looked down. I'd found my friends. Everyone (save Trevor) was in the oversized hot tub, drink in hand.

"Why didn't anyone tell me you were hot tubbing?" I didn't bother to hide the hurt in my voice. I was always the last to know about fun stuff, and it was almost always because I was working or acting responsibly when the exciting plans were hatched and discussed.

"Stop complaining and get down here, Kit," said Meg. "It's very relaxing and God only knows, you need to relax."

I wanted to go to the place Gary had mentioned for happy hour. We still had an hour before we'd have to leave to be there during prime time, which likely occurred as the sun set over the sound. I took a deep breath. "Clarence and I will be down there in five minutes."

Clarence raised his ears and cocked his head.

No hot tub for me, lady.

I scratched the top of his head. "Don't worry, buddy. You can hang out by the pool."

Clarence seemed to accept this explanation. His tail wagged as I changed into my swimsuit and headed downstairs. I realized that although I'd worn my suit several times since I'd been on vacation, I hadn't actually been in the water since our vacation started. Maybe Meg was right. I did need to relax.

"Before you get in, pour yourself a glass of vino." Meg pointed in the direction of the outdoor table. A bottle of Prosecco, Meg's favorite libation, was inside a silver chiller bucket. I grabbed a red plastic cup and poured myself a drink before hopping in the hot tub next to Doug.

"Wow, this is nice," I said. The hot water swirled around me like a giant body massager. I eased back into the seat and took a sip of the Italian bubbly.

"You work too hard, Kit," said Sebastian. He took a long sip out of his beer bottle. "Everything is going to be fine. The universe will right any wrongs."

My brother had to be the most chill murder suspect on the planet. He'd better hope his suppositions about karma weren't off base.

"Where did you go when we were taking a nap?" asked Doug. The heat from the hot tub had steamed his glasses. Could he even see anything?

I recounted our excursion to the Yappy Hour. Lisa perked up when she heard about my conversation with Lacy.

"That can't be a coincidence," said Lisa. "It proves she had a bottle of that specific type of wine in her possession. Maybe Gary had just given her the extra wine, and she ended up getting into a fight with Ronan Godfrey. If she was carrying it with her, it would have been a convenient weapon."

"It's certainly plausible," I said. "But don't you find it odd that she was serving the wine at a public event? Nothing like drawing attention to yourself."

"Perhaps not," said Trevor, who had joined us at the edge of the hot tub. I doubted Trevor had ever been in a hot tub, and he wasn't going to start now. It was way too plebeian for his tastes. Trevor had progressed a long way socially since our days in the Senate together, but everyone had limits.

"What do you mean, Trevor?" asked Doug. "Kit is right. If Lacy killed Ronan with a bottle of wine given to her, why advertise that she was in possession of that particular vintage?"

"Think of it from Lacy's perspective," said Trevor. "Most of the people who come to her happy hours . . ."

I interrupted. "You mean *Yappy* Hours, Trevor."

He waved his hand dismissively. "Whatever they're called. As I was saying, I would venture to say that most of Lacy's guests at her dog parties are vacationers, correct?"

"Well, I did speak to a local resident," I said. "Interestingly enough, he told me that Ronan had vacationed in Duck as a kid, and that's why he came back here to live after he left the tech business."

"That's one mystery solved," said Lisa. "But I don't think it helps us figure out who murdered him."

"I doubt it," I said. "But to answer Trevor's question, the man I spoke with did say that most of the people at Lacy's summer events were tourists."

"That proves my point. If Lacy wanted to get rid of the evidence, so to speak, it makes sense to serve the wine to a bunch of people who wouldn't care what vintage they're drinking," said Trevor. "Even the resident you spoke with probably didn't know what type of wine was used to kill Ronan Godfrey, right?"

"It wasn't in the newspaper accounts of the murder," I said. "There's no reason for anyone to have recognized the wine except for me, I guess."

"That was Lacy's bad luck, then," said Doug. "She wasn't counting on you coming to her dog happy hour. It was the first one after the murder. In other words, the first opportunity to get rid of the wine that ties her to the crime."

I took another sip of Prosecco and thought about Doug and Trevor's observations. "It does seem like a strange coincidence, now that I'm considering it," I said slowly.

My work iPhone buzzed on the picnic table, and Trevor glanced down at it. "Kit, you might want to take this call. It's Maeve Dixon."

Drat. Trevor was right, though. If Maeve was calling me during her vacation time, it had to be important. I began to hoist myself out of the hot tub when Sebastian gently grabbed my arm. "As long as you don't drop the phone in the water, you can take the call from here," he said. "No need to ruin your fun."

It didn't seem exactly right to take a call from my boss while I was in a hot tub, but Sebastian had a point. I was on vacation, right? Of course, I would be enjoying myself. I motioned for Trevor to bring the phone to me. He shook his head at me as he handed it over. Clearly, Trevor did not approve.

I swiped across the phone to answer the call. "Good evening, Congresswoman."

There was a pause on the line before Maeve Dixon spoke. "Kit, what's that noise in the background? Are you taking a bath?"

For heaven's sake. There was no way I could engage in subterfuge with my boss. "Please wait one moment." I climbed out of the hot tub. Sebastian gave me a pouty look as I walked toward the other end of the outdoor patio.

I got back on the phone. "Sorry about that. We were outside, enjoying the pool and hot tub. How is your vacation going?"

"It's been very enlightening, I suppose."

That was cryptic. It gave me zero insight about whether she had decided to run for the United States Senate.

"In a good way?" I asked.

"Yes, of course," said Maeve crisply.

It was clear my boss was not ready to divulge any decisions about her political future. By the way, her future was essentially on a parallel track with my career. I believed she understood this reality, but I also knew it wasn't determinative in her decision-making calculus. As good a public servant as she was, Maeve Dixon did what was best for her. As her top aide, I either benefited from or suffered the resulting consequences of her decisions.

"I didn't call to exchange notes about our respective vacations, though," said Dixon. "I wanted to follow up with you about the murder of that mayor in the Outer Banks."

"You mean Ronan Godfrey," I said. That made sense. After all, Maeve had visited with him right before he died. I wondered if she'd gotten any press calls about the homicide. She hadn't appeared in any newspaper articles about it.

"Have the police caught the killer?" she asked.

I gave her a quick summary of the investigation. I didn't mention that Sebastian was a prime suspect. No need to worry her. Furthermore, the cardinal rule of being a congressional staffer is to never make headlines. I assumed that axiom applied to siblings of staff, too.

"Didn't we meet a man named Tobias Potter at the town hall?" asked Maeve.

"We did. He's on the town council. Without Ronan Godfrey in the picture, he would have the inside track to become mayor."

"That's what I thought," said Maeve. "I spoke with a prominent political consultant in the state yesterday. She mentioned Potter's name because she knew I'd recently visited Duck."

"Why did she mention his name?"

"Because she's worked with him," said Maeve. "I thought that might be relevant. Perhaps Potter wanted to try to defeat Godfrey in the next election."

"It seems a little silly to use a political consultant for a small-town mayoral race," I said.

Maeve chuckled. "I've heard of much worse. If a politician

wants to win badly enough, they'll use a hammer on a thumbtack every time."

"It's useful information. Tobias told me he wasn't interested in becoming mayor anymore. Obviously, he was lying."

"Maybe the consultant told him he'd never beat Ronan Godfrey," said Maeve. "If so, he would have a clear motive for wanting him dead."

That made sense. Consultants didn't take on races they couldn't win. They ran the analytics for clients but weren't the patron saints of lost causes. After all, they bolstered their reputations when they won and experienced adverse effects if they lost big. Hence, they tended to avoid the latter scenario like the plague.

"You're right," I said. "Maybe Tobias realized that the only way he'd become the mayor was if Ronan disappeared. He had to take matters into his own hands."

"Well, I figured you should know about it," said Maeve. "I have no doubt you're investigating. It's not like you could let a vacation get in the way of solving a murder."

My boss really did know me too well. "I have been chatting with several suspects. But we're still trying to find time to relax."

"One more thing before I let you go," said Maeve. "Don't make any commitments on that horse legislation."

I wracked my brain to place the reference. "Oh, you mean the proposed bill that would protect the wild horse population in Corolla. Funny you mention it, because we went with the president of the foundation today to see some of the horses." I paused for a beat. "Wait a second. Why *wouldn't* you support that legislation? The herd needs help. Do you know those horses have been in the Outer Banks for centuries?"

"We can talk about it when we're back in the office. All I know is that Ronan Godfrey told me privately that I should think twice before supporting that legislation. He seemed to imply he'd changed his mind about it. I want to have time to think about it and learn more."

I scratched my head. That didn't make any sense. After all, Ronan was good friends with Gary Brewster. Why wouldn't he support the legislation Gary's organization was trying to enact?

"Okay," I said slowly. "I haven't made any concrete promises. I still think it's a good idea to protect these horses. They're a *North Carolina* treasure, after all." If Maeve wanted to become a senator, she needed to start thinking like one. Senators represented the whole state and needed to spread their goodwill around geographically. At least the smart ones did.

"Fair point. We'll discuss this when we're back in Washington. Goodbye, Kit."

I clicked off my phone. Just when we thought we were closing in on Lacy as a likely suspect, Maeve's information about Tobias and his political aspirations had complicated matters. I returned to the hot tub and relayed the information to the Scooby gang. Even Clarence seemed to listen intently.

"We really can't forget Jean Rizzo," said Meg. "If anyone has a clear motive for killing Ronan, it's her."

Doug took off his steamed glasses and wiped them with a beach towel. "Along those lines, Thalia is still a suspect. She doesn't seem broken up by her husband's death. Besides, didn't you think she might be having an affair with Tobias?"

I threw my hands up. "The relationships between these people keep getting more and more complicated." I glanced at my phone. "It's forty-five minutes before sunset. Gary mentioned earlier today that since his bar is closed, everyone would likely gather at the Sunset Grille tonight. Should we go?"

"I'm up for it," said Sebastian. "Twenty minutes in the hot tub is more than enough."

Everyone else seemed to agree. "Sunset Grille is on the other side of Duck. Let's get ready and meet downstairs by the cars so we can drive there."

A half hour later, we walked alongside the long boardwalk that extended into the sound. The restaurant's footprint was huge, including an outdoor tiki bar, gazebo, winding walkways, and plenty of tables. We were able to grab a few stools inside the bar area.

"I'm starving," said Meg. "Can we order food along with our drinks?"

Before we knew it, our server had delivered plates of tuna nachos, chilled smoked salmon dip, fried pickle chips, and calamari. We ordered a variety of tiki drinks in souvenir cups, ranging in colorful names from Jaws Attack to Jurassic Punch. The sun was getting ready to set over the Currituck Sound, and since the day had been a clear one, it was quite a spectacular show of colors. Before digging in, we pulled out our phones and snapped away. The night before, I'd been too distracted by an intoxicated Jean Rizzo to enjoy the sunset. But this evening, with an Electric Margarita in my hand that actually lit up when you drank it, I was completely focused on the wondrous display of nature in front of me. Doug put his arm around me and clinked his Tiki Parrot glass with mine. I was so entranced by the moment, I almost forgot we'd come to Sunset Grille to interrogate suspects—almost.

My fleeting moment of peaceful bliss was interrupted by a familiar voice. "You decided to take me up on the offer of the beautiful sunset?"

I turned my head. It was Gary Brewster, and he was joined by Thalia Godfrey and Jean Rizzo. I did a double take on Jean. From what I could ascertain, she seemed sober, although she did have a glass of red wine in her right hand.

I put down my blinking margarita glass and swiveled around to face our visitors. "We take the recommendations of locals seriously. You said this was the best place in town tonight for the show."

The sun had just disappeared over the horizon and the buzz at the outdoor restaurant increased considerably as everyone stopped clicking photos and returned to their table conversations. "I never come here," said Thalia Godfrey. "These two convinced me to leave the house. They said it would be good for me."

"You shouldn't be at home alone during this difficult time." Jean winked inconspicuously at Thalia.

The wink was suspicious, but I ignored it and pressed on. "Have the police uncovered any more leads concerning Ronan's killer?"

"I haven't heard anything," said Thalia quickly. "Of course, I'm busy with memorial planning. We'll have a service here next week in Duck and there will have to be something scheduled in Silicon

Valley. After that, I'm not sure where I'll be."

Still sipping his tropical drink out of his oversized parrot glass, Doug joined the conversation. "Oh, you aren't going to stay in Duck?"

"There's no reason for me to stay," said Thalia. Jean bristled at her comment. Thalia added, "If I can figure a few things out, that is."

"Like selling your house?" I asked.

Thalia waved her hand dismissively. "I might keep it as a vacation getaway. But I need to figure out where to go. Atlanta? New York? Boston? It hasn't been decided."

"I imagine you'll inherit the bulk of Ronan's estate, then?" I asked. It was a bold question. Given Thalia's blasé attitude about moving on, it spoke to motive, so I needed to ask.

"I'll inherit enough to remain suitably comfortable," said Thalia, apparently unbothered by the bluntness of my question. Perhaps she'd gotten used to people asking her about money.

"But not everything?" pressed Doug. It was uncharacteristic of my husband to be so downright nosy. It must be the Tiki Parrot drink talking. Who knows how many shots of rum it contained?

Thalia didn't miss a beat. "Ronan had a past, like most successful people. It requires payback. Fortunately, his assets were vast, and it won't impede my lifestyle one bit."

Was that a reference to an affair with Lacy Madison? Perhaps there had been a relationship with her previously and now it was over, but to keep her silence, Lacy would get a payout in the will.

The only way I'd know would be to ask. I lowered my voice and moved closer to Thalia. "Are you referring to a prior relationship between Ronan and Lacy?" I asked. "I saw a photo of them that Lacy keeps at her store."

Thalia stared at me, her eyes as dark as the deepest recess of the ocean. It wasn't a glower of hatred or anger, though. Instead, it was an expression of surprise.

"Things aren't always what they appear to be," she said. "If you're going to continue poking around in an attempt to clear your brother, you'd better remember that."

Doug must have sensed the tension in the air. He quickly changed the conversation. "Will Sonoma Sunsets reopen soon? Or are you thinking about closing it now that Ronan is gone?"

Gary spoke immediately. "Keeping it open, of course. It's the only organic wine bar in the Outer Banks and we'd been doing a brisk business. There's plenty of environmentally-conscious people who live in OBX, and it's my responsibility to give them options."

Jean bristled again and took a big sip of her wine. She wasn't very happy about the substance of this conversation.

"It looks like a lot of your business has come to this place," said Doug. The outdoor area was packed, despite the conclusion of the sunset.

Gary shook his head. "I know. That's why I'm hoping we will be open soon. I need to talk to the police tomorrow morning about removing the crime scene tape."

"Jean, we enjoyed lunch at your restaurant today," I said. "I wanted to ask you about a detail concerning the night of Ronan's murder."

She took a final sip of her wine and set the glass next to our plates. "Ask away. It's a free country."

Such a charming personality. "You said you only had one drink that night because Sonoma Sunsets didn't have your favorite wine, a Cabernet Sauvignon."

Gary narrowed his eyes but didn't say anything. I kept going. "When I talked to Detective Gomez earlier this morning, she said the murder weapon was a bottle of the Cabernet Sauvignon served regularly at Sonoma Sunsets."

"And your point is?" Jean placed her hands on her hips.

"If there was a bottle at the bar that was used to kill Ronan, then clearly the bar had the wine in stock," Doug explained. "Are you sure you only had one drink that night and went straight home?"

Jean's nostrils flared. "Are you calling me a liar? I think I can remember what I did the previous night. Like I said, the bar didn't have the wine I normally drink. I had something else and didn't care for it that much, so I called it an early night and went home." She pointed at Gary. "Why don't you ask him about it?"

"Jean is right," said Gary swiftly. "We took that wine off the menu. I don't know if we had an extra bottle behind the bar or not, but we weren't serving it any longer."

"Thank you for clearing that up." I looked back at the plates of appetizers we'd ordered. Sebastian, Lisa, Trevor, and Meg had made quick work of them. I sucked at my straw and discovered my margarita was now gone. Not a bad time to make an exit. I stood from my stool and wobbled a bit. A couple of glasses of wine and then a strong drink at Sunset Grille with no food was not an auspicious combination. I needed to get something substantial in my stomach.

"I see my friends have finished our food," I said. "We'll have to head back to our beach house for dinner. It was a pleasure talking to you."

Doug nodded politely, and we told our friends we were leaving. After paying our bill, we made our way across Highway 12 to the packed parking lot.

"Sorry about eating everything," said Meg. "We didn't want to interrupt you. It seemed as though you were having quite a conversation."

"We certainly did." I recounted all the details, including the fact that Gary corroborated Jean's story about the wine.

"That points the finger right at Lacy," said Sebastian. "If the bar wasn't serving that wine anymore, then where else would it come from?"

"I don't disagree," I said. "Although Gary said he didn't know whether there might have been a stray bottle sitting around somewhere."

"That seems rather coincidental. Why would the killer grab a bottle of wine that wasn't even being served that night? Years ago, I worked in a bar. You keep the most heavily trafficked types of wine up front so your bartenders can keep pouring glasses. Something that wasn't on the wine list anymore wouldn't be easily available."

Trevor rubbed his chin. "That's a pretty good point, Kit. If Lacy had those bottles of wine in her possession because Gary gave them to her, it explains why the Cabernet ended up as the murder weapon, even if there wasn't a bottle available at the bar."

I took a deep breath. "We'll figure out what to do about Lacy tomorrow. Right now, I have more pressing concerns that must be dealt with."

"Did Gary give you another clue?" Meg had a glint of excitement in her eyes. "Are we off to follow up on it? A nighttime interrogation? Snooping around for clues at the scene of the crime?"

"No, it's something much more basic," I said. "I'm famished. Is there anything to eat at the house?"

Chapter Fifteen

Sebastian offered to grill a steak he'd bought earlier today for me and Doug. Trevor was not to be outdone. He insisted that Sebastian also cook up his catch of the day.

"Surf and turf," said Trevor proudly. "You can't beat fresh seafood right from the ocean." Given the tiny fish Trevor had caught, it was more like steak and sushi.

We piled into the two cars and drove back to the beach house. I couldn't help thinking about our conversation this evening with Thalia, the widow who'd apparently forgotten to grieve for her dead husband. She was already planning to move away from Duck and take control of his assets. In fact, she said there was no reason to stay in town. Was she having an affair herself, maybe with Ronan's political rival, Tobias? If so, why would she want to bolt? Or was her statement about leaving town a ruse to cast suspicion elsewhere?

Sebastian and Lisa had already arrived at the house when we pulled into the driveway. Lisa had Clarence and Murphy on the dual leash for a potty break. As we got out of the car, Meg pointed in the direction of the street.

"Why is the red flag up on the mailbox?" she asked.

"You raise the flag to let the mail carrier know you have a pickup," I said. "Was it raised when we left?"

Meg wrinkled her brow. "I don't think so. Wouldn't we have noticed it?"

I spoke loudly. "Did someone put mail inside the box for delivery?"

No one said anything.

"Well, *someone* is messing around with our mailbox." Meg marched over, opened it up, and reached inside.

"Meg, be careful!" I exclaimed.

I was too late. Meg screamed as she pulled out what appeared in the dark to be a dead bird of some sort. She immediately dropped it on the ground, but her hand was covered in an icky red substance.

"Is that blood?" asked Trevor, whose face had turned completely white in three seconds flat.

Lisa and I rushed over to Meg. Unfortunately, so did the dogs. Murphy picked up the winged creature from the ground, but Clarence was not to be outdone. As he attempted to grab it from Murphy's mouth, the two rascals rolled around on the ground, each trying to lay claim to what they both considered a first-class bounty.

"Stop it!" I yelled. Whatever they were fighting over was evidence, and we needed it in one piece.

Lisa put her hand on me. "Let me take care of this." She opened our car's front door and laid on the horn. Both Clarence and Murphy immediately stopped fighting, and Lisa quickly scooped up the bloody bird.

"Nice work!" I said. "Meg, are you okay?"

Meg was examining her hand. "I don't think this is blood. It's some sort of yucky red substance." She sniffed her hand. "It smells like something familiar." Before I could tell her not to do it, she licked her thumb, which was covered in the ooze.

"It's what I thought," she said. "A red wine. Seems like more of a dry varietal. Definitely not on the sweet side."

"What was inside the mailbox?" I asked. "Is it a dead bird?" What kind of deranged person would do something like this?

Even in the darkness, I could see Lisa shaking her head back and forth. "It's a bird, but it was never alive." She crossed the driveway and showed me what she held in her hand. It was a stuffed mallard duck, like the kind you'd buy in a beachside souvenir shop.

At this point, Trevor, Sebastian, and Doug joined us. We gathered in a tight circle. "Who would take a stuffed animal, soak it in red wine, and put it inside the mailbox?" asked Doug.

It was a perfectly reasonable question. There was no doubt I knew the answer to that question.

"The murderer is sending us a message," I said.

"Kit, perhaps you've been watching too many Agatha Christie movie adaptations on BritBox," said Trevor.

"Do you have a better explanation, Trevor?" I marched over to the mailbox and peered inside. It was too dark to see anything, and I didn't relish the idea of plunging my hand inside. I pulled out my phone, turned on the flashlight, and pointed it inside. Sure enough, there was a piece of paper shoved in the back of the box. I pulled it out and shined the light on it.

"Should you touch that Kit?" asked Lisa. "In case there's fingerprints?"

"Given that you touched the duck, along with both Clarence and Murphy's mouths, I'm not sure we're going to get high marks for handling evidence," I said.

There were only five words on the plain piece of paper, written in large block letters:

YOU'RE NEXT. DUCK DUCK DEAD.

I showed the note to everyone. "Now can we agree that the killer has sent us a direct message?"

"I think that's a safe assumption," said Doug. "Covering the stuffed duck in wine ties it directly to Ronan's death."

Meg's eyes sparkled. "We must be getting close to uncovering the truth. That's why he's threatening us."

"Or she," I said. "We might have uncovered a lot of motives, but I'm not sure we know who is responsible for Ronan's death."

"It points again to Lacy. She's the one who's clearly in possession of red wine, even today. She probably took one of the half-empty bottles from her doggie happy hour, snagged a stuffed duck from one of the nearby tourist shops, and put it in our mailbox," said Lisa.

"How would she have known where we were staying?" I asked.

Lisa scoffed. "The way these Duck residents talk to each other,

I don't think it's hard to fathom that Lacy easily found out. Or she followed one of us back to the house. There's six of us running around, so it would be easy to tail someone to find out."

I had to agree. "Good thinking."

"Not to mention that your car has a Maeve Dixon for U.S. Congress bumper sticker on it," said Trevor. "It wouldn't take Nancy Drew to figure out this house is where you're staying for the week."

I laughed. "Lay off Nancy Drew. She's one of my favorite all-time detectives."

"Well, even Nancy Drew would know that we'd better call Detective Gomez about this," said Doug. "Don't you think it will help to clear Sebastian?"

"We'll see. I wouldn't count those ducks before they're hatched," I said.

Everyone groaned at my mixed metaphor. Lisa pulled out her phone and placed the call to the police, and we headed inside. Doug and I were still famished, so Sebastian agreed to fire up the outdoor grill for a steak and Trevor's size-challenged fish.

Ten minutes later, police lights bathed the otherwise dark street. As I walked out to greet Detective Gomez, I noticed the vacationers across the street peeking through the blinds. They probably wondered what we might have done to necessitate a nighttime visit from the local police. Maybe I should remove that Maeve Dixon for Congress bumper sticker until this murder got solved.

Gomez got out of the car. This time, she was alone. Probably not a lot of money in the budget for evening overtime. She motioned for me to go inside.

"Let's move this discussion off the street," she said. Maybe she'd seen the nebby neighbors, as well.

The detective followed me upstairs to the living room, where everyone was gathered, except Sebastian, who was diligently grilling the food outside. Gomez pulled out her trusty notepad and got right to the point. "Dispatch told me you received a threatening message this evening. Who can tell me what happened?"

Meg waved her hand. "I should tell the story," she said emphatically. No one challenged her. "We came back from the sunset bar place, and I noticed the mailbox flag was raised. It definitely wasn't that way when we left."

"Why are you so sure about that?" Gomez's body was rigid as she stared down Meg. Because she was so attractive, Meg was often underestimated by authority figures. She gleefully surpassed expectations each and every time. I'd grown accustomed to it and even enjoyed watching it.

"Because we backed out of the driveway, and I distinctly remember looking at the mailbox," said Meg in her most authoritative voice. "I wondered why there was a mailbox for a rental property."

Gomez must have accepted her explanation. "Go on," she said. "What happened next?"

"I reached in and pulled out *that*." She pointed to the stuffed animal duck sitting on the dining room table.

Gomez walked over to the table and peered down at the duck. Instead of touching it, she took her pen and poked at it, almost like she was wondering whether it would come to life and fly away. "What is this thing covered with?" she asked, wrinkling her nose.

"It's red wine," said Meg. "I tasted it."

Gomez's knuckles turned white as she tightened the grip around the pen in her hand. "You contaminated the evidence even further by doing that."

Meg flipped the hair of her blonde bob from one side to the other. "I tasted it from my finger, but I wouldn't worry too much about it. After I pulled the stuffed duck out of the mailbox, the two dogs fought over it before Lisa recovered it."

"Let me get this straight. There's not only human saliva, but also canine saliva on this thing?" She pointed to the duck.

"Plus, the murderer's DNA," said Meg. "But I imagine he or she was smart enough to wear gloves when handling it."

Gomez pinched the bridge of her nose. If she didn't have one already, I imagine we'd given her a grade A-sized headache.

"Anything else?" she asked.

"There was a note with the duck," I said. "It's also on the table." Sebastian entered the kitchen from the outside deck. "Kit and Doug, your dinner is ready!"

Gomez scowled. "Please, don't let me interrupt your dinner."

Doug and I sat down at the breakfast bar and began to eat Sebastian's grilled feast. It had been a long time since the pizza at Jean's restaurant. Both the steak and the fish smelled wonderful.

Gomez put on evidence gloves and picked up the sheet of paper. "The killer is allegedly threatening you because he or she knows you're asking too many questions?" The detective asked it more as a question than a statement of fact.

I put down my knife and fork. "That seems the most plausible explanation," I said. "We should tell you about what we learned today about Lacy Madison and the wine bottle that was used to kill Ronan." I recounted my story of the doggie happy hour, along with the detail about the type of wine Lacy had served.

"And now there's red wine all over the duck that was placed inside the mailbox." Gomez gave an audible sigh.

"Maybe you could figure out if it's the same wine that killed Ronan," said Doug.

Gomez threw up her hands. "Why not? I've already asked the vineyard to help us analyze the crime scene," she said. "Although they've been less forthcoming than I've liked. Pretty tight-lipped about everything. I guess that industry is really competitive. They don't seem to want anyone investigating the composition of their wine."

"It might have something to do with the fact that they're organic winegrowers," said Sebastian. "A lot of vineyards are trying to get into that market because they forecast that sales will continue to rise. More people are eating only organic foods for their health and environmental reasons."

Gomez closed her notebook and placed the note and stuffed duck in evidence bags. "Sorry this happened, folks. I'll let you know if our labs discover anything."

"Wait a second." I put my hand on Detective Gomez's arm. If looks could kill, I would have certainly been a dead duck. I immediately removed my hand.

"Is there something else you want to tell me?" she asked. Her voice was even, but I could tell she'd strained to keep it that way.

"Doesn't this exonerate Sebastian?" I pointed to my brother. "He was with us the entire time at the Sunset Grille."

Gomez shook her head. "I wouldn't go that far, Ms. Marshall."

Her response must have irked Lisa. "Why not? The murderer is clearly trying to intimidate us. Sebastian wouldn't do that. It doesn't make any sense."

Gomez put her pen inside her pocket. "I know I don't need to explain this to you folks. You're smart people. Maybe a little too smart."

"Enlighten us," said Meg. "We're not as intelligent as we look." That was a real keeper coming from Meg.

"Sebastian could have put the duck in the mailbox before you left," she said. Meg started to protest but Gomez put up her finger to silence her. "I know you said the flag was down, but he might have done it after you noticed it."

"And Sebastian would threaten us for what reason?" asked Lisa.

"To divert suspicion away from him," said Gomez matter-of-factly. "It's actually quite ingenious. Since you undoubtedly chat amongst yourselves all day long, I'm sure he knew about the story of Lacy Madison and the wine she served at her store event earlier today. Dumping wine all over the duck only strengthens the supposed case against her." The detective looked around the living room and kitchen. There was a fair share of barware strewn about the space. "I'm sure there's no shortage of red wine inside this house."

She had us there. She was one tough customer, making her mini speech without batting an eyelash. Carla Gomez was a hard-nosed police officer who considered everyone was guilty unless proven innocent. Sebastian wouldn't be getting a reprieve anytime soon unless we caught the killer red-handed. And with the involvement of the Cabernet, it was altogether likely we *would* catch the murderer red-handed.

"Very well, then," I said. "I certainly hope you catch the real criminal soon."

"That's what we all want, don't we?" Gomez gave us a half-hearted salute with two of the fingers on her right hand. She began to walk down the steps and then stopped abruptly.

"By the way, you'd best heed the advice of whomever sent that mailbox message. Stay out of police business. I'll try to protect you, but the Outer Banks is a big place. Law enforcement can't be everywhere." She paused for moment before continuing. "If no one here is guilty, then you have nothing to worry about. We'll bring the right person to justice."

For some reason, Detective Gomez's words didn't comfort me. I didn't like playing "Duck Duck Goose" when I was a kid. The so-called "goose" always seemed tap me, which inevitably meant I had to run around in circles until playtime was over. Now, instead of putting up with an annoying childhood diversion, we were dealing with a much more dangerous and deadly game.

Chapter Sixteen

I SLEPT FITFULLY THAT NIGHT, most likely the result of eating a steak right before bed and thinking about Ronan Godfrey's murder. I dreamt of bloody ducks, shattered wine bottles, and Sebastian restrained by handcuffs—not exactly the sweet dreams I'd hoped for during vacation. Given everything that had happened in the Outer Banks, Washington, D.C. seemed like a walk in the park. I rubbed my sleepy eyes as I thought about our situation. Even if we wanted to return home, we couldn't. My brother was a murder suspect and there was no way Detective Gomez would give permission for his departure until the crime had been solved.

Clarence sensed that I was awake, and he wasted no time. He jumped off the bed and sat next to me. He took his right paw and gently clawed at my arm.

Get up, lazybones! Time for my morning walk!

Dogs were a reliable motivator for exercise. I could ignore Clarence for five or ten minutes, but there was no escaping the fact that he had to go out. And that meant my butt needed to get out of bed. After throwing on some beach shorts, a tank top, and flip-flops, we left a snoring Doug behind.

Clarence moved toward the stairs, which he knew was the way out. "Wait a second, buddy. Not so fast."

I flipped on the Keurig, brewed a cup of coffee, and put it in one of those fancy rambler mugs that kept its liquid contents hot all day. There was no way I could even begin to face the day without some caffeine. Unlike the other mornings, no one else appeared to be awake. It looked like it was just me, Clarence, and my steaming cup of java.

As we stepped onto the front porch, it appeared as though it would be another scorcher today. The sun had already risen and was blazing over the ocean horizon. In an hour or two, it wouldn't be enjoyable to drink hot coffee outside.

"What do you say, Clarence?" I asked. "Should we give the beach a try again?"

Clarence didn't seem to protest when I led him in the appropriate direction. When we got to the wooden steps that led to the ocean, he hopped up them without hesitation. However, when we got to platform at the top of the access stairs, Clarence jumped up on the wooden bench and sat down. He looked at me with his big brown eyes. I knew what he was thinking.

This is the end of the road for me, lady. I'm not going any further.

I shook my head and sat down next to Clarence, sipping my coffee. What was that old saying? You could lead a horse to water, but you can't make him drink. I guess my version was: You could take a beagle to the ocean, but you can't make him swim. To make sure I was intuiting Clarence's body language correctly, I tugged gently on his leash, which was attached to his harness.

"Let's go, buddy. Do you want to explore in the sand?" I nudged him in the direction of the descending stairs to the beach.

Clarence didn't move a muscle in his body. He sat absolutely rigid and stared in the opposite direction. I sighed and gave up. After all, I had a prime view of the ocean from the access platform. Compromise was a good thing, even outside of the Beltway. I could drink my coffee, enjoy the sight and sound of waves lapping in the distance, and allow Clarence to maintain his distance from the threatening beach he abhorred.

I sipped my coffee as I thought about the murder. In previous instances, the guilty party had occasionally sent a "warning" message of sorts. That usually meant I was getting close to solving the mystery. However, the problem with this case was that if I was barking up the right tree, so to speak, I didn't know which tree. I'd managed to put pressure on all the suspects by interrogating them. That included Thalia Godfrey, Jean Rizzo, Lacy Madison, and Tobias Potter. I'd had pointed conversations with all of them.

It was time to return to basics again. Again, in a murder investigation, the ingredients were means, motive, and opportunity. Each suspect had an opportunity to kill Ronan. None of them had an airtight alibi for the evening in question. Likewise, each of them had a compelling motive, especially if it turned out that Lacy and Ronan were involved in a relationship. What about means? My zealous hobby of reading crime fiction had taught me that "means" referred to the capability of committing the crime. Did the suspect have access to the murder weapon? Could he or she have physically committed the crime?

The bottle of wine used to kill Ronan still remained a puzzle. If it wasn't being served at the bar, was there still a remaining bottle behind the counter, as Gary suggested? Or did the use of that particular vintage point to Lacy Madison, since she'd clearly been in possession of it. Gary had provided Lacy with the extra bottles. Maybe it would be a good idea to talk to him about it. Gary seemed deeply interested in the business of Sonoma Sunsets and its continued success, particularly within the environmental community.

I didn't have Gary's phone number to text him and Sebastian was still sleeping. Given everything he'd been through and the added stress of Lisa considering the FBI job with Murphy, it was best to let him get his rest. My stomach growled as I drank the last of my coffee. Suddenly, I had the perfect idea.

"Clarence, we're headed to Duck Donuts," I said.

The famous early morning breakfast spot would be teeming with tourists and locals even this early in the morning. Surely, someone there could tell me where Gary lived. In the meantime, Clarence and I could happily split a doughnut.

Clarence wagged his tail in excitement as we walked down the steps and away from the beach. I dropped off my coffee cup at our rental house, and we set off for the walking path that led us into town.

The sweet aroma of Duck Donuts was a powerful guide. Clarence's nose went right up in the air as soon as he caught a whiff. Luckily, Duck Donuts was a canine-friendly establishment, so there was no problem entering the crowded storefront where orders were placed. I stared at the multitude of options. After only a moment, I knew precisely which combination I must order, particularly with Clarence in tow.

"One maple bacon doughnut, please," I told the teenager behind the counter. "Plus, a small coffee and a bottled water." He rang me up and handed me a receipt.

"You can pick up your order across the way." He pointed across the boardwalk.

"Thank you. I assume you're a local resident?" I asked.

He nodded, adjusting his Duck Donuts baseball hat.

"I'd like to get in touch with a friend of mine, Gary Brewster. He co-owns the wine bar down the boardwalk. Do you know him?"

"Everyone knows Gary," he said.

"Would you be able to tell me where he lives?" I asked. "I don't have his phone number, but I need to speak to him." I lowered my voice. "It's about the murder of your mayor."

His eyes widened. "Are you a police officer?"

I leaned in closer. "No, but I'm helping the police solve the murder. Can you help me?"

"Like a private investigator?" he asked.

"Sort of." I wasn't lying. I was like a PI, except I didn't get paid for my investigations. I was a PBPI. *Pro bono private investigator.* I might start using that title.

"I don't know where Gary lives, but I do know Tobias Potter's house. He works with Gary over at that fancy wine bar." He pointed in the direction of Sonoma Sunsets.

The woman behind me in line scowled and crossed her arms. She turned toward the man in line with her, and I heard her mutter, "How complicated is it to order doughnuts?"

I had to speed this up before I had a riot on my hands in the Duck Donuts line. "That would be helpful."

He gave me directions to the right house, which thankfully

wasn't too far from where we were. I noticed the countertop tip jar wasn't exactly overflowing. I pulled a ten dollar bill out of my wallet and stuffed it inside.

"Thank you for your help." Thalia Godfrey was a bit of a flake, but I agreed with her on the importance of karma.

I scurried across the way to retrieve our order, which was already ready. Clarence immediately reacted to the piping hot doughnut, his chunky butt wiggling as he eagerly licked his lips. We found an empty bench, and I pulled off a small bite for Clarence. Apparently, he approved of the combination of maple sugar icing and crispy bacon. He promptly sat down and waited for me. Between the two of us, it didn't take long for us to finish off the doughnut. I pulled out Clarence's portable water bowl from my purse and gave him a drink of water as I sipped my coffee.

"Ready to get to work, buddy?" I asked. Clarence, who had been staring at the sanderlings swooping over the water, immediately got to his feet. He knew when our break was over.

Tobias Potter lived on the sound side of Duck, so we only had to walk past the town shops and then turn down a quiet road off Route 12. Our friend at Duck Donuts had explained that Tobias lived in a condo complex and if I looked at the mailboxes, I could figure out which one. Sure enough, I scanned the row of silver compartments and found one with the name "T. Potter" on it. I knocked on the correct door and waited.

Tobias answered the door, still dressed in what I assumed was pajamas. His hair was ruffled, and his eyes were crusty.

"Sorry to disturb you, Mr. Potter," I said. "Clarence and I were up early this morning and I thought you might be able to answer a few questions about Ronan's murder."

Tobias looked less than thrilled. "I guess since you came all the way here, you might as well come in." He moved out of the way and motioned for us to enter.

It was a two-story condo, with the living room and kitchen on the first floor. The place looked like a bachelor pad. There were newspapers, dirty dishes, and clothes lying about. It was messy but not a full-scale disaster.

"Sorry. I didn't expect visitors." He removed a pair of shorts and a baseball cap from the couch to make room for me to sit. Clarence, who had a bad habit of jumping on furniture when uninvited, appeared content with the floor. He curled up at my feet and promptly fell asleep.

"I'm the one who should apologize for coming by unannounced," I said. "I have several questions to ask you, and I hope your honest answers can help me figure out who killed Ronan Godfrey." As soon as I said it, I realized that I'd probably encouraged him to lie if he was the murderer.

Tobias flinched. "I think I'd better make some coffee. Would you like a cup?"

"Sure. I never turn down coffee," I said, trying to lighten the mood. Tobias walked inside the kitchen and turned on his Keurig. As he waited for the water to heat, I casually surveyed his home. His small dining room table was covered in papers and official-looking documents. On the edge of the table was a bottle of wine. I couldn't quite see what kind it was, but it looked familiar. Tobias's back was turned towards me as he waited for the "ready" light to illuminate on the coffee machine. I carefully got up from the couch and took a few steps in the direction of the table. Clarence sensed my movement and woke instantly. His doggie dream interrupted, he barked in protest. Tobias whipped around and caught me in mid-stride.

"Is something wrong?" He frowned.

No sense in lying since I'd been caught snooping. "The bottle of wine on your table. What type is it?"

Tobias made a face. "It's a red, but I'm not sure of the vintage. I had a glass a few nights ago while watching the sunset. That's the advantage of living on the sound side of the island." He grabbed his glasses, which were tethered around his neck, and picked up the bottle.

"It's a Cabernet Sauvignon," he said. "We used to serve it at the bar, but Gary told me to take it off the menu. He gave me a few extra bottles of it."

That jived with the story we heard last night at Sunset Grille. It also meant that in addition to Lacy, Tobias was also in possession of the wine that was used to kill Ronan. The plot thickened.

"The mayor was hit over the head with that particular type of wine," I said. "Bottles of it keep turning up in all kinds of places."

Tobias handed me a cup of coffee and we sat down on his couch. "There's a reason why everyone had plenty of this Cabernet."

I took a sip of the coffee, which was smooth and rich. "This is delicious," I said.

Tobias smiled. "I use a Keurig because I'm lazy and live alone. No sense in making an entire pot. But the coffee is from a local Outer Banks roaster in Kill Devil Hills."

"Back to the wine," I said. "You were going to say something about the Cabernet."

"Oh, yeah. Everyone had bottles of it because Gary got rid of the stock."

"Doesn't a restaurant or bar typically use everything they have and then take it off the menu?" I asked. "Seems like a bad business move to give the wine away."

"Normally, I would agree," said Tobias. "But Gary wanted that wine off the menu, pronto. I think it had something to do with the fact that the vineyard wasn't really organic."

That might be why they were ducking calls from the police, no pun intended. If the vineyard claimed to produce organic wine but they were actually producing regular wine, they were probably breaking a federal law, since the product had crossed state lines.

"How did Gary figure out the wine wasn't organic?" I asked.

"Dumb luck. I found a case of the wine in our storeroom. It had been delivered about a year ago. I showed Gary, and he said it would taste horrible, since organic wines don't have a long shelf life," explained Tobias. "We opened up a bottle and presto! It tasted really good."

"What happened next?" I asked.

"Gary got pretty angry and stormed off. A few days later, he told me to take the wine off the menu," said Tobias.

"Did Gary pick the wines in the first place?" I asked.

Tobias shook his head. "I don't think so. Ronan liked that part of it. He enjoyed making trips to Sonoma and Napa to pick out particular selections for the bar. I think he'd visit his old Silicon Valley buddies when he was out there."

"Then what did Gary do for the business?" I asked.

"He promoted the wine bar to the environmentally-conscious crowd," said Tobias. "Gary drummed up a lot of clientele beyond tourists. We had local people last year coming to our bar in the off season. That made it quite profitable. Most of the businesses in the Outer Banks have to make all their money during the summer months. But Sonoma Sunsets had a crowd almost year-round."

I thought about the wine catalog in Gary's Corolla office. Maybe Gary felt like he'd have to take over Ronan's duties concerning wine selection and wanted to get up to speed. "Can I see the bottle?" I asked.

Tobias shrugged and handed it to me. The producer's name was on the back of the bottle. I pulled out my phone and took a photo of the label so I wouldn't forget.

While the details about wine was interesting, I didn't want to forget to ask Tobias about the political consultant Maeve Dixon told me about. After all, Tobias had a good reason to want Ronan Godfrey dead. He wanted to be the next mayor of Duck, and Ronan was a permanent roadblock.

"My boss called me yesterday and told me that you hired one of the top political consultants in the state. Were you trying to unseat Ronan Godfrey in the next election?"

"I gave up becoming the mayor of Duck a while ago," said Tobias. "I'm a political realist. I knew Ronan would have that job for as long as he wanted it."

"That sounds like a motive for murder," I said. "If the consultant said that you couldn't beat Ronan, you might have to figure out another way to win. With Ronan out of the picture, now you can run for the job without any serious opposition."

Tobias shook his head. "You really don't give up easily. If you must know, I'm working with the political consultant in Raleigh so I can run for a state legislative seat. The local state senator has retired and there will be an opportunity to run in a crowded primary. With a professional's help, I might stand a decent chance."

Tobias's story would be easy enough to verify. If he wasn't

telling the truth, then it was an awfully elaborate lie.

"One more thing. Last night, my friends and I found a threatening message inside the mailbox outside our rental house." I told Tobias about the "Duck, Duck, Dead" message and the stuffed animal soaked in red wine.

His eyes widened. "That sounds deranged."

"It's disturbing," I agreed. "You weren't at Sunset Grille last night with Gary, Thalia, and Jean. Where were you?"

He chuckled. "You think I stuffed a fake duck in your mailbox? I don't even know which house you've rented."

"This is a small island. I was able to get your address pretty easily," I said.

"That might be the case, but I didn't have anything to do with it. I was at home last night, doing online research for my upcoming campaign." He pointed at his laptop computer. "You can check my web searches, if you like."

"That won't be necessary." I'd finished my coffee, so I stood. "Thank you for speaking with me. Good luck with the race."

"By the way, that's why I came out of retirement to manage the wine bar for Ronan and Gary. The money I've made has gone toward putting the political consultant on retainer for my upcoming state legislative campaign." He paused for a beat. "The bar is opening back up tonight, and I'm thankful for it. I need a few thousand dollars more before I have enough to start my campaign."

"Then you must really want to win," I said. "By the way, do you know that several people think you're having an affair with Thalia Godfrey?" *Several* might be an exaggeration, but at least it would catch his attention.

Tobias chuckled. "What would the wife of a multi-millionaire want with me?" He gestured with his hand. "It's not as though I live in the lap of luxury."

"A wealthy woman like Thalia might not care about the financial status of a lover," I said.

Tobias scratched his head. "You got me there. All I can say is that you're barking up the wrong tree." He glanced at Clarence. "No offense, buddy."

Chapter Seventeen

As we walked back to the beach house, I thought about my conversation with Tobias. It seemed coincidental that the same type of wine that had been pulled off the menu had also been used as the murder weapon. I wondered if Jean Rizzo had a bottle of it at home. Since it had been her favorite wine at the bar, maybe Gary had given her a bottle, too. If that was the case, then I couldn't cross her off the suspect list, either.

Tobias had vehemently denied having an affair with Thalia. He'd implied that I was completely off base - that I was "barking up the wrong tree." What did that mean? Was Tobias implying that he was having an affair with someone else? Or perhaps Thalia had another lover? Or that their friendship was merely platonic? The cryptic comment was now lodged in my brain, and I had a nagging feeling I wouldn't be able to get rid of it until I figured out what it meant.

Clarence and I arrived at the house and climbed the stairs. Meg and Lisa were relaxing in the living room, each with a steaming mug of coffee in her hand.

"And where have you been this morning?" demanded Meg.

"Clarence and I walked to Duck Donuts and then ended up at Tobias Potter's house," I said. "There were a few questions I needed to ask him."

Lisa's face became animated. "Did you uncover any important clues?"

"Tobias had a lot of good answers for everything I threw at him," I said. "But he also had a bottle of that Cabernet on his dining room table. He said Gary gave him several bottles when it came off the menu. Apparently, it might not have been organic wine."

Lisa's head jerked back. "They weren't serving organic wine at Sonoma Sunsets?"

I told them how Gary discovered the problem. Lisa shook her head. "I bet that went over like a lead balloon. I'm sure they charged a premium for the wine. Some people will only drink and eat organic. It's like false advertising."

"I don't think it was their fault," I said. "It seems like the problem was with the vineyard."

"Sonoma Sunsets would need to let their customers know what happened," said Lisa. "The environmentally-conscious community does not like it when they're told something is green and it's not."

"All this talk about wine is making me thirsty," said Meg. "What are we going to do today, ladies?"

Lisa frowned. "I think I need to stay out of the sun for a day. I'm getting a little burned, even though I put on sunscreen."

Meg scrunched up her forehead, deep in thought. Then she snapped her fingers. "I've got it. Let's go to the spa! We deserve a treat, especially after what happened last night."

"Don't you think we need to figure out who killed Ronan?" I asked. "Before the killer follows through with another threat? Next time, it might be more serious than a stuffed animal inside a mailbox."

"Kit, you have a one-track mind. You need to *relax*." She drew out the last word to make her point.

The door to our bedroom opened and Doug emerged, his wavy dark hair sticking up in several different directions. As he yawned and stretched, he gestured towards Meg. "I agree. A little relaxation would do you good, Kit."

Meg gave me her most serious "I told you so" look.

I shrugged my shoulders. "I know when I'm beat. Let's go to the spa."

Meg jumped up and gave me a squeeze. "Perfect. I'll call and get us appointments." She ran down the stairs in search of her phone.

Lisa smiled as she rubbed Murphy's head. "I think a change of scenery is in order. Who knows? Maybe it will even help us clear our heads about this murder."

"That's not a bad point, Lisa," I said.

Meg bounded up the stairs. "Everyone needs to get dressed. We have an appointment in an hour at the Sanderling for spa pedicures. I wanted to book massages or facials, but there weren't any openings."

"After that month of campaigning all over the state with Maeve Dixon, I wouldn't mind a foot massage," I said.

Meg's eyes sparkled. "That's the spirit, Kit!"

"Sebastian and Doug can be in charge of the dogs," said Lisa. "Let's get ready."

Less than an hour later, we pulled into the parking lot of the Spa at Sanderling, which was right across the street from a hotel resort. The whole complex looked fancy. "What kind of spa is this?" I asked. "For the rich and famous?"

"It's one of the best spas on the east coast," said Meg. "Don't worry. I didn't go overboard. We're getting the fifty-minute pedicure and that's it."

We checked in at the front desk and minutes later, we were lounging inside the so-called "whisper zone," wearing our fluffy white robes and sandals, and sipping chilled water infused with fruit.

"This is delicious," I downed the entire glass. "Maybe even better than wine." I winked at Meg.

"Let's not get *too* crazy, Kit." Meg flipped through the latest issue of Vogue.

Before long, we were lined up next to each other, our feet relaxing in a seasonal salt soak. Meg had somehow managed to order a glass of Prosecco and was sipping away from her long flute glass of bubbly.

"Now, this is vacation," said Meg. "I needed this after that terrible trauma from last night." Our treatment moved into the exfoliation phase, which tickled my feet while also feeling luxurious.

"Did Trevor go fishing again today, Meg?" asked Lisa.

Meg's expression, which had been smiley, immediately darkened. "Yes," she said, barely above a whisper.

"What's up with him?" asked Lisa. "He's even more anti-social than his usual self."

Meg stared at her hands. "I think he's trying to decide if he wants to leave his current job so he can find something that's more lucrative."

"Does he need more money for a particular reason?" asked Lisa.

Meg squirmed, which resulted in her foot splashing the manicurist in the face. "Oh, I'm sorry." Meg's face turned red.

I rescued my friend, who obviously was uncomfortable talking about the situation. "Meg is worried that Trevor might want to get married soon."

Lisa's eyes widened. "Did you talk to him about it?"

Meg shook her head. "I don't know what to say."

"The key to any relationship is communication," said Lisa. "When I decided to apply for the FBI, I told Sebastian right away."

"Lisa is right," I said gently. "You should talk to Trevor. You don't want him to make a change in his career without understanding how you feel."

Meg nodded, but I could see tears welling up inside the corners of her eyes. "I don't want him to dump me," she said.

Lisa reached out and patted Meg's hand. "Better to talk now than wait until there's a bigger problem to solve."

Big tubs of warm purple paraffin wax were brought over, and we each got to dip our feet several times in the scented liquid. After several layers, our feet were wrapped in plastic bags and then covered with hot towels.

"This feels really nice, but what good does it do?" As much as I tried, it was hard for me to shake my utilitarian beliefs.

Meg downed the rest of her Prosecco. "It opens up the pores and removes the dead skin. You'll see how nice your feet feel after they remove the wax."

I had to give her credit. Meg knew her beauty treatments, and she was dead right on this one. My feet felt soft and silky after the paraffin, which was only enhanced with a foot and leg massage.

"Speaking of problems, has our morning of pampering done anything to help us solve the murder?" I asked.

Just as I spoke, the door opened. Lo and behold, it was Thalia Godfrey and Jean Rizzo. They were dressed in white spa robes and looked very relaxed.

Jean spotted us immediately. "I see you discovered one of the best places in Duck."

"We did," I said. "Meg suggested we come here for some rejuvenation."

Thalia reached out and touched Jean's arm. "Same for us."

A spa employee approached Jean and Thalia. "We'll start with your pedicure first, and then we'll head over to a private room for the couple's massage treatment. Sound good?"

Both Jean and Thalia nodded and said nothing further. I glanced at Meg and Lisa. Both of their mouths were open. I silently put my hands to my lips, but Meg either didn't see my signal or decided to ignore it.

"Are you two, you know, *together*?" Meg wiggled her eyebrows.

Jean fixed a hard stare at us. "There's no need to pretend any longer. Right, Thalia?"

In response, Thalia beamed. "No, there isn't. It was probably the worst kept secret in town."

I thought about Tobias's comment that I was barking up the wrong tree when I implied that he and Thalia were having an affair. I understood what he meant. Wrong tree, indeed.

Now it was Lisa's turn to ask an inappropriate question. "By any chance, were the two of you together the night when Ronan was killed?"

Thalia nodded. "We told the police our whereabouts, of course. That's why neither of us is considered a prime suspect by Detective Gomez."

"Well, enjoy your pedicure and massages," I said. Our manicurists were finishing up by painting our toenails with the polish we'd selected.

Five minutes later, we left the nail salon room and retreated to the solarium, which featured a peaceful view of the sound. Sea birds flew overhead in the distance as we sipped herbal tea and waited for our pedicure to dry.

I leaned over towards Meg and Lisa. "You guys are the nosiest people I know."

"It's a good thing we are," said Meg, who had somehow managed to score another glass of Prosecco in addition to her herbal tea. "We found out they have corroborating alibis."

"It does complicate matters. But we can't completely cross them off our list," I said.

"I agree," said Lisa. "They might have worked together to kill Ronan, and then lied about their alibis."

"Besides, now we know they have an additional reason to want Ronan dead," I said. "With him out of the way, Thalia has access to his money, Jean gets her revenge, and they both can enjoy their relationship without having to sneak around."

"Although Thalia did say that everyone knew about it," said Meg.

"There's a difference between a poorly kept secret and being out in the open about something," said Lisa.

"Good point," I said. "With Ronan out of the picture, they can pursue whatever type of relationship they want. They didn't have that type of freedom when he was alive."

Our toenails dry, we paid our bill and headed south on Route 12 back to the beach house. Meg announced, "I'm starving. Can we stop for lunch?"

"Let's pick something up we can take back with us, so Doug and Sebastian have something to eat, too," I said.

"We can stop at Tommy's Market," said Lisa. "It's a specialty grocery store that has made-to-order sandwiches. On Tuesdays, they have a lot of free tastings of food and drinks."

Meg's eyes lit up. She never passed up free tastings. When she was a congressional staffer, Meg had always known about the best receptions in the House and Senate. I had no doubt that she'd already identified and attended the best events at the Library of Congress in her new position.

As we went inside, Lisa headed to the deli counter. "I'll order an assortment of sandwiches for everyone. You guys should take a look around the store."

Meg made a beeline for the wine tasting. An older guy with grey hair dressed in a bright Hawaiian shirt was pouring a sampling of wines. "We have two California vintages and two wines from our home state of North Carolina," he said.

Meg held out her plastic sampling glass. "I've never tried North Carolina wines before."

"You're in for a real treat," he said, with a slight southern drawl. He poured us both generous samples. "This is Wild Pony White from Sanctuary Vineyards. One of our most popular blends. Every bottle helps benefit the wild horses of Corolla."

"We know about those horses, don't we, Kit?" Meg sipped her wine.

"Gary Brewster took us on a tour of Corolla to seem them," I said. "Do you know him?"

"Of course, I do," said our wine pourer. "I've lived in the Outer Banks my entire life. There's not too many people I don't know."

"You knew Ronan Godfrey, then?" I asked.

Our pourer ignored my question and offered us the next sample. "This is from the Biltmore Estate in the Blue Ridge Mountains of North Carolina. It's a red blend that's fruit-forward." He poured himself a sip. "Very drinkable."

Shouldn't all wines be "very drinkable?" I decided not to ask. But I did press on Ronan.

"You didn't know Mayor Godfrey?" I asked after I'd tasted the wine. My mouth watered a bit as I imagined drinking it with a meaty piece of fresh fish. There were a lot of excellent restaurants in Duck, and we hadn't really tried them out because we'd been so focused on finding the killer.

"You bet I did," he said. "And not just when he was rich."

"What do you mean?" I asked. "I thought Ronan moved here after he left Silicon Valley and was already a millionaire."

"Here's a buttery Chardonnay from California." He poured us another hefty sample. I put mine aside on the table, too focused on getting my question answered.

After pouring himself a taste of the Chardonnay, he returned to our conversation. "He did move here after his time in the tech business. But he came here every year with his parents for vacation. I remember him as a teenager."

Interesting. That corroborated the comment the man at the Yappy Hour had made about Ronan.

Meg stuck her hand out for the last wine, which he quickly poured. "Pinot Noir from Sonoma," he said. "You either love it or hate it. Personally, I love it." He drank another sip, and I started to wonder if he partook in all the tastings. If so, wouldn't he be awfully tipsy by the end of his shift? It seemed like the perfect retirement job.

"What was he like as a teenager?" asked Meg. "By the way, can I have some more of that Pony White?"

He nodded and poured Meg almost a half glass. "He was a hellion. You gotta remember Duck wasn't built up in those days. There wasn't much around here, except for the Wee Winks convenience store, a couple fishing supply stores, and a few vacation houses. Hell, it wasn't even Duck then. It was part of Kitty Hawk." He took a breath. "Back in those days, the locals actually knew the vacationers. That's why I remember Ronan."

"He misbehaved?' I asked. It might not be relevant to his murder, but it was fascinating to hear gossip from a local.

"Nothing that got him into trouble with the cops or anything, but he was always running around, getting into someone's business," he said. "When he got older, he was popular with the girls in town. That made a lot of the fathers angry, as I recall."

Maybe Ronan had always had a thing for the ladies. If that was the case, Thalia might have had enough. She could have used her romantic relationship to convince Jean she had to help her get rid of Ronan permanently.

"So that's why he moved to the Outer Banks after he sold his tech company," I muttered.

"He had a lifelong connection to this place, but the funny thing is, he never mentioned it, even when he ran to become the mayor.

I always thought it was strange he never talked about spending his summers here as he was growing up. Not many people knew about it."

"When did he stop coming here for the summer?" I asked.

He rubbed his chin as he pondered my question. "I can't quite recall the year. But I remember he was here one summer after he graduated from high school. Then I never saw him again until he moved back here."

Something was rattling around in my brain about this timeline. I couldn't quite put my finger on it, yet my intuition told me it was important. My past experience told me I shouldn't ignore that little voice in my head. The subconscious portion of the brain often figured out the answers to tough problems before it became apparent to the conscious. That's why it was critical to pay attention to persistent hunches.

"How much time between his last vacation and when Ronan and Thalia relocated to Duck?" I asked. "Even a rough guess."

Our wine-lover friend used his fingers to help him with the calculations. "Let's see. I can't be exactly sure, but I bet it was at least twenty-five years in between." He snapped his fingers. "Wait a minute. I can tell you for sure."

He dashed off and returned with an iPad. "I read Godfrey's obituary in the *Outer Banks Voice* online." After a few taps on the screen, he found the article. "Ronan was fifty years old when he died. And the writeup says he moved to Duck two years ago. That means it was about thirty years between his last vacation here and his return."

"That was impressive," said Meg, who had finished her second serving of Pony White. "By the way, I really like this wine. I'm going to buy a bottle."

Our local wine connoisseur beamed. "The boss can't get angry at me for talking to you for so long since you ended up buying a bottle of wine. Don't be a stranger, and I hope you enjoy your vacation."

Lisa had just finished up at the deli counter. She had an assortment of sandwiches, chips, and drinks and was headed to the checkout. "Did you enjoy the free tastings?" she asked.

"Definitely," I said. "I've got a good idea who we need to speak with after lunch."

Chapter Eighteen

We arrived back at the house and there was no one inside to greet us. I opened the sliding glass door that lead to the third-floor balcony and peered down. Sebastian, Doug, Clarence, and Murphy were sound asleep in the shade by the pool. So much for Sebastian thinking about who might have killed Ronan or Doug coming up with the topic for his next book. It was vacation, after all. Even doggies needed a break.

"We brought home lunch!" I yelled. Four heads lolled to attention. I don't know about the rest of them, but Clarence definitely knew the magic words "breakfast, lunch, dinner" meant that there was the potential for food.

Doug stretched his arms and rubbed his eyes. "We must have taken a nap. We'll be up in a second."

Lisa had already unwrapped the sandwiches and placed them on a large serving platter. She'd bought an assortment of selections, including turkey, ham, tuna salad, vegetarian, buffalo chicken, and roast beef. Meg had already poured herself a glass of Pony White. Besides eating anything she wanted and not gaining a pound, she also had the amazing fortitude of being able to sip drinks endlessly and not become intoxicated. I was the first to admit that my best friend possessed superwoman powers that even I did not fully understand.

After Sebastian, Doug, and the dogs joined us, we dug in. Between mouthfuls, Sebastian asked, "How was your spa treatment?"

We told them about Thalia and Jean's couple's massage. Doug stared without blinking. "Does that eliminate them as suspects?"

"It gives them corroborating alibis, but it doesn't completely exonerate them," I said. "They might have teamed up to kill Ronan."

"Tell them what we learned during our wine tasting." Meg lifted her glass.

"First, we learned that there's some tasty North Carolina wines," I said, smiling. "But more importantly, we found out more about Ronan's history with Duck." I told them the details we'd learned from our conversation at Tommy's Market.

"It solves the mystery about why Ronan left Silicon Valley for Duck, but I'm not sure it's relevant to the murder," said Sebastian.

"That's what I thought at first. But then I started to put the pieces of the puzzle together," I said.

Doug leaned in. "Stop keeping us in suspense, Kit! Tell us."

"I'm not sure if my hunch is right, but maybe we can find out this afternoon. Lacy Madison's secret photograph with Ronan Godfrey never made sense. No one could confirm that they were romantically involved. Lacy seemed to stick to her guns about it, too. Look at Thalia and Jean. When there's no reason to hide a relationship, most people prefer to have it out in the open."

"Okay." Sebastian drew out the word. "I follow your logic, but I'm still lost."

Lisa chuckled. "There are other possible relationships besides romantic ones."

Doug and Sebastian pondered Lisa's hint for several moments. Doug figured it out first. "Do you think that Lacy is Ronan's daughter?"

"Bingo," I said. "The timeframe is right. By my guess, Lacy is almost thirty years old. I think what happened is that Ronan had a relationship with Lacy's mother that last summer he spent in the Outer Banks. Remember Lacy told us that she inherited her mother's house, who lived in this area her entire life."

"That would explain why Ronan's family never came back to the Outer Banks on vacation again. Perhaps there was some arrangement between the Godfrey and Madison families concerning the child," said Meg.

"After Ronan made his millions, he decided to leave California. Why not return to the place where he knew his daughter was living and try to establish a relationship with her?" I asked.

"Of course, this is all speculation." Meg stuffed the last piece of her sandwich in her mouth and washed it down with a big sip of the Pony White.

"But we're going to find out if my hunch is right this afternoon," I said. "Meg and I will head over to Lacy's store and ask her."

"If Lacy is Ronan's daughter, then maybe he was going to leave her a sizable amount of money in his will," said Sebastian. "That would give Lacy a firm motive to want him dead."

"Not to mention he was complicating matters for her by proposing a change to the dog policy on Duck beaches," I said. "That must have rubbed her the wrong way, especially if Ronan was her biological father."

"Good sleuthing, Kit," said Doug. "Just be careful when you approach Lacy this afternoon. If she did kill Ronan, she won't be happy to find out you've uncovered her secret."

"That's why we're going to her store," I said. "This way, we can confront her in public."

After cleaning up the remnants of lunch, Meg begged for pool time before walking to Lacy's store. "All work and no play is dull," she said. I decided not to remind her that we'd gone to a world class spa earlier that morning. But we were at the beach, and at least some of that time should be spent submerged.

Refreshed from our dip, we dressed so we could walk to Lacy's store. Meg wore a red floral wrap dress with flat white sandals, and per usual, I went casual in blue running shorts, a tank top, and Birkenstocks. The sun was blazing as we headed down the pedestrian path towards the shopping center.

"Trevor is still fishing?" I asked.

Meg nodded. "It's good for him to have time to think."

"I didn't want to press you in front of Lisa at the spa, but did you talk with him?" I asked.

"We're not making any decisions at this moment," she said quickly. "I'm distracted with solving this murder, obviously."

"That seems prudent." I knew my best friend inside and out. She didn't want to talk about Trevor and if I pushed her, she'd clam up. Beach pun fully intended, of course.

"Let's talk about the plan with Lacy," said Meg as we approached the shops where Duck Dogs was located.

"We don't want to spook her, but on the other hand, we can't really beat around the bush," I said.

"A direct approach is best," said Meg firmly. "It's not like we're going to draw it out of her. If that was the case, she would have told you when you let her know you discovered the photograph underneath the counter."

We walked into the store and scoped it out. There was a teenager with stylish strawberry blonde pigtails manning the cash register while scrolling through her iPad, but no sign of Lacy. "Is Lacy Madison here today?" I asked.

The girl snapped her gum before answering. "She took a few hours off." She looked at us. "Do you need me to help you find something?"

I didn't want to buy Clarence yet another dog accessory he didn't exactly need. "No, we're friends of hers and wanted to talk with her. Will she be back later?"

She shook her head back and forth, so her pigtails almost smacked her in the face. "Don't think so. Tuesdays are slower days, so she takes the afternoon to go kayaking in the sound. She usually closes the store but today she asked me to watch it."

"She uses the public boat launch?" asked Meg.

The girl nodded. "I think so. Duck Village Outfitters keeps a kayak for her."

"Thanks a lot," I said.

She snapped her gum again and returned her gaze back to her tablet as we walked out of the store. Meg already had her phone open. "That kayak place is just up the road a bit," she said. "Maybe a five-minute walk."

"Let's go," I said. "Do you know how to kayak?"

Meg was examining one of her perfectly manicured light pink fingernails in the sunlight. "Kit, do I look like I know how to kayak?"

Touché, Meg. Touché.

Chapter Nineteen

WE APPROACHED DUCK VILLAGE OUTFITTERS and walked inside. I'm not sure we had a plan, except that we needed to speak with Lacy Madison.

A suntanned, slim man in his twenties with bushy hair and a surfer dude vibe manned the counter. Before we could say anything, he greeted us. "Welcome to Duck Village Outfitters. How can I help two gorgeous ladies this afternoon?"

Meg ate it up instantaneously. She sauntered over to the counter. "We're interested in kayaking." She licked her lips. "Can you help us?"

The salesclerk snapped to attention. "Yes, I certainly can." His hands fidgeted as he grabbed the iPad in front of him. "My name is Sean. I can check to see what might be available."

"Sean, I hope you can be *particularly* helpful to us this afternoon." Meg reached across the countertop and stroked his hand gently. "My friend and I have an important mission. And I know you can help us with it."

Sean gulped, his Adam's apple protruding. "Whatever you need. I think we have several openings if you would like a kayak."

Meg pulled her hand back. "Sean, I need a kayak, but I also need your *assistance*." She drew out the last word much longer than normal.

"How can I assist?" asked Sean in a quaking voice. Meg had this effect on heterosexual men. I was used to it, but our latest victim was an ingenue, I suspected.

"We need to speak with Lacy Madison," said Meg. "We're friends and we have a matter of utmost important to discuss with her."

"Lacy really enjoys this time alone on her kayak," said Sean. "She only gets a few hours a week to paddle on the sound. I don't know if you should interrupt her."

Meg drew back her hand, then fluttering to her throat and décolleté. "This sounds very dramatic, Sean. We only have one question to ask of Lacy. But I'm afraid it cannot wait. So, your help is *critically* necessary." Meg's smile stretched as wide as the Currituck Sound.

Sean's face turned pink, which was a real feat given how tan he was. "Well, I guess if you only have to ask her one question, that wouldn't bother her too much."

Meg reached back across the counter and touched his hand again. "Fantastic, Sean. I really appreciate your help." Meg smiled seductively at the poor clerk, who gulped hard.

"I can take you over to the kayak launch," he said. "I should be able to point out where Lacy is on the sound."

After paying for a double kayak rental, we followed Sean across Route 12 and onto the boardwalk. "One problem with the plan," I whispered.

"What?" Meg hissed. "I think that was one of my best performances yet."

"It was, but the issue is that *neither* of us knows how to operate a kayak."

"That's your problem, not mine," said Meg. "I got us this far."

Luckily, Sean must have foreseen our plight. After giving us each a life vest and a paddle, he instructed us about operating the kayak. It didn't sound too hard. Steady, alternating strokes to move forward and then a sweep stroke to turn the kayak. Hopefully if we steered clear of other paddlers, we wouldn't need to stop on a dime, but the reverse stroke would halt us if we needed it. Once we understood the optimal position of our hands on the paddle, we were ready to launch.

Sean pointed directly ahead towards the horizon, which, according to my calculation, was due west. He used binoculars to spot Lacy.

"If you head straight out, you'll eventually see her," he said. "It looks like she paddled out and is resting there. She's not moving at the moment."

What luck. If we could get out there, we wouldn't have to chase her all across the sound. I had a feeling I would be providing a lot of muscle. Meg wasn't exactly known as a big fan of physical exertion. Sean got behind the kayak on the launch and gave us a shove into the sound. He shouted something to us as we drifted away from the dock, but since I was in the front position of the kayak, I couldn't understand what he said.

"Could you hear what Sean was shouting?" I asked Meg.

"I heard the phrase 'watch out' but then I couldn't hear the next couple of words," she said.

That was ominous. We were supposed to watch out for something, but we didn't know what it was. The water on the sound was quite still. "Maybe the Outer Banks has a version of the Loch Ness monster or something." I gave a nervous chuckle.

"I don't know," said Meg warily as she peered out over the water. "If I see something, I'll let you know, and you can whack it with your paddle."

I turned around to look at Meg. "If you see something, don't wait to tell me to hit it," I said. "You should take care of it." But then I saw that Meg had already rested her paddle perpendicular to the kayak.

"Okay, Kit. Whatever you say." Meg examined one of her fingernails and then pointed ahead. "That's Lacy's kayak straight ahead. It doesn't look that far away."

I started paddling with even strokes in the right direction. It was challenging to keep the kayak on the precise path we wanted, but at least we were moving forward. It didn't take too long to realize two things. First, kayaking was a major workout. Second, Lacy had appeared a lot closer than she actually was. Still, we made progress, and miraculously glided across the water at a faster pace when Meg decided to dip her paddle into the water and row with me.

Lacy's kayak was slowly getting bigger in the distance when I spotted something on the surface of the water ahead. It seemed to be moving.

"Meg, did you see that?" I turned around as much as I could.

"What are you talking about?" She put her hand over top her eyes to shield her view from the western sun.

"Is something moving on top of the water?" I'd seen it again and there was no mistaking what it was, but I didn't want to say it. Instead, I pointed in the distance.

Meg followed my direction and I turned around to gauge her reaction. I immediately saw the fear in her face. Her shoulders tightened and her elbows pressed into her sides. With a tremor in her voice, she spoke softly. "Is that what I think it is?"

I gulped hard. "Afraid so."

We pulled our paddles out of the water and drifted slowly. "That's what Sean was trying to tell us when we left the launch. Watch out for *snakes*!" Meg took her hand and dug it into the back of my arm.

"Ouch! You're hurting me," I said. "Listen, let's be rational about this. They aren't renting kayaks if the sound isn't safe. That snake isn't going to bother us one bit. In fact, I think it's gotta keep moving to stay on top of the water."

"Let it slither far away before we move any closer," said Meg. "If that thing throws itself in our kayak, I'm jumping ship."

It probably wouldn't be a good idea to willingly enter the water where the snake would undoubtedly want to return, but I kept my mouth shut. We both silently watched as the snake passed by us, never giving us as much as a glance.

"See? I was right. He's headed back to the marshy area over there." I pointed with my paddle.

"Let's get moving." Meg dipped her paddle into the water.

"Have you decided to row now?" I asked.

"The quicker we can reach Lacy and talk to her, the better. I bet Mr. Snake isn't a loner, and I don't want to meet his friends."

We doubled down on the paddling, and in under ten minutes, we were within shouting distance of Lacy Madison, who was stretched out inside her kayak, apparently soaking up the afternoon sun.

"Lacy!" I shouted. "We'd like to speak with you."

Either Lacy didn't hear us or ignored my overture. She continued to recline inside her kayak. We were now fast approaching Lacy's boat. "Meg, use the reverse stroke so we can stop this thing!" I said.

"Kit, I have no idea what a reverse stroke is. But I'm about to have a real stroke if we collide with her kayak!" she exclaimed in a high pitch voice. "And then we'll be in the snake-infested water!"

"Take your paddle out of the water," I commanded. Instead of paddling forward, I reversed the stroke, which put the brakes on the kayak, so to speak. We slowed down a few feet from Lacy's kayak. She was still sprawled out, with no sign of apparent recognition.

Meg tapped me on the back and leaned closer. "Do you think she's alive?"

I looked closer. Her chest seemed to move up and down. I pointed my paddle at her boat and tapped her on the arm with it. In an instant, she sat up.

"What's going on?" She looked around, clearly disoriented. "Who are you? What are you doing?"

"Sorry to wake you," I said. "It's Kit Marshall and this is my friend Meg. We needed to ask you a question."

"You needed to ask me a question." Lacy repeated the words back to us. "And so you thought it was a good idea to paddle out here on a kayak to ask me? It couldn't have waited until I returned?"

"As you know, we're trying to solve the murder of Ronan Godfrey," I said. "My brother Sebastian is a suspect, and we can't clear his name until the real killer is brought to justice."

Lacy sighed. "Go ahead. Ask me your question. It's not like I can escape." She waved her hands around, reflective of the fact that the three of us were bobbing in kayaks in the middle of the Currituck Sound. It had to be one the strangest locations ever for a murder interrogation.

"I've been puzzled about your relationship with Ronan Godfrey," I explained. "In my mind, you were a prime suspect. You had access to bottles of wine just like the murder weapon and you clearly had some sort of attachment or affection for the victim. People don't keep photos with total strangers in private locations that only they can see."

Lacy clenched her jaw and remained silent.

"In fact, you seemed like the leading suspect. No alibi, a legitimate motive, and the appropriate means to commit the crime. Especially if you'd had an ongoing relationship with Ronan Godfrey and he wasn't interested in leaving his wife," I said.

Lacy started to speak, but I cut her off. "Let me finish and it will become clear. Something didn't make sense, though. No one told me you were involved with Ronan Godfrey. Duck is a small town. If you were having an affair with the mayor, I would have had busybodies lining up to tell me about it. That didn't happen."

Lacy shifted uncomfortably in her kayak. I kept going. "We went to Tommy's Market earlier today and one of the clerks chatted with us about Ronan Godfrey. It turns out he didn't just show up in the Outer Banks out of nowhere. Although he kept it quiet, Ronan had visited Duck many times as a kid and teenager. He and his family were regular summer renters."

"That's where it really gets interesting," said Meg.

"I remember you said your mother was a local and that you inherited her house. Based upon Ronan's age when he died, I was able to guess that Ronan had previously visited this area about thirty years ago," I said. "I don't like to presume women's ages, but my guess is that you're almost thirty."

Lacy gulped hard.

"I think Ronan Godfrey was your biological father. I also think that when he left Silicon Valley, he decided to return to the Outer Banks in the hope of reconnecting with you. I assume his parents had prevented him from further contact with your mother after she found she was pregnant. The clerk at Tommy's Market said that Ronan and his family abruptly stopped coming to Duck and never returned for another summer."

I looked pointedly at Lacy. Now it was time for me to stop talking and find out if my deductive reasoning was correct.

Lacy bowed her head and then stared directly at us. "You figured it out and I'm not going to deny it," she said. "Ronan Godfrey was my father."

Chapter Twenty

WE DIDN'T SAY ANYTHING for what seemed like an eternity. Finally, Meg broke the silence, speaking in a low voice. "Do you want to tell us about it?"

Lacy wiped sweat off her forehead. The late afternoon sun had hit, and it was sweltering on the water. "You got a lot of it right," she said. "Ronan had a summer fling with my mother. But his family didn't want his future ruined with a girlfriend and a baby. So, Ronan went off to college and my mother had me." She took a breath. "The Godfrey family did provide my mother with resources. It enabled her to purchase the house I live in now. They sent monthly checks to her for my welfare, and I got to pick the school of my choosing for college."

"Did your mother ever tell you about Ronan?" I asked.

She shook her head. "It was part of the agreement. Even when my mother was sick, she didn't tell me the name of my father. She said it wasn't possible and it didn't matter. The family supported me, but they didn't want to be involved beyond that."

"You never tried to find out the identity of your father after your mother passed away?" asked Meg.

"At that point, I already had opened my store. I inherited my mother's house outright. I didn't need any further support and I figured it would be impossible to find him," said Lacy. "My father's name wasn't on the birth certificate, and since my mother was dead, who would have known?"

"Then what happened?" I asked. I had to admit this had all the trappings of an Emmy winning soap opera.

"Ronan moved to town," said Lacy. "It caused a minor stir, since most people knew he was a tech millionaire. People wondered why he chose Duck, but Ronan had a pretty convincing schtick about it. He'd talk all about how he searched up and down both coasts for the perfect beach town and he decided on Duck."

"He didn't contact you before moving to Duck?" asked Meg.

"Nope," she said. "One day he showed up at my store and asked if we could get a drink or coffee." She wiped beads of sweat off her forehead. "I told him I wasn't interested in married men. He laughed and promised he wasn't hitting on me." She paused for a second. "I think he actually said he had a business proposition for me."

"A business proposition?" I asked. "To persuade you to spend time with him?"

"As it turns out, that's exactly what he wanted to talk with me about," said Lacy. "After a few pleasantries, Ronan didn't mince words. He explained that he was my father and what had happened. He apologized for not being involved in my life."

"You must have been shocked," said Meg. "And angry."

"I was surprised, as you might imagine," said Lacy. "But I wasn't really angry. Sure, I didn't have a father in my life. On the other hand, I was supported well. I loved my mother. She was enough for me."

"What was the business proposition you mentioned?" I asked.

"You have to know that Ronan was always working an angle. He didn't want a snuggly father-daughter relationship that would make up for lost time. Instead, he was intrigued that I was a business owner at such a young age. He thought I'd inherited the Godfrey gene for business."

"What did he offer you?" asked Meg.

"He was planning to start a small business of some kind in Duck, like a restaurant or bar. Once it was profitable, he'd turn over his part of the ownership to me, so I could have a stake in it."

"Do you know why he wanted to do that?" I asked.

Lacey shrugged. "Probably guilt. He also wanted to become part of my life, and I think he decided the best way to do that was through a business deal."

"He didn't tell anyone you were his daughter," said Meg.

"That was because of me," said Lacy quickly. "Ronan wanted to tell everyone. I put the brakes on that."

"Did his wife know about it?" I asked.

"Thalia knew," said Lacy. "People noticed that Ronan was spending more time at Duck Dogs than you would expect. After all, he doesn't own a dog. Thalia expected that people might talk about it, but she knew the truth."

It was time to inquire about the most sensitive matter. "Do you know if you're in his will?" I asked.

"Ronan said I would inherit his ownership of Sonoma Sunsets," she said. "It had recently become profitable. He was quite proud of that. In the beginning, it struggled. Organic wines cost a lot of money because they don't produce mass quantities at those vineyards. They also don't keep for a long period of time, so you need to move the inventory."

"Ronan had figured out a way to turn it around?" asked Meg.

Lacy nodded. "He was the money-making brain behind that operation. Gary understood the environmental community and was helpful with that crowd, but he didn't have the business savvy that Ronan had." Lacy sighed. "After all, my father did make millions in Silicon Valley."

"Was he going to turn his portion of the wine bar over to you soon?" I asked.

"Whenever I wanted him to do it," said Lacy. "Of course, at that point, we would need to go public about the fact that he was my father. Otherwise, people would find it really strange that Ronan had given me his share of the business."

"Were you ready to do that?" I asked.

"I was getting there," said Lacy. "Since the bar had become profitable, I could take that money and reinvest it into Duck Dogs. Maybe consider opening stores in Kitty Hawk, Manteo, or even Nags Head."

Suddenly, Meg swiveled from the right to the left. The kayak teetered in response to the jerky movements.

"What are you doing back there, Meg?" I tried to crane my neck to see what was going on.

Almost in a whisper, she said, "I thought I saw something. You know what."

Lacy used her paddle to direct us. "Do you mean a snake? One just went by us."

"That's it," said Meg in a voice much louder than a whisper. "Kit, we're returning to land."

"They won't hurt you," said Lacy in an even tone. "It's not like they're going to throw themselves in the kayak."

I could feel Meg shudder behind me. "I was never able to get over the fear of snakes on a plane. And now I have a new worry."

I giggled. "Snakes on a kayak. A new motion picture movie starring Meg Peters."

"You think this is funny, Kit?" asked Meg.

"Sort of."

I turned my attention back to Lacy. "Thanks for answering our questions. It has been extremely helpful."

"I didn't kill Ronan," said Lacy. "To tell you the truth, with my mother gone, it was comforting to know I still had someone else who cared about me. Even if he hadn't been in my life when I was younger."

"I believe you," I said. "Come on, Meg. Let's paddle back to the dock."

We managed to turn the kayak around and point it in the direction of the dock where we launched. This time, Meg was motivated to row, so the kayak moved swiftly over the water.

After we had established a brisk pace, Meg spoke. "You let Lacy off the hook. You don't think she's still a suspect?"

"No, I don't believe she is. She might have had the means and the opportunity, but there's no motive there," I said. "If she wanted Ronan's half of the bar, she could have asked for it. There was no need to kill him to get it. Besides, the photograph under her cash register tells me she was warming to the idea of Ronan as her father.

There's no indication she wanted him dead."

Sean had been talking to a few guys along the pier, but when he saw us approach, he met us at the launch to help us haul our kayak out of the water. "I looked with my binoculars and saw that you talked to Lacy," he said. "Have I made you a kayaker?"

He looked pointedly at Meg, probably imagining the two of them drifting on the sound under the gorgeous colors of the Outer Banks sunset. A romantic scene, but it wasn't in the cards for poor Sean.

Meg handed him her paddle. "Thanks, but no thanks." She pointed in the direction of the water. "There's snakes out there!"

"I tried to warn you." Sean's face turned red. "Did you hear me?"

"No, we most certainly did not," said Meg. "Kit almost had a heart attack."

I shook my head but didn't respond to her patently false version of events. Instead, I placed my hand on her arm and gently guided her in the right direction. As we walked away, I shouted back at Sean. "We appreciated your help today!"

Once we were out of earshot, Meg jabbed me in the ribs. "You could have let me have a little fun with him. Like old times."

"You mean before you were in a serious, committed relationship." Sometimes I had to remind Meg about Trevor. She wasn't used to flying solo with one guy. It might not be in her DNA.

Meg sighed. "Kit, did anyone ever call you a killjoy?"

"Many times." I linked my arm in hers. "I wear it as a badge of honor."

Meg doubled over in laughter. "Only you would think it as a *compliment*."

"Before we talk murder again, have you decided what to do about Trevor?" I asked.

Meg squeezed our intertwined arms. "I'm going to tell him not to quit his job," she said. "If he likes his current situation, I don't want him to change it."

I patted her forearm. "Good decision. Trevor is devoted to you. I'm sure you know that."

Meg nodded, her face more serious than usual. "I know it." She smiled at me. "One step at a time."

"Agreed," I said. Meg's phobia of commitment wouldn't be solved overnight, but at least she was considering Trevor's future as well as her own. That was progress.

We turned down the street where our house was located. Per my iPhone, it was almost five o'clock. I hoped someone had started dinner, or at least snacks.

When we opened the door to the house, we could hear voices from above. Sure enough, everyone was gathered in the living room. Happy hour was just getting started. Sebastian and Doug were serving as bartenders, while Lisa and Trevor were nibbling on cheese and crackers.

"How did it go?" asked Doug. "And can I interest you in a Caribbean rum punch?" He had a recipe book open on the countertop and was clearly intent on mixing up something more sophisticated than a vodka tonic.

"Sure, that sounds good," I said. "Meg probably wants one, too. We were almost devoured by snakes."

Trevor raised his eyebrows. "I assume this is an exaggerated statement in an attempt to convey humor."

"Yes, but you've just ruined it by stating the obvious," I said.

I looked around the room. Something was off. It took me a moment to figure out what it was. Then I had it. With cheese and crackers in the mix, we were missing two interested parties.

"Hey guys, where are the dogs?" I asked.

Sebastian stopped chopping fruit for the tropical drinks and glanced behind him. "They were in the kitchen about fifteen minutes ago. I haven't seen them since then."

That was strange. Besides pepperoni, Clarence adored cheese. His little black nose could sniff out cheddar from miles away. It was unlikely he'd miss an opportunity to sample an assortment of *fromage*.

I heard a faint tinkle of a collar coming from our bedroom. I pushed open the half-closed door and couldn't believe the sight in front of me. Clarence and Murphy had gotten into our suitcases and tossed every piece of clothing in a scattershot across the floor. Our laundry, which had been in a basket in the corner of the room, was now mixed in with our clean attire. If that wasn't enough, they'd also managed to tear up one of the pillows, so big puffs of cotton rested on top of our clothes, almost like it had miraculously snowed in the Outer Banks.

Clarence and Murphy sat on the other side of the bed, looking guilty as charged. Their ears were plastered against their heads and their puppy-dog eyes were as big as quarters.

For once, I was speechless. Lisa must have recognized silence as an indicator of a major problem. She walked into the room and gasped.

Lisa immediately marched over to Murphy to look at him in the eyes. "Bad boy. BAD!" Murphy bowed his head in shame. Clarence, on the other hand, promptly licked Lisa's leg.

"I wonder who the instigator was," I said.

Lisa shook her head. "It doesn't matter. If Murphy pulls something like this at the FBI Academy, we'll both get tossed out."

I put my arm around Lisa and gave her a squeeze. "Don't worry. I'm pretty sure Clarence is the guilty one and Murphy was simply the accomplice. Without a bad influence, Murphy will do just fine at the academy."

"What's going on in there?" asked Doug. "I'm finished mixing the drinks!"

"We'll be out in a second," I yelled back. Then I turned to Lisa. "Tell Doug what happened. I'm going to straighten up in here, and I'll be right out."

"Are you sure you don't want my help?" she asked. "You shouldn't let Murphy off the hook so easily."

"It looks worse than it is," I said.

"Murphy, come!" Immediately, Murphy got up and followed Lisa out of the room. Clarence had a look of triumph on his face. *He got in trouble and I didn't.*

"Don't act so smug, Clarence. I know you were behind this." Clarence promptly laid down and put his snout between his paws. Who said dogs couldn't understand English?

I picked up the cotton from the pillow and piled it up next to the trash can. I would have to report the damage to the beach house rental company. How much could a pillow cost? Actually, when I thought about it, I didn't want to know.

I separated the clothes into a "dirty" and "clean" pile. The former could go back into the laundry basket and the latter would return to my suitcase. I picked up the pretty blue dress I wore on Saturday, the first day of our vacation. It seemed like an eternity ago. When I folded the dress, something fell out of the pocket.

It was a business card. I turned it over in my hand and looked at it. Suddenly, everything clicked. A moment later, my heart sank. I had a theory about who killed Mayor Ronan Godfrey. However, proving it would be no day at the beach.

Chapter Twenty-One

Thirty minutes and one Caribbean rum punch later, we'd devised the plan for the evening. Doug, an amateur mixologist, had really outdone himself on the punch. Since I was on vacation, I would have indulged in a refill. But tonight would require my full faculties, and I doubted wine on top of rum resulted in favorable outcomes.

Sebastian ran his fingers through his sandy hair. Even though he'd lived for a year in northern Virginia, remnants of his California persona persisted. Nonetheless, nascent worry lines appeared across his face. We were playing a high stakes game to catch a killer, and we had no idea if our gambit would work or what risk we might incur.

"It's all set," I said. "Sebastian and I will head to Sonoma Sunsets, and we'll text you if everything is going according to plan."

"When we hear from you, we'll spring into action," said Lisa.

"Are you sure we shouldn't call Detective Gomez and tell her what we've cooked up?" Doug wrinkled his brow.

"We discussed this," I said. "She's going to tell us to stop meddling. I'm afraid if we don't set a trap, then we'll never be able to prove my hunch. Right now, the evidence is circumstantial."

"At best," said Trevor as a smirk emerged. "Otherwise, it's delusions of grandeur."

"Thank you, Han Solo," I said, without missing a beat. "If I'm wrong, then nothing has been wasted other than an evening we could have spent in the hot tub."

Meg sighed. "That's a substantial cost, Kit."

I reached across the dining room table and patted Meg's hand. "I promise I'll buy you another bottle of Pony White if we catch the killer tonight."

Meg's face brightened considerably. "It's a deal!"

In a few minutes, my brother and I were ready to depart. Doug caught me in the bedroom as I placed my iPhone and wallet inside a small purse. He grabbed my arm and squeezed it gently.

"You need to be careful," he said.

"I know, Doug. It's not like I haven't done this before." We'd set plenty of traps to solve previous murders. Everything had always worked out, although oftentimes not *exactly* as planned.

"I understand that, but you've had the police involved before," he said.

"Gomez wouldn't be interested in helping, so it doesn't matter. You will be there. Meg will be there. Trevor will be there. And Lisa, a future FBI agent, will be there." I took both of my hands and placed them on his shoulders. "Nothing will happen. We might not even get that far. It may not work."

"I don't know whether to hope your hunch is right or wrong," said Doug.

"We want it to be *right*," I said emphatically. "So that Sebastian can be cleared, justice is served, and we can enjoy the rest of our vacation."

Doug pulled me in for a tight hug. "Do not take any chances. Remember the codeword Trevor suggested."

We'd used codewords before when trying to catch a killer. When the rest of the gang heard the word, they knew it was time to spring into action.

"Fishing," I said emphatically. "If that comes out of my mouth or Sebastian's . . ."

Doug cut me off before I finished the sentence. "We'll take care of the situation."

I had no doubt they would. Solving a murder, I'd learned, required a team effort.

I walked out of the bedroom into the living room, where Sebastian was waiting for me. "Ready to go, little brother?"

He nodded. "Let's get this over with."

Meg gave me a quick squeeze. "Don't forget to text to let us know how it's going."

After Sebastian said goodbye to Lisa and I gave Clarence a farewell pat on the head, we began our walk to the sound.

"Nervous?" I asked Sebastian. He'd been involved in two other murders I helped solve, but never as bait to lure a suspect into a confession.

"A little." He blinked a few times rapidly. "Shouldn't I be?"

"Of course. I'm nervous, too."

We walked along in silence for several minutes before he spoke again. "Lisa is going to accept the offer to attend the FBI Academy with Murphy."

"I figured as much." I squeezed Sebastian's shoulder. "It's her lifelong dream. It doesn't mean you have to break up."

"We won't," said Sebastian quickly. "I'm going to have to get used to her being in dangerous situations all the time, though."

"That's true already with her job as a police officer on Capitol Hill, Sebastian."

"I guess so," he said. "She's worried about tonight. At least she'll know how I'll feel on a regular basis."

"It will get easier over time," I said in the most reassuring voice I could muster. Doug was a historian, so I couldn't say that I'd been in a position to feel the same way.

Sebastian nodded and then changed the subject. We were approaching the boardwalk area where Sonoma Sunsets was located. "Let's go over the plan again."

We stopped walking down the ramp that connected the outdoor bar area of Aqua to the boardwalk. It was a steamy summer night and vacationers were everywhere, reclining in the Adirondack chairs outside and enjoying drinks and dinner.

"This part is simple," I said. "We need to ask questions about the wine served at Sonoma Sunsets."

"At a certain point, you'll reveal what you know about the

vineyard in question," said Sebastian.

"Yep. I'll show my cards, so to speak. After that, we'll make our exit," I said.

"Then, we'll see what happens."

"Either our little ploy will work, and the killer takes the bait..."

Sebastian interrupted. "Or we get a few thousand more steps with our nighttime walk."

"Exactly," I said. "And remember that everyone will be there to help us if we need it."

"Maybe we should have called Detective Gomez." Sebastian's forehead wrinkled in uncertainty.

"Lisa is a police officer. She'll know what to do," I said. "Gomez wants to pin this murder on *you*. She's not going to help us try to trap the real killer."

"Whatever you say, big sister," said Sebastian. The worry lines were gone from his face and had been replaced by a reassuring smile.

I gave him a hug. "Just keep your cool and follow my lead."

A minute later, we approached Sonoma Sunsets. The outdoor bar wasn't quite filled. I suspected that tourists had learned about the murder and decided to steer clear. However, as predicted, the locals were there.

I whispered so only Sebastian could hear me. "I see Jean Rizzo, Thalia Godfrey, Tobias Potter, Lacy Madison, and Gary Brewster."

Sebastian winked. "The gang's all here."

I fired off a quick text to Doug and the rest of our friends back at the beach house.

Everyone is in place.

A few seconds letter, Doug responded with a "thumbs up" sign to acknowledge my message.

"Ready?" I muttered under my breath, but loud enough that Sebastian could hear.

"It's now or never," he whispered.

We ambled up to the bar and found two empty seats. Tobias and Gary were behind the bar, serving customers. Lacy was at the far end of the bar, while Jean and Thalia were a few seats away from us.

Gary approached us. "Where are your other friends?" he asked.

"They decided to stay in for the night," I said. "I don't know if you heard, but we got a threatening message from Ronan's killer last night. It was waiting for us when we got home from our happy hour."

Gary tilted his head. "Can't say that I heard about it. But I've been busy all day getting ready for our reopening."

He put two wine lists in front of us. I scanned it quickly before speaking.

"There's no Cabernet Sauvignon," I said. "Wasn't that the type of wine which was used to kill Ronan?"

"I think so." Gary jerked his head in the opposite direction. "If you excuse me, I need to pour a refill for a few customers." He scuttled off to the other end of the bar.

Jean Rizzo must have overheard our conversation. She walked over to where we were sitting. "Gary hasn't replaced the Cabernet yet," she said. "I already asked him about it."

"Did he explain why it came off the wine list in the first place?" asked Sebastian.

Jean shook her head. "I don't think so."

Thalia Godfrey joined us. "What are you talking about?"

"The Cabernet and why it was removed from the selection of available wines at the bar," I said.

"You'd have to ask Gary about that," she said. "I wasn't involved with the daily management of this place." She sighed. "I hope *that* doesn't change."

Gary meandered back to our direction. "Have you made a selection?"

"I'll try a glass of the Chardonnay," I said.

"I'll go for the Pinot Noir," said Sebastian.

Gary scuttled off to fill our order. Jean leaned closed to us. "Any updates on solving the murder?"

"Nothing concrete, but I found out something curious. Tobias told me that Gary discovered the Cabernet Sauvignon wasn't really organic," I said. "I did a little online digging and found out the vineyard had been passing itself off as organic but hadn't adhered to the requirements."

Gary returned with our two glasses of wine. "Enjoy your drinks." He pivoted to walk away.

Before he could, Jean spoke up. "Gary, what's this I hear about Sonoma Sunsets not serving real organic wine?"

Gary cleared his throat. "What do you mean, Jean? Is this another pathetic attempt to discredit us so you can take over this space again with your pizzeria?"

Jean chuckled. "Not at all. I'm headed to greener pastures," she said slyly, stealing a furtive glance at Thalia. "Our guest from Washington, D.C. just mentioned you took the Cabernet off the menu because it wasn't authentically organic."

Gary looked pointedly at me. "And how did you arrive at that conclusion?"

I pointed to Tobias. "He told me earlier today," I said. "Then I did some research. Sure enough, the vineyard is bogus."

"It was a mistake," said Gary. "It was removed from the menu as soon as we knew."

Lacy Madison snuck up behind us. "What are you talking about? It seemed like a lively discussion, so I thought I'd walk over to join you."

"We're talking about the Cabernet Sauvignon wine," I said. "Gary gave you extra bottles of it, right?"

"He did," she said. "It tasted great, so I wasn't about to complain."

I took a sip of my wine. "Very nice. I found out from reading up on wines that some people don't think the organic wines are quite as good as the traditional varietals. They also don't keep well in storage very long. They are considered 'buy now, enjoy now' products."

Gary's face reddened. "That's completely untrue."

"I wonder if the police think it's a coincidence that the Cabernet that was removed from the menu ended up becoming the murder weapon that killed Ronan." asked Sebastian. It was more of a statement than a question.

I waved my hand. "That's for Detective Gomez to figure out, I suppose. I'm sure I'll catch up with her tomorrow to share updates on the case. I can tell her then what I discovered about the vineyard."

Sebastian picked up his glass and clinked it with mine. "It's beautiful weather this evening."

"A perfect night for a walk on the beach. Are you up for it after we're finished here?" I asked.

Sebastian appeared to consider my offer for a moment. Then he said, "Sure, why not? I suppose we can walk off the wine."

Thalia, Jean, and Lacy made small talk with us as we sipped our drinks. I tried to appear as casual as possible. The trap had been set. The question was whether the mouse would take a bite at the cheese, so to speak. When the others weren't looking, I gave the high sign to Sebastian, indicating we should leave soon. We both finished our glasses of wine a little faster than normal and threw several bills down on the bar to cover our tab.

"We're headed out," I announced.

"A nice walk on the beach will be a perfect end to the evening." Sebastian's comment was directed to no one in particular. I elbowed him gently in the ribs. He was overplaying our hand. We didn't want to be too obvious, after all.

After saying goodbye, we walked to the boardwalk and began to retrace our steps. "I'm going to text everyone back at the house to let them know we've left the wine bar," I whispered.

Headed to the beach now.

My text message was met with a "thumbs up" sign from Doug. I sent another message.

Put all systems in place.

This time, Doug texted an actual reply.

Good luck & don't take any chances!

It was my turn to give a "thumbs up" sign in response to Doug's message.

"Everything all set?" asked Sebastian as he watched my fingers fly over my phone.

"We're on. They'll be there by the time we arrive," I said.

"Do you think it worked?" asked Sebastian.

"We'll soon find out," I said.

Sebastian and I continued in silence until we reached the ramp leading to the beach. It was well past sunset, so the entire beach was bathed in darkness. I looked to our left in the general direction where our friends were supposedly hiding. Because it was pitch black, it was impossible to see them or spot their silhouettes. However, a moment later, I saw three bright flickers in quick succession. That was the flashlight signal to indicate everyone was situated properly. The plan had worked. Our conspirators had carefully camouflaged themselves by hiding on the rolling dunes amongst the tall seagrass.

I took a deep breath and turned to my brother. "Ready to do this?"

Sebastian, never one to show too much emotion, shrugged his shoulders. "No time like the present."

We made our way down the wooden stairs and onto the sandy beach. I turned around and looked behind us. No one was standing on the platform that I could see. Of course, it was almost impossible to make out any discernible figure. Some of the houses along the beach had lights on, but the illumination didn't extend to the beach itself.

Without much light, it was hard walking in the sand. "Let's walk closer to the water," I said. "The sand is more compact so it will be easier." I turned on the light of my phone so we could at least figure out the reach of the tide. We didn't have to go far.

"It must be high tide," said Sebastian. "With beach erosion and rising ocean levels, the water is coming closer and closer to the dunes and the first row of houses."

We walked alongside the water, which was lapping at our feet. "Ronan must have been worried about that," I said. "He was no environmentalist, but I'm sure he cared about the economic impact."

Before Sebastian could reply, we both heard the rustle of sea grass behind us. A familiar voice spoke. "It didn't take you too long to figure out Ronan Godfrey. Too bad you're not going to live to tell anyone about it."

The voice was familiar, but we both turned around to confirm our suspicions. I shined my iPhone light directly in front of me. Gary Brewster was standing five feet away, and he had a gun pointed right at us.

Chapter Twenty-Two

I TOOK A DEEP BREATH TO CALM MYSELF. Our plan had worked perfectly, except we hadn't counted on Gary bringing a gun. That was an unanticipated wrinkle.

"Gary, what are you doing?" exclaimed my brother. He couldn't have been completely surprised to see him, since we suspected Sebastian's longtime friend as the guilty party. But like me, Sebastian hadn't counted on Gary brandishing a firearm.

Gary laughed at us, a wicked chuckle that rattled me even further. "I'm going to kill both of you, of course."

"Wait a second." I put my hands out in front of me. "You're overreacting."

Gary's face remained placid. "Am I? You wouldn't stop poking around, even when I sent you a clear warning there would be consequences."

He was obviously referring to the stuffed duck in our mailbox. I had to keep him talking, or all of this would be for naught. In the meantime, we needed to avoid getting killed.

"Consequences for what? We haven't figured anything out." I concentrated on keeping my face as neutral as possible. When engaged in a lie, most people had a notable "tell," such as an eye tick or facial expression.

My efforts didn't matter. "Don't lie to me," he sneered. "You've snooped around the entire town, asking about the Cabernet and why it was pulled from our serving list. You made a point of letting everyone know about your suspicions tonight."

"Then it's ridiculous to kill us," said Sebastian in a reassuring tone. "The police will talk to witnesses and pin our murders on you."

Gary waved the gun around, which made me nervous. Sebastian and I both took a step back. "That's where you're wrong," he said. "On the walk over here, I figured out an ingenious plan. Even better than Ronan's murder, which I admit, I had to come up with on the fly."

I had to keep him talking for a little while longer. "What puzzled me was why Ronan got shoved into the marshy water. Especially when we found out that the blow to his head killed him."

Gary chuckled again, his malevolence readily apparent. "You figured that out, huh?"

"Pretty ingenious, actually," I said. In my experience, ego-stroking never hurt, even when dealing with maniacal killers.

"The whole thing was more or less an accident. I'd already left the bar for the evening, but then I realized I had left my wallet there. I walked back to get it and found Ronan alone. Tobias had closed up, but Ronan couldn't sleep so he came back for a nightcap." Gary motioned with the gun in the direction of my brother before continuing. "I didn't plan on killing Ronan that night. Sebastian knows that I'm a lover of the Earth. I'm not a fan of killing animals or people."

"You still smashed Ronan over the head with a bottle," said Sebastian. "Even if it wasn't planned, you did it."

Gary shrugged. "That's true." He emitted a tired sigh before continuing. "Ronan was a smart man, but he wouldn't listen to reason. He wanted to turn a profit off the wine bar and then turn it over to Lacy. He confessed to me that she was his daughter when I pressed him about it. There was a problem with his business model, though."

Sebastian spoke up. "Organically produced goods are expensive and the organic standards for wine in the United States are high."

"Bingo." Gary pointed the gun in our direction. He was making me increasingly nervous. "Tourists don't want to pay fifteen bucks for a glass of wine. Furthermore, you have to be careful about your inventory. It needs to move fast, or you have to toss it out. There's no extra preservatives or additives to organic wine."

"Ronan didn't care about these details. His goal was to start a business and turn it over to his long-lost daughter as a way to repay her for not being in her life when she was growing up," I said.

Gary's nostrils flared. I'd hit a nerve. "He *didn't* care about selling or promoting sustainable wine. It was all just a ploy for him. But there was no way I could be associated with a business that was buying wine from less than reputable vineyards and passing it off as organic. If someone had found out, my reputation would be ruined."

"My guess is that you got into an argument with Ronan and he insisted that the Cabernet come back on the menu," I said.

Gary interrupted. "Not just that wine. I would have never killed him over one indiscretion." Gary took a deep breath. "He had others that he wanted to buy that were cheaper. From the same types of suppliers that cut corners but passed themselves off as organic producers. If I didn't play ball, he was going to use his influence to endanger the Corolla wild horses by telling members of Congress the protection legislation was useless." Gary bared his teeth. "He was going to destroy me and threaten our most precious Outer Banks legacy."

"In a fit of anger, you hit him over the head with the bottle of wine you were arguing about," I said. "Before that, I'm guessing there was pushing and shoving."

Gary now had the gun pointed directly at us. "Go on," he said. "I'm enjoying this."

I took a big gulp. "You were a biology major. You told me that when you took us on the wild horse tour in Corolla. You knew that your DNA would be all over Ronan's clothing because of the tussle. Once the police dove into the evidence, you would be the prime suspect."

Sebastian picked up where I left off. "Even though Ronan was dead, you needed to get rid of the evidence. You knew that if the body was submerged in water for several hours, it would make the recovery of identifying DNA on his clothing almost impossible. So, you dragged Ronan over to the kayak launch and shoved him into the marsh, wiping away all evidence of you as the killer."

Gary clapped his hands together while still keeping the gun pointed at us. "Bravo, bravo. Under the right circumstances, you both would have budding careers as detectives. It's a shame none of that will come to pass, I'm afraid."

"If you kill us, you're not going to stand a chance. Our friends know you did it. They'll tell the police what happened," said Sebastian.

Gary chuckled. "Give me a little credit, Sebastian. Like I said, I came up with a plan. I grabbed my gun from my car and decided I'd take this opportunity to provide a fitting ending to this story." He paused for a moment before continuing. "You're both victims of an unfortunate murder-suicide. Kit figured out that her brother was guilty. When she confronted him on the beach, Sebastian murdered her and then killed himself. A tragic ending, almost Shakespearean, if I do say so myself."

"Sebastian doesn't own a gun," I said. "They'll trace it right back to you."

"It's quite convenient that I reported my gun missing on my way to the beach," said Gary. "A brief phone call to the police and I've already set the scene for the story."

Geez. This guy had thought of everything. Now I was officially worried. It was time to call in the cavalry. Hopefully, it wasn't too late. I doubted that our friends, who were sequestered behind the sand dune grasses, could see that Gary had a gun. Maybe they'd heard the conversation and realized it was time for help?

Then, I remembered our code word. I couldn't think of a subtle way to work it into a sentence. Also, I needed to make sure everyone heard it. Why hadn't we thought of a better signal?

"But if you kill us now . . ." I stammered, my brain churning for the next words. "We won't be able to go FISHING!" I screamed the last word at the top of my lungs.

My bizarre behavior caught Gary off guard. He jerked his head and shuffled backwards. After that, everything happened in a blur.

Trevor yelled from a distance. "Kit and Sebastian, get out of the way!"

Reflexively, we took several steps backwards. A second later, a fishing hook caught Gary right in the neck.

He screamed in pain and dropped the gun. "What in the hell?" He desperately tried to remove it. But before he could, Gary found himself attacked on another front.

Out of the blackness, Clarence appeared. He charged towards Gary and abruptly bit him on the leg. As he did it, the water from the ocean spilled over his four paws. Nonetheless, Clarence appeared unfazed. He growled, showing his sharp, white teeth.

Moments later, our entire clan appeared. Meg held out her iPhone. "I'm calling the police right now!"

Sebastian, Trevor, and Doug took over for Clarence and grabbed Gary's arms. For good measure, Murphy circled and waited for Lisa's command.

"One false move and I'm going to unleash this police dog on you," she said. "I guarantee you it won't be the love bite Clarence just gave you." Lisa bent down and secured the gun, which Gary had flung to the side after Trevor hooked him.

When Gary saw that Lisa had his gun, he stopped struggling. "Okay, okay. Call your dogs off."

Lisa motioned for Murphy to heel. He sat immediately and stared at her for further instruction.

"Clarence, come here," I said. Displaying a striking level of obedience never exhibited before by our beagle mutt, Clarence walked over to me, turned around, and sat down next to my feet.

"The police are on their way," said Meg, waving her phone. "I called them as soon as I heard you say the code word."

"Sebastian, did you get everything we needed?" I asked.

My brother nodded. "All good."

"What are you talking about?" snarled Gary.

"Sebastian hit the 'record' button on his phone once you showed up on the beach. We wanted to make sure others could hear your confession," I said. "Not that it matters much, since two counts of attempted murder is serious enough."

We heard the familiar whirl of a police siren and moments later, the darkness of the ocean was bathed in red and blue light. Detective Carla Gomez and a team of cops literally stormed the beach.

"Gary Brewster! Put your hands in the air where we can see them," she ordered.

Doug, Sebastian, and Trevor released their grip on Gary, who immediately raised his arms. Three guns were aimed directly at his chest.

Doug hustled over, encircling me in his arms. Never one to miss an opportunity for affection, Clarence whimpered until we picked him up and gave him a doggie snuggle.

Doug touched his paws. "Clarence is soaking wet," he said. "I guess his concern for you superseded his fear of the ocean."

Clarence must have agreed. He responded by giving me a sloppy kiss on the cheek. We finally had our beach-loving beagle.

Chapter Twenty-Three

"KIT, CAN YOU HAND ME THE PACKAGE OF HOT DOGS?" I grabbed them from the picnic table and handed them to Doug, who was manning the charcoal grill adjacent to the pool area. It was Saturday night, and we were celebrating vacation with a traditional backyard barbecue. After answering hours of questions at the police station and then facing a similar interrogation from the local North Carolina press, we had finally settled down to enjoy our remaining time at the beach.

A pile of cheeseburgers, veggie burgers, potato chips, and macaroni salad covered the large dining table on the balcony. Once we added the hot dogs, we'd be ready for our evening feast.

I heard a familiar female voice above me on the balcony. "I hope I'm not too late."

Meg answered. "Not at all, Congresswoman Dixon. Kit and Doug are just finishing with the grilling."

I moved towards the pool so my boss could see me. "I'll be up in a few minutes."

There was nothing that could beat the smell of a barbecue on a warm summer evening. Doug motioned to me with the grill tongs he was holding. "You can join the congresswoman and Meg on the balcony, Kit. I've got this covered."

"Okay." I smiled appreciatively. Doug knew I was eager to find out what Maeve Dixon had to say. In fact, she'd invited herself tonight during a brief phone call yesterday.

It was one of the first times I'd seen my boss not dressed in a power suit. Instead, she wore a gingham short-sleeved blouse and tailored matching shorts with a sport belt. Her brown hair was pulled back into a ponytail, and she was sipping rosé wine out of a glass.

"I'm glad Meg found you a drink," I said. "Thanks for driving all the way out here to the beach."

"When I heard you had the chance to extend your vacation for a few days, I figured it would be a good idea to stop by," she said. "After all, you have not had the typical stay in the Outer Banks."

Meg was also sipping on the rosé and raised her glass. "That's the understatement of the year, for sure."

"When the owners of the beach house found out we helped the police with Ronan Godfrey's murder, they said we could stay a few additional days for no extra charge," I said. "There were no renters scheduled for next week, so it was a hard offer to refuse."

"You deserve the break," said Maeve Dixon. She looked at the food piled up on the table. "Are you expecting other guests?"

"Yes, the Duck residents we got to know will be coming for dinner, too," I said. "You don't mind, do you?"

Dixon winked. "I always like getting to know future constituents."

A wide grin spread across Meg's face. "Does that mean you've decided to run for Senate?"

My boss beamed. "I wanted both of you to know first," she said. "But you have to keep it a secret. I'll make an official announcement in several weeks."

I walked over to my boss and gave her a hug. "Congratulations!" Then I added, "*Senator* Dixon."

She waved her hand dismissively. "I'm not counting my chickens before they're hatched. It will be an incredibly tough race."

"I have no doubt you're up for it," said Meg. "Even though I don't work for you anymore, count me in as a campaign volunteer for the evenings and weekends."

"Enjoy your extra days off, Kit," said Dixon. "When you get back to work, we will be hitting the road at a breakneck speed."

"I'll be ready," I said.

Our conversation was interrupted by the opening of the sliding glass door leading to the deck. Sebastian, Trevor, and Lisa appeared with our guests.

"Congresswoman Dixon, you've met these folks at the town hall meeting in Duck, but let me reintroduce you," I said. "Thalia Godfrey, Jean Rizzo, Tobias Potter, and Lacy Madison."

Maeve shook hands with everyone. "A pleasure to see you again. As I understand it, my chief of staff and her friends proved quite helpful in solving the murder of your mayor."

Thalia spoke up. "I'm sure the police would have eventually figured out Gary was responsible for my husband's death, but Kit and her friends pushed it along. I'm very grateful for their assistance." She smiled and put her arm around Jean.

"I read a couple of newspaper articles about it," said Dixon. "The man who killed Godfrey was his business partner?"

I nodded. "It was a complicated story to unravel. Ronan moved to Duck because he knew his long-lost daughter lived here," I said. "That's Lacy."

"After Ronan told me that he was my father, he wanted to try to help me in a meaningful way. I didn't want charity from him. So he decided he would open a business in Duck and once it was profitable, he would turn his share over to me," explained Lacy.

"And you were okay with this plan, Thalia?" asked Meg.

Thalia smoothed her long, wavy hair. "Of course. After all, I understand the importance of karma. Ronan had done a bad thing by running away from Lacy and her mother when he was a teenager. But he wanted to make amends, and I was fully supportive of it. I also respected their privacy and didn't tell anyone about the relationship."

"The problem was that Ronan wanted to make Sonoma Sunsets as successful as possible in a short period of time," said Tobias. "Organic wines are more expensive than regularly produced wines, and they also have a shorter shelf life. Ronan was a shrewd businessman. He figured out the challenges almost immediately and decided to purchase wines from suspect vineyards."

"In other words, he was cutting corners," said Sebastian. "And Gary is a true enviro, much like me." Sebastian pointed to his t-shirt, which read: "Keep the Sea Plastic-Free."

"Gary wouldn't tolerate Ronan's business decisions," I said. "Eventually, he figured out something fishy was going on."

"According to what Detective Gomez told us, Gary decided to confront him at the bar last Saturday night," said Meg. "Gary claims he didn't plan on killing him, but things got out of control when Ronan threatened to endanger the wild horses of Corolla if Gary didn't go along with his business schemes. There was a scuffle, and Gary ended up hitting Ronan over the head with a bottle of wine."

"We'll never know if it was planned or not, but it probably wasn't. After all, Gary had to scramble quickly to cover up the fact his DNA would be all over the victim's clothing," I said.

"So that's why poor Ronan ended up in the marsh," said Thalia.

"Unfortunately, that's right," I said. "It was an important piece to solving the murder. I couldn't figure out why someone would go to the trouble of submerging Ronan's body if there wasn't a valid reason."

"I know how you figured out that Ronan was my father, but how did you finally come to the conclusion that Gary was the murderer?" asked Lacy.

"It was a strong hunch more than anything," I said. "Gary was certainly unnerved when he caught me snooping around his office. He didn't want me to know that he was taking a closer look at the wines ordered for the bar. There was also the question of why Ronan ended up in the water after the blow had killed him. But then I found a clue."

"Actually, it was Clarence and Murphy who helped you discover it," said Doug.

I laughed. "You're right. I shouldn't shortchange them."

"What did the dogs find?" asked Thalia.

"Clarence and Murphy got into our laundry and tossed our room," I said. "When I was cleaning up, a business card fell out of the pocket of the dress I wore at the town hall. It was from Gary."

"And that reminded you of the fact that Sebastian's business card had been discovered at the scene of the crime," said Lisa.

"It did. I remembered that Gary had asked me for my business card before the town hall began. His card was the only one in my pocket," I said. "Trading business cards is almost like second nature. Most days, I couldn't tell you who I shared my card with."

"And that made Kit think that if Gary had been handing out business cards before the town hall, maybe he'd somehow gotten his hands on Sebastian's," said Doug. "After all, he was introducing Sebastian to a lot of people."

"I don't think it was part of a premeditated plan. But after Gary killed Ronan, he knew he had to divert suspicion to someone else," said Sebastian.

"You were a convenient scapegoat. You'd caused enough of a ruckus at the meeting and you were from out of town. He must have realized he had one of your cards on him, so he dropped it on the ground to plant a false clue for the police," I said. "He probably planted it after we discovered Ronan's body. He showed up with Tobias at the scene, and Sebastian's name was raised as a suspect. He could have easily tossed the card behind the bar. When I found the broken wine bottle in the same spot, Sebastian's card wasn't there. Yet the police found it when they examined the scene."

"That means that someone had to place the card there within a very short window of time," said Lisa.

"To make matters worse, it turned out Sebastian didn't have an alibi for that night, which worked out to Gary's advantage, at least until Kit figured it out," said Meg.

"What's going to happen to the wine bar now?" asked Congresswoman Dixon.

Thalia smiled at Jean and then Lacy. "I'm going to follow Ronan's wishes. I'm turning over his half of the business to Lacy. She'll continue to work with Tobias, who will now become a full-fledged partner."

"That's fantastic," said Sebastian. "Are you going to keep the environmental, organic focus?"

"It's going to remain part of our wine menu," said Lacy. "That way, we can give our customers options."

"Spoken like a true businesswoman," said Jean, who leaned closer to Thalia. "We have our own plans to announce, too."

"Don't keep us in suspense," said Meg, who was eyeing the pile of cheeseburgers and hot dogs.

Jean took a deep breath. "I'm keeping my restaurant in Duck open. My family has been in the Outer Banks for a long time and I don't want to lose that connection. But I am going to expand to the Raleigh metropolitan area."

Thalia piped up. "I'll keep my house here. I'm also going to find a place in Raleigh so we can split our time. I'm thinking about opening a yoga business there. I never could break into the yoga scene on the Outer Banks, except for my free classes on the lawn. Now it's time to spread my wings and see if I can soar."

"Ronan would have appreciated both of your business ventures," said Tobias.

"And do you have any announcement to make?" asked Maeve. She was the one who had tipped me off that Tobias had been thinking about running for higher office.

"I do," said Tobias. "But I'm not ready to make a formal announcement yet. Ronan left me a tidy sum in his will, so I will be using that money for my state legislative campaign."

Doug cleared his throat. "I have made a decision about my next book."

"Hurry up and tell us," said Meg. "We can hardly wait to find out what four hundred-page tome Kit will make us read next."

Doug ignored Meg's comment. "I decided I needed a challenge. Something I have never done before."

I wracked my brain. Doug had written about Supreme Court justices, presidents, and Speakers of the House. Was there a fourth branch of government he'd missed?

"I give up," I said, my hands up in the air. "Don't keep us in suspense."

"I'm going write a book about women trailblazers in politics," said Doug triumphantly. "Sojourner Truth, Susan B. Anthony, Jeannette Rankin, Ida Wells, Alice Paul, Frances Perkins, Hattie

Caraway, Shirley Chisholm, Sandra Day O'Connor."

I reached over and hugged Doug. "That will be a fantastic book."

Meg opened her mouth to speak, but instead, she walked over and put her arms around Doug. "Now that's a book I look forward to reading."

Sebastian put his arm around Lisa. "Everyone is moving on with their lives, and I think that's a good thing. Lisa is going to head with Murphy to the FBI Academy soon."

Trevor cleared his throat. "I thought about changing jobs, but I've come to realize I belong exactly where I am, which is working in the House of Representatives." He smiled at Meg. "And we'll take things one day at a time."

I glanced over at Maeve Dixon, but she remained mute. As promised, she'd save her big news for another day.

"I saw a quote on a framed poster at a store yesterday," said Doug. "Life takes you down many paths, but my favorite ones lead to the beach."

I looked around at my dearest friends, my new acquaintances, and my boss. I didn't quite know where our paths would lead us. Right now, I was happy that we could savor this moment together with the roar of the ocean in the distance.

THE END

COLLEEN J. SHOGAN has been reading mysteries since the age of six. A political scientist by training, Colleen has taught American politics at numerous universities. She previously worked on Capitol Hill as a legislative staffer in the United States Senate and as a senior executive at the Library of Congress. Currently, she's a Senior Vice President at the White House Historical Association. A member of Sisters in Crime, Colleen splits her time between Arlington, VA and Duck, NC.

CPSIA information can be obtained
at www.ICGtesting.com
Printed in the USA
BVHW030816160721
612048BV00002BA/270